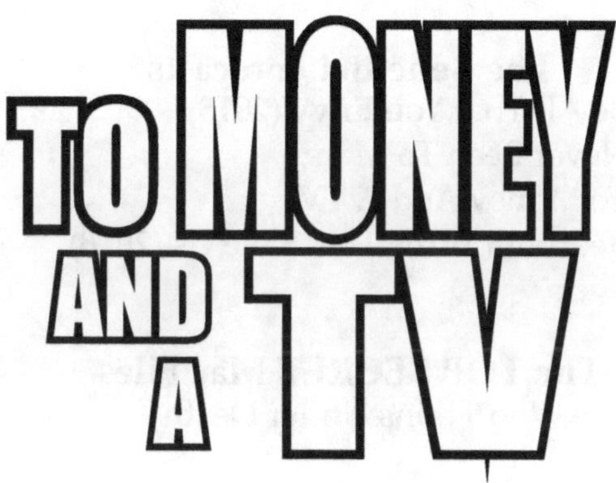

TO MONEY AND A TV

LARRY GENT

ALSO BY LARRY GENT

The Benedict Forecasts
Be All That You Envy (2018)
Never Been To Mars
To Money And A TV
Bedroom Walls That Save Us (2018)

The TOP SECRET Mac Files
She Who Trains Under Death

Avalon Lost
Lightyears To Go Before I Sleep

Vörissa's Catalyst Online
Patch 1.01:   New Game+
Patch 1.02:   Escort Mission
Patch 1.03:   Corpse Run
Patch 1.04:   In Another Castle
Patch 1.05:   Silent Protagonist

TO MONEY AND A TV

LARRY GENT

MIDNIGHT READING PUBLISHING

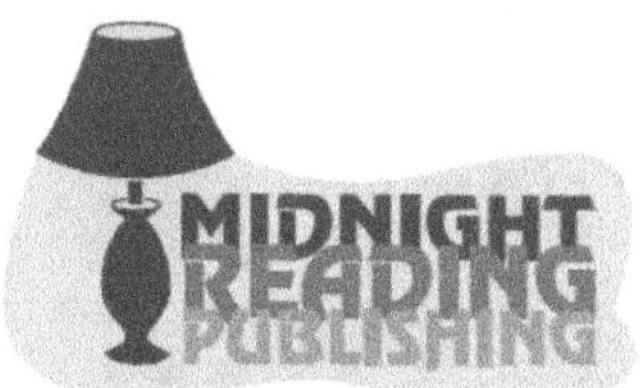

Published in Canada by Midnight Reading Publishing, Ottawa

Gent, Larry, 1983-, Author.
        To Money and a TV / Larry Gent
ISBN: 978-0-9959515-9-4
Ebook ISBN: 978-1-989152-00-3

Cover Design: Valérie Gent

Midnight Reading Publishing
511 Brittany Drive
Ottawa, Ontario
K1K 0S1

Dedicated to James Patrick Dunne

To the man who taught me storytelling, computers, table tennis and chess, just to name a few.

You, like many others, fed me book after book and then talked with me about them. You are a major peice of the puzzle that made this book happen.

You are a man of many titles but to me there was only one important one.

Thank you, Grandpa.

I miss you.

The Benedict Playlist

Music has always been a big part of my life. I use it for everything. I use music to sleep, I use music to play video games, I use it to read, to exercise (as if), play Magic and above all else I use music to write.

When I want to write a certain character I need to get into his mindset, I need to feel what he's feeling. I do that by music. A happy song has the power to energise me, a sad one to turn my mood foul and a raunchy song will.....well you see where I am going with this.

Sex. I was talking about sex.

So below is what I am calling The Benedict Playlist (because I can't call this I Stole This from Carrie Vaughn PS I love your work Carrie). These are the songs that I listened to over and over in the writing process of the Ben Books. They are the songs that, while not always being lyrically appropriate, had verses in them that related to what Ben is doing now.

I don't own any of these songs, sadly paying $0.99 on iTunes doesn't count as owning them; they belong to the talented people who wrote them. So to them I give as many thanks as I would anybody else who helped me out. For without your lyrical skills I wouldn't be where I am today.

Here to the Cowboy and his music.

Songs

- Is Anybody Home? – Our Lady Peace
- Here's to Us – Halestorm
- Where My Heart Will Take Me – Russell Watson
- Blind Mary – Gnarls Barkley
- Frank's 2000" TV – Weird Al Yankovic
- Hammerhead – The Offspring
- The World can Use a Cowboy - Adam Gregory
- You Can't Always Get What You Want – The Rolling Stones
- Blood in the Cut - K.Flay
- Try Try Try - Rachael Sage
- Sometimes When We Touch - Dan Hill

Chapter 01
Century of Magnificent Beds

For as long as there have been humans, there have been beds. We need a place to lay our head, we need a place to sleep and we need a place to fornicate when the airplane bathroom stall is occupied. Beds are important. Bed-based history majors have called the 17th century the *century of magnificent beds*, but personally I think it comes, at best, to a close second. These days we have adjustable beds, bunk beds, futons, Murphy beds, vibrating beds and even waterbeds; but the best bed that ever existed in all of history was my bed. It wasn't a special bed that altered based on my needs and it wasn't a bed with dozens of features; it was just a regular old bed that recently had the uncanny ability to produce a naked woman beside me when I woke up.

Honestly, in my mind that ability trumps all others.

"Your phone is ringing."

I stirred at the sound of her voice, rolled over and smiled as my hand wrapped around her naked body. Her name was Rachael Puzo and she was a member of the FBI. While she would stanchly claim that FBI stood for *Federal Bureau of Investigation*, I often claimed it stood for *Foxy Bodied Individual*. She never agreed with that but she never disagreed with it either. Puzo didn't look like those actresses from TV that played FBI agents, perfect and flawless in every way; instead she looked like a good ol' girl: smooth skin with a tear or two, a well worn hand, and a thin scar that ran the length of her neck. She was the type of girl who could have a beer, toss a bale of hay and kick your ass all in the run of a day and best of all: she was naked in my bed.

"Meh, let it ring," I muttered, desperately wanting to ignore the Rocky ringtone, the *awesome* Rocky ringtone, and stay right where I was: naked in bed with her. "I'm good."

She elbowed me in the chest as she reached for my phone. "Answer it."

I winced, louder and stronger then the blow actually allowed -- I was playing it up for sympathy -- as I sat up. "Man, I thought cuddling was a benefit of being in a rel--."

Her head snapped towards me like a whip, I could honestly hear the crack, as she stared at me with an accusing look and wide eyes. I suddenly caught my mistake. I almost said the forbidden word, the dreaded R-Word.

"A benefit of being in a... a... a... really nice bed with a hot naked woman." I'll admit it wasn't my nicest save, but it would have to do. She rolled her eyes and handed me my phone.

Relationship: the R-Word.

Rachael and I weren't in an R-Word. We'd been together for six months, enjoying each other's company, messing around in a carnal fashion and even doing couple-things, but despite all of this we weren't in an R-Word. She didn't want one and she didn't have time for one. I, on the other hand, wasn't sound enough, in body or mind, for anything long term, so instead we just hooked up, repeatedly, while staunchly declaring, over and over, that we weren't in an R-Word. We weren't even allowed to say the word. If either of us even muttered the word we owed the other twenty dollars. I was a gimp on a military disability pension; she was a high ranking federal police office. Neither of us had twenty dollars to burn.

It wasn't the most functional R-Word, but right now it worked; it gave me someone to talk to, someone to embrace in the morning, and someone to bump uglies with.

FYI: Never refer to your woman's sexual organs as 'uglies' to their face. They tend not to enjoy it, and when your not-girlfriend carries a gun, *not to enjoy it* often turns shooty.

I took my phone from her and grudgingly answered it. "Hello?"

"I'm looking for SRG Security?" Crap. Those words meant I was getting out of bed whether I wanted to or not.

A year ago I was just your regular war vet, a dead-beat shmuck who watched way too much TV and sat around doing crap all. Then one day, an envelope was couriered to me. I ripped it open and watched as my future poured out like a college football team from a school bus. I watched as documents and paperwork poured onto my kitchen table followed by a private investigator license and ownership of a company called SRG Security. In less time than it took to tie my shoes, I became a PI, a gumshoe, a detective. Actually, that's a bad example. My bum leg actually makes it really hard to tie my shoes. Two days after the package arrived on my doorstep, my phone started ringing. People somehow knew SRG existed and, even more surprising, they wanted to hire me. So despite every urge and attempt by the old reluctant me to ignore these calls, I became a private eye.

I was living my childhood fantasy

I'd always grown up wanting to be a detective. I wanted to star in my own film noir world where it was always a dark and stormy night, and when a woman walked through the door my first thought was always *I knew right away she'd be trouble*. But like most adults, I gave up my childhood dreams when I grew up. I gave up my hope of being a detective the moment I joined the Army Rangers and left to go to war, and I gave up my hopes of damn near everything else when I came back with a leg full of shrapnel.

Growing up sucked.

I got calls from Fortune 500 corporations, businesses and companies, museums, and from other such people who needed my help. I'd helped save a man's career after his best friend tried to sabotage him, I found a stolen painting and even stopped an alien invasion. No big, it's all part of being you average PI.

Truth Time: The alien invasion turned out to be a fake -- go figure -- but the art theft was totally legit and I stopped it. I would go so far as to say that said case's legitness was so great that quitting was not an option. MC Hammer would be proud.

So as I stood before yet another big business building, all I could do was think of how much I missed my TV. If there is one thing I enjoy doing more than anything else it is -- it is – well, it's Rachael, but if there is a *second* thing I enjoy doing more than anything else, it's watching TV. I love everything about TV. I love the semi-predictable plots, the cheesy TV mysteries, the laugh tracks, the cop shows and even the To Be Continueds. When there was nothing in my life, there was TV. My TV and I hated to be apart.

This building was home to Skit-Tech, an up and coming Technology Company that was looking to make it big in the mobile world, and they had the building to prove it. It was one of those glass skyscrapers that looked like it would come crashing down at the next errant stone or baseball that happen to strike it. The inside looked as high tech as the out, with minimalistic furniture but screens and scanners as far as the eye could see. What I know about computers can best be described as basic+. I know how to use the internet -- I mean, who doesn't these days -- and I know a couple extra tricks the Rangers taught me, but when it comes to how technology works, I draw a blank bigger than an unfinished metaphor. So when I stepped inside and like thirty small lights start rapidly blinking, I knew I was being scanned but I had no bloody clue how.

When a company decides to hire SRG Security, i.e. moi, they will always start the same way. I show up at a building, I stand around in awe in the lobby, and a young guy in desperate need of help comes rushing down saying my name.

"Benedict Thompson?" Just like I said he would. I gave the man a nod and offered my hand. He took the hand, with a firm grip, and gave it a shake. "I'm Frederick Déshant. Come this way please."

The next phase would happen the same way. The man would glance back at me, nervously like he'd made a *bigger* mistake, and ask the next question, the one that showed his uncertainty of the entire situation.

"Are you sure you're the best SRG has to offer?" Right on cue. "You sure don't look like corporate security."

I never could fault anybody when they asked that question; I really didn't look like corporate security. Most investigators were tall men who wore slick suits, had stern faces, and were the statuesque examples of toughness. I, on the other hand, was nearly always seen wearing jeans, a pair of leather gloves, a collared shirt, a brown winter jacket, and a cowboy hat. I also hobbled along using a cane to walk. My cane was a wooden walking stick with derby handle made from a blend of silver plate and faux ivory. The handle had a mustang horse carved in basso-rilievo. The only guy who looked less like security then me was the janitor, and he was unionized.

"I am, sir," I assured him with three words. There wasn't a need to go into more. This just left the final question before we got down to work, the one I got not only from anybody who hired me, but also from damn near anybody who ever met me.

"Is your name really Benedict?"

Benedict Butler Thompson; I get this question a lot.

Amongst all of our similarities, the Thompson clan shares one major trait: an unwavering love of westerns. Our fondness of the genre was passed from my Grandfather to my Mom and then down to my sister and me. My mom's love of the cowboy way was so big that she named all her kids after famous cowboys. It's like those parents who are so obsessed with *Harry Potter* and *Game of Thrones* that they named their kids Ginny or Khaleesi. The only difference is cowboys are by far much cooler then ginger wizards or the dragon's version of Teen Mom.

I was named after the famous Ben Thompson. Mom always said he was a gambler and gentlemen, a man who'd only fight to protect others, and even though he walked with a cane he never let it keep him down. Sadly, Mom didn't know how prophetic that name would become.

My sister Annie Belledin, nee Thompson, was named after Annie Oakley, the legendary cowgirl who was a famous sharpshooter and exhibition shooter. The obsession didn't stop there; it just got passed to another generation. Annie ended up naming her firstborn son Robby after the cowboy photographer Robert E. Cunningham and her daughter Alice after Alice Ivers, a Colorado cowgirl best known as Poker Alice.

Then there was Clint.

He didn't exist, yet.

Frederick led me into a room, got me to sign a non-disclosure agreement, then moved me to another room with little else but a desk, a chair, and a brown envelope sitting on the surface. This room was creepy. I felt like this was a murder room.

There was one thing that always bugged me about murder rooms, well two if you counted the actual murders, and that was how dark and dreary the rooms actually were. If I have planned enough about a murder to actually go and construct a room to commit said murder in, then why not make it a room I'd enjoy being in? Why not let in some light or add some colour? I'd suggest red; it wouldn't stain. Most people build rooms for things they enjoy. I enjoy TV so I have a TV room. It has a couple couches and one awesome ass La-Z-Boy chair that is for me and me only. My TV room is a room I enjoy being in. So why not do it the same for a murder room? But maybe I'm just old fashioned that way.

Against my better judgment, I stepped inside and slowly pulled off my gloves. I wear gloves not as a fashion statement, although I make this look Will Smith good, but as a means of protection. I'm not a germaphobe who fears life, the universe and everything; I need the gloves to protect me from something much worse.

If I'm about to get attacked here, which wouldn't be the first time, I wanted to know. So with an emotion that seemed like the aftermath of Self-Preservation getting knocked up by Reluctance after a drunken one-night stand, I dragged my fingers across the wall. A familiar shiver shot up my back, and my eyes began to twitch, and the world began to shift. Frederick faded away and the room shifted back to show this room not two hours earlier. Frederick stood there with an attractive woman wearing a skirt three sizes too small. Note: Frederick wasn't complaining and neither was I.

"Are you sure of this?" the woman asked as she handed him the brown envelop.

"Yeah. A buddy of mine at Starmoore Entertainment swore by this guy. He said this guy saved his career."

"All this for a hunch?"

"It's more than a hunch. It's my project that put us in this dogfight, my wheeling and dealing that gutted the next two companies for their parts and my *brilliant* scheming that put us head-to-head with the big boys. We need to win this. There's no backing down now. I need this guy."

I pulled my hand back and allowed reality to return. Well, at least they weren't here to kill me. That's a plus. The superhero lives to fight another day. Yeah, you heard me, superhero.

I am Benedict Thompson and this is my life, the life of a superhero.

I'm not a great superhero. I'm not super strong, I can't fly or climb walls -- hell, because of my bum leg I'm forced to hobble everywhere with the assistance of a cane, so I'm not likely to be fighting crime anytime soon -- but what I can do is read items.

The technical term is psychometry. According to Wikipedia, it's the ability to relate details about the past or future condition of an object or location, usually by being in close contact with it. It was on Wikipedia, so it must be true. In the normal tongue of everyday people, if I touch an object, I see a moment from its past. It doesn't work on anything that lives or breathes, and it is always a moment from the past, never the future -- almost never.

The problem with visions is that I never get a clear picture of anything; I mean, the reception is good, 1080p at 120 frames per second, but I never know what's going on. Tuning into my vision is often like being dropped halfway into a *Law and Order* rerun. I spend half the time trying to figure out who's who and what's going on. Occasionally I get information in a manner not dissimilar to VH1's *Pop-Up Video*, but most of the time I get nothing but more questions then answers and a crap load of awkward apparitions.

"Please be seated." I moved to the chair and plopped my ass down, eyeing him the entire time. Frederick Déshant was a high level associate, I figured that by his fancy-smansy suit and his douche haircut, but aside from that I knew next to nothing. My vision told me he had no problem tearing someone down to get his way and that he'd win no matter what, but those were the limits of my deductive skills. I'm no Sherlock Holmes, never have been, never will be, and never could be. I'm not smart enough. I can't take one look at a guy and figure out that he's a banker, that he's come back from overseas, and that he boinking his secretary and the mail room boy. I can, however, look at a guy in an expensive suit and deduce that he's a crap ton richer then I am. Maybe he'll co-sign a car loan for me.

While what I knew about Frederick Déshant was next to nil, what I knew about Skit-Tech was a little more in depth. They were a tech company that started with computers. They made cheaper laptops and desktops, and had annoying commercials in the 90s. *Dude, you're getting a Skit!*

Research on my laptop, which actually was one of theirs, told me more about them. They spent the next decade going through financial problems, tried to get out via a loan or bailout and were eventually bought out by one company or another until some massive parent company picked them up midway through '06. They went mostly silent, still selling average computers at below average prices and selling parts to whomever wanted them, until they showed up at major tech show a year ago with a new image, a new look, and with intent of stepping into the mobile/tablet ring.

Tech experts around the world criticized their decisions. Why were they stepping into a dogfight already being won by Samsung and Apple? It was a fight that HP lost with their TouchPad, Asus lost with their Eee Pas, Google with their Nexus, and even Microsoft all but bailed out with their Surface Pro. How did this fourth rate company hope to survive? One review I read called Apple and Samsung giants in the playground and every other company were the smaller beings that they were stepping on, unaware of their presence. Then Skit-Tech revealed the specs. It blew people away. Not since Apple introduced their first iPad had the tablet market been so shaken up. Their flagship project, the Sketchbook, was revolutionary. It shook up the tech world so much that George Washington returned from the dead with a Sketchbook in his hand and proclaimed it to be the biggest revolution he'd ever taken part in.

Six months later, the Skit-Tech showed up at another convention with another new product, a smartphone called the ScratchPad, and reviewers questioned their logic. Why fight a war on two fronts? Android and iPhone owned the market, why challenge them on that front when they hadn't even released their tablet yet? Then they saw the specs and the crowd went wild. The internet fell in love with their phones. Somehow Skit-Tech had hit gold and their product wasn't even out yet.

"I'd like for you to look into something for me," Frederick began as he slid the file over. "Hopefully it's not outside your area of expertise." Truth was, I never had an area of expertise (still don't), so whatever it was he asked, it was guaranteed to be outside my domain.

I opened the envelope and started to read, listening as I scanned each page. "In almost two weeks Skit-Tech takes its biggest risk ever and launches two major products in field dominated by two major companies. This is David and Goliath." The pages were mostly Greek to me, graphs based on predictions and estimate, flow charts built from trend following, and an estimated level of where the market and their stock price should be. None of it made sense to me. If I had the smarts required to read those pages I would've had the smarts not to join the army. What I did understand was the big red line that flew way below the others. "Early reviews of our product are good, tech gurus are speaking our name and we've basically gotten the tech-head market locked down. Our stock prices should be through the roof, but they're not."

I flipped the page and saw a stock comparison of their competitors. Apple, Samsung and even Microsoft, still limping in the fight with their Surface Pro and Windows Phone, were showing massive jumps in their stock prices.

"We should have the stock boost, but we don't; instead people are betting against us."

"Perhaps they're being cautious?" I added playing the devil's advocate. "It's not that uncommon right?"

"It's not." He continued to explain with, "But our bean counters apparently calculated that in. What is weird is the percentage." I took another look. Each of Skit-Tech's opposing companies showed a 17.36% increase in price. It meant different numbers for each company, but they all went up the same percentage. Well, colour me curious.

"Somebody knows something that I do not," Frederick declared. "And I have too much at risk for that. We have millions of units sitting in our warehouses. We ship them out in one week so they'll be ready for our launch in two. If you can find out what it is that I don't know by the shipping date, I'll double your fee."

Well, damn.

Chapter 02
Do You Really Teabag Guys in the Army?

I stared out of the backseat window as the cab sped through the city, my mind lost in thought. This was, as he said, outside my realm of speciality. I was trying to find secrets, trying to find something that was intentionally hidden. This was normally my forte, psychometry lets me see secrets, but without anything to actually *touch* I'd have to rely on my major weakness as a detective: detective work.

Life was so much easier when you could touch whatever you wanted.

That might have sounded dirtier then I intended.

Psychometry wasn't always the blessing it seemed to be. I'll be honest; I don't know why anyone would think that it was a blessing because it's not. It's a curse, a damn bloody curse. Imagine touching an object and seeing its past. You could touch a pencil and see everybody who's ever used it. You could touch a Nike sneaker and see everything that went into making said kick. You could touch a twenty dollar bill and see the path that bill had taken, from printer to bank and from person to person; and while all that seems cool and interesting, let me paint the reality of the situation. My powers are uncontrollable. I don't choose what I see -- somebody else, be it Fate, God, or Spongebob, chooses for me. Imagine touching a fork and seeing nothing but wave after wave of people shovelling food into their mouth; imagine touching a urinal or a toilet and seeing nothing but people crapping over and over; and imagine, if you would, touching a hotel bed and seeing -- seeing -- well, seeing the things people do in a bed that they don't own.

I did that once.

Ewwwwwww.

Even as I sat in the cab, my hands safely tucked away in my gloves, a small patch of skin on the back of my neck brushed the back of the chair as I sat down, and my body reacted. A shiver shot up my back and my eyes began to twitch as the world faded away, and I was left with an image of the cab, a month earlier, at 2 am Saturday morning with a man, a *drunk* man, seated in the backseat, blitzed out of his mind after a Friday night of binge drinking. Then he decided to relieve himself exactly where I am sitting.

God, I hate my powers.

I exited the cab and hobbled to my front door, using my cane for support as I awkwardly ascended the stairs. I live in a downtown house that was converted into a duplex. I live on the bottom floor with some hipsters living on the top. My apartment is weirdly laid out. I enter the door and have a massive spare room on my left and a long hallway that leads me to my second spare room on my right. At the end of the hall are my living room/kitchen combo and a small door that leads into my bedroom. I hung up my jacket and hat, and dropped my cane into its holster, and limped inwards.

I love my cane, well as much as anybody can love an inanimate object that they are required to use to walk, but luckily I don't need to use it 24/7. My leg is bad, this is a fact, but for simple movements around the house I don't need it. I spend most of my time with my ass in *the world's greatest chair* watching TV, but take me out of the house, on a case or for whatever unthinkable reason, and I bring my cane. My chair is, sadly, based solely in my living room. I pulled off my gloves and tossed them on the table, happy to let the air cross over my bare hands. I don't need my gloves in my apartment.

When I said I couldn't control my powers, I meant it,

more or less. I have learned four things about my powers:

1. Visions are emotion based. The more emotion that went into an event, the stronger the vision will be.
2. My visions are a random crapshoot, but if I really focus I can -- at best -- suggest they show me something relevant. They rarely listen.
3. My body can become numb to the visions.
4. These rules don't mean shit.

My apartment fell under Rule 3. I have seen the visions within my apartment so often that I have become numb to them. It's like working in a retail store and hearing the same thirteen songs playing on the speakers all day long. Eventually you don't even notice them anymore; and I don't even notice the visions in my apartment. Everything I owned, within this apartment anyways, rarely triggered a vision.

Rachael's stuff was different.

Ever since she and I started knocking boots -- which, by the way, is a rural euphemism for sex and not, in fact, a way to get mud off your footwear -- I'd been finding some of her stuff in my apartment. It started with the occasional bra or panties she'd forget, but then it became some extra clothes.

But we weren't in an R-Word.

One day, I blinked and she had a toothbrush and some supplies in my apartment. She even had her type of coffee on my counter and apple juice in my fridge. I hate apple juice; I'm a staunch OJ dude.

But we weren't in an R-Word.

Hell, the more I thought about it, the more I realized that there were things in my apartment that were never there before. There were extra pillows on my bed, there was some decretive western blanket draped over my couch and my private investigator's license was framed and hung on my wall instead of being lost in some drawer.

But we weren't in an R-Word.

I didn't care; I actually liked having super hot naked

women around my apartment. I know I'm weird, but it's the way I was raised by my Dad. So as I stared at my chair, the world's greatest La-Z-Boy, I spotted her official FBI suit jacket draped over the back and I was caught in a conundrum.

What do I do?

My woman -- who I am not in an R-Word with -- is Senior Special Agent Rachael Puzo of the FBI. She is a big-shot who has solved missing children cases, fought crime and took down the baddies. This meant that she was tasked with important and classified federal cases to handle. Classified files meant I couldn't know what she knew. It was a security risk. This was especially difficult for her, as an FBI agent, when she was sleeping with a psychic. So we had rules, we had an agreement. Okay, to be honest she had rules, and if I wanted to ever see her naked again I had to follow them.

I remember the day my Dad gave me the best advice I'd ever gotten. We were both outside. He looked me in the eye, placed his hand on my shoulder and spoke:

"Son, if she's naked do whatever the hell it takes to keep her that way! Do you understand?" I looked at my Dad and nodded. He smiled at me. "Good, now go to school and enjoy kindergarten."

Basically, I had to respect her career and her privacy. This mean I couldn't visionize (her word not mine) her work clothes or gear. It was a fair cop, and I tried really hard to respect it, but I'm curious to a fault. So as much as I hated my powers, I knew that if I touched her jacket, even briefly, I would be 'blessed' with images of whatever exciting missing child case she was on.

Just a single touch.

It's not that I didn't respect Puzo, quite the opposite, but sometimes it felt like we were holding back from each other. Perhaps we could go past our non-R-Word and maybe move into something I could actually say out loud without having to pay her twenty bucks. Perhaps she *likes* bat-crap crazy ex-soldiers like me.

The sound of my door opening, and the cheerful hello

that filled the apartment pulled my gaze from her black jacket. It was sweaty time! Standing at my door was Elaine Moeller, my physiotherapist. She was the type of person who always had a smile, one so infectious that the CDC has procedures to deal with its inevitable outbreak. She was a beautiful woman with curly hair that hung by her shoulders, a round face, and stunning eyes. This woman also happened to be the girl I was seriously crushing on.

"Hey, Cowboy," she smirked. "Let's pump you up."

Elaine and I had been working together for a while, which was why she never knocked anymore; she was helping my leg get better and I was being the charming man I was. Truth was, it was a little bit of a one-sided partnership as I was the one getting the most from it.

"So how goes things?" Elaine used to ask me about work, she was as much of a TV detective show fan as I was, but six months ago my life got real when she followed me to a case and saw a dead body before her. After that, she couldn't handle it. Honestly, part of me expected never to see her again but there she was, the next day, ready to talk.

She showed up with her super-perfect, super-douchey boyfriend.

"Things go." I went with a no-committal answer. "More work, hanging out with Robby tonight. Aside from that, I'm spending most my time with Rachael." She does her best to hide her discomfort at the mention of Puzo's name, but it doesn't work.

My relationship with Elaine could only ever been called weird. I was crushing on her for months, and I mean crushing hard. I was like a nerdy guy crushing on the hot blonde from *8 Simple Rules for Dating my Teenage Daughter* who lives across the hallway. She was always with her boy-friend, Steve Rapoza. The man was one of those perfect male nurses. He was super athletic, super kind and was actually kind of good looking.

Like I said: douche.

So during all of my crushing I met this woman, this

gorgeous woman who could kick my ass and actually got *really* scary when she was pissed. We hooked up and things started going well. Then Elaine started getting weird, and not just *I-saw-a-dead-body-weird*, but legitimately weird. Her smile became strained whenever I mention Rachael and she seemed to get uncomfortable. If I didn't know better -- and let's be honest, I rarely do -- I would think she liked me back. I always believed she liked me, but this was different. Annie, my only source for deciphering the mystery wrapped in an enigma known as women, came up with an interesting hypothesis. Elaine liked me, she always had, but I was her fall-back guy. If things didn't work with Captain America: Male Nurse Division, then she would come to me. I was her plan B and when I was, somewhat, off the market she didn't like it. This made no sense to me but Annie was the ovary-based life form expert.

"So things are good between you two?" she sheepishly asked as we stretched out my bum leg. I just nodded in reply. "That's good. That's really good. I'm happy to hear it."

"What about you and the nurse?"

"You mean Steve? It's going alright, I guess." I know I'm a detective and I know I'm not very good, but even I caught her tone. Things weren't great.

This is where I looked horrible.

I'm with Rachael, kind of, but I still pined for Elaine. Was I just some dumb ass guy who never understood how to love what he had? That wasn't me, not really. I loved being with Rachael, she was fun, but I had been crushing on Elaine something serious for months. She was fun, she was always smiles, and she had this weird ability to get me, but she was taken. She had been since I knew her.

Then there was Puzo. The woman was tough, bad-ass, and was a commanding chick in a suit, a turn-on of mine: blame the army. Best of all, things with Puzo were easy. But Puzo wasn't without her own conundrums. Puzo was a businesswoman, a career babe who was climbing the FBI ladder at a stunning rate. She didn't have time for an R-Word, and if she did, she deserved better than me. I never knew what would happen with her. So in the meantime, instead of putting dozens of labels on what we were, we just had fun and it was easy.

I tried to dodge, pulling up my gloved fists up to protect my face as my torso shifted away, but my body moved too slow and the ninja's blows struck like lightning. I grunted loudly, desperately trying to defend myself, to get out of the way or to strike back, but the ninja moved too quickly. Robby whooped loudly as his fingers moved like blurs, striking a series of buttons before leaping to another, each one forcing the on-screen ninja to land another pummelling blow to my health bar. I sighed loudly as my avatar, T.J. Combo, an ex-heavyweight champion boxer expelled for cheating, dropped to the ground in defeat.

Damn, this kid was good.

We were playing *Killer Instinct*, a video game for his Xbox One where weird warriors pummelled each other, and I was losing, repeatedly. I glanced at my character and frowned. I had chosen him because he looked, somewhat, like Stalone had in *Rocky* (in truth he looked more like the love child of Stallone and Mr. T) but this man, T.J. Combo, got his ass kicked. Realistically, it was probably *my* fault but that would require me admitting I sucked and that wasn't going to happen anytime soon.

"You're getting better, Uncle Ben," Robby reassured me with a wide-eyed grin and a mop of blonde curls. "You don't suck nearly as much as you used to."

Luckily if I never want to admit I suck, my nephew will step up and take care of it for me. Isn't family amazing?

I don't have kids -- yet -- so I don't have any youngling to spend time and/or money on, so any urge I have to spoil a kid goes to Robby and his six month old sister Alice.

Robby's a twelve-year-old kid and loved everything that kids his age did. If it was an action packed show or a violent video game, he was all over it. On top of that, he was a walking encyclopaedia for all things geeky. If there was a superhero film, he'd seen it; if there's a monster in *Lord of the Rings*, he could name it; and if there's an alien race in a *Star Wars* film, he could describe every social cue in their existence. The kid's awesome. He looks up to me. I'm the cool uncle.

Robby belongs to my older sister Annie. When she was twenty years old, she met a man named Greg Hazeltine, fell in love, and got pregnant. Six months later, the man panicked, packed his stuff, and ghosted like Swayze (man, that saying is totally different now). So at twenty-one years of age, Annie gave birth and named me the godfather. Ever since then I've done my best to be part of this child's life. The day I first saw my nephew, leaning over his crib staring down at his newborn body, I made him a promise that no matter what happened I would be there for him and his mother. I never thought that promise would require anything more than a video game or a cheat code, but then six months ago our lives exploded.

Six months ago, I answered a call from Annie to find out Robby had gone missing. The FBI showed up, lead by Rachael -- our first meeting -- and quickly they named it a kidnapping. So while the FBI ran around searching for leads, I did some investigating of my own. No superhero, be they as heroic as Superman or pathetic as me, can just sit around while innocents are in trouble, especially when those innocents are family. So I started touching things, I touched whatever I could get my hands on, I touched things like mad.

I always knew I was a freak, I had psychic visions that manifested after an IED decided to generously pump a fist full of shrapnel into my body, but I thought I was the only one. Spoiler: I wasn't. Turns out there is an entire world out there filled with powers, evil corporations, super spies, and malicious private militaries; all of them versus me. Yeah, that seems fair.

So when one company, WhiteStar Securities, decided

they wanted brand new child super-soldiers they kidnapped Robby, and a dozen others, and tried to smuggle them out of the country. I came after him, I called in every favour I had, and I went after him. I learned a lot that day about the world, about my family, and about me, the most important of which was that I did not like who I was. Six months ago I was an injured war vet who hated what he was and was so ashamed that he pushed everybody away, including his kick-ass nephew. Then Robby vanished and I came running... er... hobbling to the rescue. The old me died that day, leaving in its place only me. I'm not fully back to the super-cool uncle I was before my deployment but I'm getting there.

I saved my nephew and got him home only to have the bad guys show up at our front door, literally. Turns out my family are basically Jedi. There is a superhero gene, the Lycotta gene or something, and my family produces so much of it that we basically crap diamonds in the super-power world.

Sorry if these medical terms get confusing.

So not only am I a superhero, but so is Robby and so was the unborn baby in my sister's womb. The bad guys wanted them and a firefight broke out, one that triggered Annie's labour. We didn't know if the child was going to make it, but six months in and both Annie and her daughter Alice are going strong.

I looked over at Robby as he switched games and frowned slightly. I could see it in him, how those two days still hung on his shoulders. Most kids would hopefully forget that event, the human brain is remarkable that way, and get over it, but it wasn't going to be that easy for my nephew. According to my super-spy guy, because I *totally* have a super-spy guy, Robby has perfect memory recall. Once his powers kick in, he'll remember every detail of everything he ever witnesses, ever. His recall will be so total that both Arnold and Colin will be fighting over it. Most powers, so I'm told, take full effect at puberty but show symptoms as they grow older. Robby already had an amazing memory for the geekery stuff he loved but nothing else. Yet somehow I knew those events would be etched into his brain forever. It's hard enough for a kid to get over an event like that on his own let alone adding in super-powers.

"Hey, Uncle Ben, do you really teabag guys in the army?" I suddenly snorted and burst out into a fit of laughter. Robby had switched to a war game and was currently playing online.

"Obviously," I explained. "It's an army tradition. We have classes on it. You have to learn how to snipe the guy, hear him call you the worst names ever, have him question your sexuality and only then can you teabag him. It shows respect."

Robby just smirked.

"Let me tell you, m'boy," I continued, switching to an 'old man' accent as I pick up the second controller and joined him. "In the army you have to learn many-a-thing including how to st- oh son of a bitch!" I blinked as the camera panned around to show my Spartan dead on the ground with a fresh hole in its skull courtesy of a passing sniper round.

Robby laughed, partially at my horrible luck but mostly at the fact that I just swore. "You really need to get better at this, Uncle Ben."

"I thought I was," I admitted sheepishly. I glanced at my nephew and decide to test him. "Maybe I should quit?"

"I didn't hear no bell, Uncle Ben." And the kid passed life. "Mickey loves ya'," He passed with flying colours.

"Okay, enough of this crap. We're pairing up. Did you see where that guy shot from?" Robby nodded. "Good. We'll circle around him and fill him with futuristic Spartan lead." I re-spawn my character and dash across the field. "You can be my wing man."

"Bullshit, Uncle Ben, you can be mine."

"Atta boy!" I said triumphantly, "But don't let your mother hear you swear. She'll kill me."

What happened next varied by who told the story; I tell it how we stormed the futuristic planet, slaughtered all who opposed us and came out on top using proper military strategy, coordinated attacks and good ol' fashion home-grown gumption. Robby told the story a little differently. In his version I died every thirteen seconds by the most dodgeable shots ever and was, in his words, embarrassingly noobish. But since I'm telling the story, we'll go with my version.

For the next couple hours we played together, slaughtering the hellish legion of evil fifteen-year-old boys who swamped Xbox Live, victorious in our war campaign and never once did I, despite what Robby said, fall off a cliff or crash an alien jet into myself.

"Hello!" Annie yelled. She always let herself into my apartment, normally with a knock as she stepped through the door. "Anybody home?"

Robby jumped to his feet and dashed to the door. "Hey, Mom! Guess what? Uncle Ben crashed a jet into himself in *Halo*."

It totally didn't happen. I told you not to listen to him.

I exited the game, climbed to my feet, and limped to the front door. My sister, Annie, stood there awkwardly hugging her son with one hand as she carried her daughter in her other. Seeing me, she broke the first hug and moved towards me to start a second one. As that hug reached its finale and she pulled away, I was left holding the cute and adorable Alice. I didn't know how it happened exactly, a mother's hands are faster than a magician's, but I didn't mind in the least.

A chuckle filled the hallways as man stepped in behind Annie. "Hey kiddo, ask Uncle Ben about the jeep he crashed in real life." Robby's head snapped over and his eyes went wide.

Whatever you do, don't listen to David either.

Staff Sergeant David Belledin was my best-friend/ brother-in-law. He was the soldier's solider: six foot one, two hundred and ten pounds, dark hair maintained in a crew cut and a look of strength about him. Dave and I met years ago in the infantry and quickly grew to that BFF level where we sat around, did each other's hair, and talked about just how cute Derek from gym class was. Truth is that description was never far off. All you had to do with replace *sat around* with *drink, do each other's hair* with *drink, talk* with *drink* and *Derek from gym class* with *strippers* and it was a perfect match.

We were stationed together stateside until I got posted to a different division. It didn't take long until I introduced him to Annie. The two hit it off and before long he was marrying into the family. He was perfect for her, perfect for Robby, and perfect for me. Think about it, how many people would love to have physical photographic proof in which to blackmail your brother-in-law with? I know, I know, I'm a trendsetter. Y'all allowed to be jelly.

The only problem was he knew stories about me too. None of which were pleasant.

Dave closed the door behind him as he spoke. "So we were on the army base, I can't remember which one, and your Uncle Ben has to go pick up the Major's jeep."

"And Major is high up right?"

"Oh, it is very high up. Now your Uncle Ben was up very late the night before studying for a test he had." He really meant drinking. "This mean he was very tired the next morning." He really meant hung-over.

"What happened?" Robby asked as we all walked into the living room.

"Well nobody knows for sure, but your Uncle had to drive across a big desert-like field. We're talking a field the size of an airport with nothing but open space, sand, and one *single* tree." Robby nodded eagerly. "So I'm back at the base and I get a call over the radio. Your Uncle has been in an accident and needs our help. I jump into my car and speed out after him."

Robby would glance at me to see my reaction only to shoot his gaze back to his father for the rest of the story. His head shot back and forth like a cat watching a ping pong match.

"I get out to the desert field to find your Uncle has crashed the jeep into the tree. The. One. Single. Tree." Robby looked at me and laughed loudly.

Despite Dave's embarrassing bro-story (a brory? That term is trademarked by Benedict Thompson Inc.), the tale did make Robby genuinely smile. It was something I had missed. I hadn't seen it much before the kidnapping, a by-product of my attempted withdrawal from the world, and it had become a rarity after. So to watch the kid in a fit of laughter, a full on guffaw with gasps for breath and the occasional snort, was comforting. He was two steps away from the descent into a literal (real definition not the new one) *roll on the floor laughing out loud* incident. I refuse to call it ROFLOL.

I pulled Alice closer and looked into her adorable baby eyes. "When you're sixteen, I'm going to teach you so many bad habits. You and I are going to make your Daddy's life horrible. I'll even tell you stories about what he did when he was younger. Yes, I will." Alice giggled and I gave her a gentle kiss on her forehead. "Those stories will be totally inappropriate for a sixteen year old girl."

"Those stories are totally inappropriate for a daughter-of-mine at any age," David laughed.

I felt the warmth on her skin and shrugged it off. It wasn't warm like a regular kid's skin was; instead it was closer to a heat that almost bordered on a fever. Her entire body was like that, very warm to the touch. It was a cause for concern when she was younger, but after it never went away and Alice seemed perfectly healthy, the doctor's concluded that she just ran warmer.

The five of us sat in the living and chatted for a bit as Robby grabbed another game and put it into the Xbox. Annie did the mother thing, glancing at the violent game staring a Roman General and proclaiming it too violent for her son, but lost out when she turned to her husband only to find him glued to the screen and begging me to borrow it while applauding his son's latest gruesome kill.

We were interrupted when my front door opened again and a familiar female voice filled the hall. "Hey, Ben, it's me. I just need to grab the extra shirt I keep here. Your place was closer than mine. I'll be gone again in a second."

As the words hit my ears, but before I could react, I saw Rachael exiting the long hallway and standing in the entryway to my living room, her suit shirt unbuttoned, her bra-covered breasts visible, as she attempted to undress in a hurry. She spotted my family, realized we weren't alone, and rapidly pulled her shirt closed. "So *that's* whose van is parked on the side of the street."

Annie just glared at me. I was in trouble from my big sister.

Well, crap.

Chapter 03
Does Your Sister a Job as an
Interrogator 'Cause Gitmo's Hiring

At that moment each member of my family each gave me a different look. Robby gave me a look of thanks for what he just saw, a look that told me I had just made him the most popular boy in school for the next week after he told this story to his friends. Dave gave me a look that said *I want to pause time and give you a high five buddy, but my wife is literally right there but regardless -- kudos.* Alice gave me a giggling look because she currently thought that my dropped-jaw-scrunched-face look was actually a funny face I had willingly made to amuse her. Then there was the look from my sister. Her look was a far more complicated and layered. Part of it said *does this happen often in your house when my child is over?* Part of it said *you've met someone, I'm happy for you.* A third part, which I'm pretty sure I misread, said *I've just saved a lot of money by switching to Geico* and a forth part, the one I feared, said *you have a woman partially living in your house and you haven't told your big sister? I will bloody kill you for this. They won't find your body. I'll make sure of it.*

"Mr. and Mrs. Belledin, a pleasure to see you again."

"Special Agent Puzo," Annie said. "It's great to see you as well."

"I didn't know you guys were here."

"Obviously." Rachael and Annie stared at each other,

doing that female thing where one would look the other up and down and instantly deduce if they were a threat to them in any way.

"Excuse me, I need to change my shirt," Rachael excused herself, having deduced no threat. Annie, needing an extra second to deduce whether or not Rachael was good enough for her younger brother, let her go with a nod. Rachael vanished into my bedroom. I handed Alice to Dave and limped into my room.

I stepped in to find Rachael topless. I'm not used to finding topless women in my bedroom, but I'll be honest, I liked it. Puzo opened my closest and pulled out a fresh white shirt, her old one discarded on my bed, and quickly pulled it on. She eyed me in the mirror with an apologetic look.

"Sorry. I didn't know you had family over," she said with a laugh. "I even saw the van, but didn't put two-and-two together. My mind's been elsewhere."

"I'm sorry FBI-lady but what do you do again? Fight crime? Solve mysteries?" I teased. She elbowed me as she passed. I glanced down at her discarded shirt and spotted a small red stain. "Is that blood?" I asked as I reached for it.

She slapped my hand out of the way. "Ben, don't. You can't touch my work clothes." The agreement: I had to respect it, but she couldn't stop me from asking.

"Is that blood? Are you okay?"

"Don't worry, it's not mine." Her answer did two things. One was that it did nothing to reassure me and the other was that it brought a small smirk to my face because her answer was such a movie-answer. "I was at a crime scene and I got splashed. No danger, don't worry."

"Good." Damn it! At that moment I needed a better response then *good*. I needed a response that didn't make me look like the scared woman waiting at home.

She gave me a kiss and laughed. "You know, I could get used to having a scared woman waiting at home."

Crap! She can read minds. She's a witch. I'm sleeping with a witch; get the torches.

"You have your *get the torches* look again," she laughed. "Did I just say what you were thinking?"

Double Crap. "No," I lied. "Not at all. Let's change the subject. You know my family would love to see you again."

"Ben, that is more of an *R-Word* thing," she said as her smile faded. "I really shouldn't."

"They haven't seen you since the incident. They'd love to thank you."

Puzo gave me a strained smile as she checked her phone. "Sure, but only for a few moments."

We exited my room and re-joined my family. Annie gave Puzo a hug and Dave thanked her. The six of us sat down and chatted briefly. It was nice, albeit awkward. Annie wanted to know details of my R-Word and found round-about questions that allowed her to dive for details without actually asking questions; Dave wanted throw me a parade for *tapping that* (and I wanted to let him); Alice wanted more funny faces from me and started to reach across and touch my face to see if she could prompt them. Rachael, while enjoying the attention, found it crossing a line, and I knew which one. As every guy knows, meeting a partner's family is a *major* step. If you're lucky, it goes only slightly awkward. If you're a redneck, it could potentially end up with shotguns involved. Luckily I didn't have a shotgun. Yet despite all the reactions, Robby's was weirdest.

He didn't pull away or hide, neither did he approached Rachael or hug her when it was offered. Instead he seemed to be staring at her waist. Robby and I are a lot alike, we both liked to stare at Rachael hips. I chose to stare at them because her rear is attached to them and I quite enjoy her rear. Robby stared there because just as her rear hung from her hips so did her Glock 22.

Robby was uncomfortable around guns. I had caught sight of this a couple times since the kidnapping. Once he came over, earlier than I expected, and found me cleaning my M9. It scared him and I felt bad. I normally wouldn't have my guns out around children, but he showed up an hour early. What am I psychic? Oh wait...

Guns are a very real thing to be afraid of, every aspect of army firearm training is based around fearing what a gun can do, and to be honest, the kid's allowed to be afraid of them. Having a gun pointed at you while a firefight breaks out around you could easily cause such a phobia, but I didn't want the kid to be crippled by the fear. A gun was a tool, like a screwdriver, a hammer and, if an ex or two were to be believed: me, but unless you were a blond haired deity-hunk staring in five blockbuster movies, a gun could cause a lot more damage than a hammer.

Eventually the conversation came to an end and I walked Puzo to the door. She gave me another kiss as she exited. "She can really drill a person. Does your sister want a job as an interrogator, 'cause Gitmo's hiring?"

I walked back to the living room and found the glaring eyes of Annie waiting for me. "So you're living with a woman and didn't tell me?"

It got worse before it got better.

After an hour of trying to explain my *it's complicated* Facebook-relationship status, Dave finally came to my rescue and said it was time to go. God bless the man. He is a saint and deserves none of the bad things that life could throw at him. I only wish the man happiness; I still plan on making his life a living hell by spoiling his kids, but that's neither here nor there.

With the apartment back to myself, I plopped myself down before my computer and started research. I had a case, one that required attention and one that would pay double if I met a deadline. I wanted double. Be it pay, beers, women, or Ds, I always want double.

When I got my mysterious brown package in the

mail, it came with a PI license, business papers, and dozens of other government forms and payroll methods. I also received a list of contacts to call if I need help or assistance. The list was vast and had contacts for people who specialized in everything from medical information to legal matters, from automotive questions and services to even a pilot for hire who I could call on in a pinch. My friend Hotwire, a morally challenged hacker for hire and proven ally, was part of this list. He'd proven to be the most useful person, followed shortly by the lawyer, on that list, but as I scrolled down the list on my phone, I passed his name and landed on Mia Roan. Mia was a young graduate just out of school. She graduated school with Bachelor of Economics and a minor in journalism. She wanted to be, obviously, a business journalist for any major new media, and she was talented, and hot enough, to do it. She wanted to be HBO's Sloan Sabbith -- just real and not fictional. In short, she was brilliant and was climbing the ranks in the news world. She was also broke beyond belief, thanks to student loans, and loved any work I threw her. I tapped her number and listened as the phone rang.

"Hello, Benedict," she sang into the other end. "What have you got for me?"

"It's Ben," I corrected her.

"Not going to happen, you know this," she laughed. "Every time I hear your name, I picture Mr. Cumberbatch. So I'm going with that."

My full name used to be weird enough that nobody would ever call me it. Then *that* show had to become popular. Damn *that* show. It ruined a horrible name.

"I'm on a fact finding mission and I need your mind," I said as I turned on the speakerphone. "I'm emailing you the files I have. This pays double if we can solve this in a week."

"I am more than just my mind. When will guys learn that woman want to be known for their bodies as well as their minds? Guys are so rude," she joked. "Sweet mother of loveliness, Benedict; you're working for Skit-Tech, this is amazing. Drop off my resume, will ya?"

I wasn't entirely sure if she was joking or not.

"The mysterious stock jump, I had caught wind of this. I even passed it up to my editor, but so far there's nothing to write about." Mia was a researcher for the business division of some news channel. I could never remember *which* channel it was she worked for, but they were on the air 24/7 and had dozens of letters in their name. She was trudging away in the production side, paying her dues, until she could make the jump to screen time and really shine. "Right now it's all speculation."

"I don't have to worry about facts as much as you do right now," I admitted. "I'm allowed to thrive on speculation at the moment. What do you got for me?"

"Occam's Razor: Everybody is expecting the Scratch-Pad and Sketchbook to fail and they want to bet on the other team."

"That's what I suggested."

"But that doesn't explain the board wide 17.36% jump. Yeah, I get that." She hummed to herself. Back in basic, I had a sergeant who said that when woman hummed to herself it meant one thing. The rest of the joke was highly inappropriate and I won't repeat it. "Okay, top of my head isn't coming up with anything else besides insider trading and plots to bad action movies probably starring Ben Affleck."

She hummed again as she read the file. My sergeant's joke returned to my mind's forefront. It was very inappropriate. Seriously, do not let your work's HR officer hear you say this joke. "Wow, your file goes a lot further then my own research had. Standard deal?"

"Yep." The standard deal between Mia and me was simple. I'd hire her for work, basic stuff mostly but the business world always seemed beyond me. If she was researching anything for a story that was relevant to me she'd let me know, and if I had anything she could use I'd give her a holler. I avoided NDA lawsuits because she worked for SRG as a freelancer and she avoided getting in trouble at work because I was a layabout and therefore nobody important.

"I'm going to start diving into parent companies and subsidiaries. See what those come up with," she explained, "If I were you Benedict, and with my stunning body it would be slightly awkward, I would start investigating Skit-Tech to see if there's a leak or an error with the product that hasn't been released; something crippling."

"You had to throw in the crippling when talking to me." She ignored me and resumed humming. "You think somebody is selling inside trading intel to skit-tech's rivals?"

"That would be it, Mr. Detective."

I thanked Mia and hung up. I eagerly typed on my laptop and drew up a large email. I typed in Hotwire's email and fired it off. I grabbed my phone and scrolled to his name. I tapped the screen and quickly fired him off a text.

Me: Sent you an email. Can you see if anybody in Skit-Tech's mobile division has been getting any banking irregularities? Extra $$ if we find it by week's end.
Hotwire: Will do. Talk soon.

When my life exploded during the Robby kidnapping, Hotwire was there for me. He was my support, both tech wise and other, and went above and beyond in the effort to find Robby. He even risked his own life in the process, but since then he'd become different. His texts were always short and sweet, to the point, while his emails were lengthy. Hotwire was always a security expert, mainly at cracking said security, but since then he'd become paranoid. His emails came with obscene amount encryption and were bounced through literally thousands (again: classic definition not the new one) of routers and IPs before it found its way to me. I've tried asking him what happened, why he went AWOL for a while during the investigation, but he never answered me. He never explained, but whatever happened he was now doing his best to hide from someone.

I pushed the thought out of my mind and scrolled down my contact list. I clicked on the name Jack and typed off a text.

> **Me**: Need to cancel today's session. Work.
> **Jack**: Wussy.

Jack was my other trainer. He was re-teaching me how to fight. It was more than learning how to throw a punch or kick, it was also how to use the cane as a weapon and how to shift my weight so my bum leg didn't hinder me as much. Jack was a brilliant fighter and a great teacher. He was also an asshole. He was the kind of guy you assumed had a rough exterior and had a heart of gold beneath it, but the longer you spent with him the harder it was to get past that exterior. The chances were that he could have just been an asshole through and through. It was a scary thought.

I ignored my fear and went to work. If I was going to pretend to be a private dick, I had to at least act like one. I grabbed my remote and clicked on the TV. I'm the kind of detective who needs noise in the background.

"We live in a time where our past procedures are no longer enough." I glanced at the unfamiliar face. The caption said Theodore A. Koplan, MD MPH - Director, Centers for Disease Control and Prevention but what confused me the most was why my TV was on CNN? I didn't even know my TV could go on CNN. Was Puzo watching CNN -- on my TV? "We've seen outbreaks that pop up by surprise and with such a speed that it makes it difficult to form a timely response. The Guinea Ebola outbreak took the world by surprise, and that's just one example.

"The CDC is always evolving to match the evolution of the threat. The time has come to expand again. I am pleased to announce our latest upcoming initiative: The Centers for Disease Control and Prevention's Advanced Versatile Emergency Response and Tactics Team.

"The CDC's AVERT team will be compromised of highly trained military professionals, each highly skilled and highly vetted individuals, that will be able to be secure an outbreak with military precision and begin to address the situation, access the threat and even take actions to resolve the situation.

"The advantages to a military approach to this team will help eliminate the chance of errors and accidental contamination as we sadly saw World Health Organization members suffer in the latest Ebola outbreak. We are choosing not to draw from the US armed forces; we need a team that can operate on US soil on a moment's notice. Instead we will be enlisting the service of a private military company. Our decision as to which company will be released at a further date. Regardless of which PMC is chosen, each member will undergo rigorous training to make sure that pr--"

And I'm bored. With a couple taps, I flip over to the All Action Super Violence Channel. Imagine an entire TV channel that never really evolved past the actions movies of the 80s and 90s. It is exactly as amazing as it sounds. "Welcome to the all day Sylvester Stallone Marathon!"

My jaw dropped. This was TV heaven. I reluctantly changed channels. There was no way I'd get any work done if that was playing. I left my TV on the Comedy Central and went to work. I spent the next hour and half surfing on my laptop as I looked for rumours concerning Skit-Tech, minus the break or two I took for to look up Stallone film rumours, and found myself keeping two windows open on my browser. One was for the economist and business pages that I read and the other was for an online idiot's guide to business that I was using to look up the business words I didn't understand. There were a lot of words that I didn't understand.

The *Rocky* theme song pulled my attention and I scooped up my phone. Unknown Caller. I raised an eyebrow -- a weird gesture 'cause I was alone -- and tapped the screen to answer it.

"Hello, Specialist Thompson: Let's play a game," a mysterious voice said over the phone. I didn't recognize the voice. It was male and had a hint of an accent, one I couldn't place.

"Who is this?"

"If you answer my questions, I will tell you about me. First Question: What was Stallone forced to sell in order to survive before making *Rocky*?"

"His pet dog. Who is this?" I repeated.

"I am the man who will torment you. I am your charismatic villain. Next question: In a fight how many rounds would John Cena last against an Irish man?"

How many rounds? What the hell? Who was this guy and why was he bugging me at home? I'll admit that if this was a telemarketer, then they had really stepped up their procedures. Rounds: oh duh. "*Twelve Rounds*. What's with movie trivia for amateurs?"

"It feels very Hollywood, doesn't it? Chilling phone calls, mysterious voices, and quirky little trivia games that are annoying but not too difficult. It just makes my movie watching nerves tingle."

"Seriously, I'm not buying anything and I am quite content with my long distance service," I snapped. "Who is this?"

"I am the person who hates you, Benedict. I loathe you for what you did to me."

"Only my mom, and other women, call me Benedict," I corrected. "And your voice isn't deep enough to be my mother's. Please, call me Ben." There are two things about me that aren't immediately obvious. One is that when I'm scared or confused or bored, I tend to resort to sarcasm and bad humour as a defense mechanism. The other is I am so dead when my mother finds out what I just said about her.

"Ben it is then. Ben, I am the guy who is going to make your life a living hell."

"You're too late. An IED did that for me and women have finished the job. So just do me a favour and kill me if that's your end game. This will make a shitty movie if I don't try."

"I'm not going to kill you Ben, I want you alive. I want you to suffer like I do," he scoffed. "I'll see you at Lyon

Estates." And with that, the line went dead. I looked at my phone with blank look at my face. If that wasn't my mom, or an ex-girlfriend, then I had no freaking clue who the hell that was.

A knock on my door pulled my attention away from my phone and sent a small chill down my spine. I didn't know that many people, most of which had already been here, and secondly whoever this person was they knocked. My friends are, apparently, incapable of doing that. I limped to the front door and slowly opened the door.

I nearly shat myself when I glanced outside.

Standing in my doorway was Greg Hazeltine.

Chapter 04
I Loved *Lost* But That Show Was
Bat-Crap Crazier Than I Am

For a long time I'd grown up hating Greg Hazeltine. He was the deadbeat who had seduced Annie, knocked her up, then bolted, never to be seen again. I hated him and so did Annie, our parents and all of our friends. He just left and it was years before I saw him again. He briefly showed up once in my past, weeks after I returned from Iraq, and he gave me my cane. As quickly as he showed up, he vanished.

"What do you want, Greg?"

"It's Jason and I need your help, Ben." When Robby went missing and I was up to my knees in conspiracy and confusion, Greg reappeared dressed to the nines in a fancy suit and using his real name: Jason Daggett. I learned a lot about his side of the Annie-Greg story. I wouldn't call it the truth, Greg and I were far from that, but I would call it less-lies. "Can I come in?"

I rolled my eyes and let him in. Jason had brown hair, cut short, blue eyes and a solid chin. He wore a blue pinstriped tie, a sky blue shirt, and a blue tie with bluer spots on it. Part of me prayed he lived in a blue house with a blue window and a blue corvette and everything was blue for him. Jason stepped inside carrying with him a small shoebox.

"Robby was just here a couple hours ago."

"How's my so-" he paused. "How's the boy?"

"Good. A little worse for wear after everything that happened, but he's getting over it." I limped back to the living room and reached for the liquor cabinet and pull out some vodka. "Drink."

"Please."

"That wasn't an offer. So what's wrong, Jason?" I asked as I poured two shots and handed him one.

"Croxallé would like to hire you as a freelance security agent."

I nearly choked on my booze, the burn amplifying as it went down.

"Yeah, right," I hacked. "And Santa wants a crippled man like me to deliver presents."

"Ben, I'm serious. Lives are in danger and I need your help."

Croxallé was your stereotypical evil medical corporation. On the surface they seemed happy and nice, donating monthly to medical charities like the fight against cancer, AIDS and funding the battle against every illness like a medical arms dealer's, but the moment you followed the white rabbit down the rabbit hole was the moment the truth started to reveal itself. Croxallé had but one major goal in mind, to create superpowers in humans.

Under the disguise of obstetricians and paediatricians, they implanted the scientific seeds that would hopefully grow into full-fledged meta-human powers. Then they waited, checking up on the kids, first through legitimate means and when all other methods failed, illegal ones. But at the end of the day, all the children returned home safe to their parents with all their medical bills paid. Jason was their chief of security and to make matters worse he was a full-blown Chris Evans telekinetic.

"Look, Jason," I said sincerely, "You're a dangerous man and I owe you one for what you did to help Robby and Annie, but please don't kill me when I tell you to shove it."

"Ben..."

"Croxallé is evil, you know it and I know it, but whatever trouble your company is in, I know it has the resources to get out of it."

Jason stared at me. He put the shoebox on the center of my kitchen island and reached into his suit and pulled out five bills, each of which proudly displayed a 1 and two 0s. He dropped them on the counter. "There was a murder and all we found at the crime scene was this item. I need you to touch this item and see it--"

"Visionize it," I corrected out of spite.

He raised his eyebrow. " --and visionize it. Tell me what you see. It may give us a hint. I'll give you five hundred dollars for two minutes of work."

Five hundred dollars for two minutes work. Hookers had to work a full fifty-eight minutes longer to earn that much -- less if they squeezed the clock -- and they normally needed mouthwash after. With a sigh, I nodded and took off my gloves. Jason opened the box and carefully withdrew its contents. It was a pair of gunmetal Ray-Ban sunglasses with black arms and green tinted lenses. They were old, poorly taken care of, but still useable. He placed it on the island's countertop and looked at me.

"These are nice shades. I used a pair like this when I was in Iraq." I glanced at Jason, expecting a response, but got nothing in return. With a deep breath, I gently, and carefully, traced my fingers across the lenses. A familiar shiver shot up my back and my eyes began to twitch as the present day faded away.

The first sense to kick in was touch, the feeling of a metal doorknob. The funny part was I could feel it myself. It was unusual for me to *feel* anything in a vision because it was never me in a vision.

This time it was. I was watching myself in my own vision. This was a rarity for me. The only time it happened was when my couch or TV remote decided to trigger a vision and sent me into an endless spiral of vision that showed nothing more than me watching TV. It was depressing at best.

Yet in my current vision I was opening a building

door and entering a meeting room. I glanced around and saw the room filled with faces I knew and recognized: Sergeant Major Hector Blane, Specialist Andy Clement and Corporal Leo Anderson. Together with Specialist Benedict Thompson -- me -- we made up Odin Squad. We were a unit of the US Army Rangers that had proven to be a little more resilient and adaptable then others. We got mission that best suited those traits.

"Am I last one here?" I asked, hoping it wasn't true. Clement just nodded. "Crap."

There was a joke within Odin Squad that said only those that came prepared got to sit. So despite there being way more chairs then needed, I had to stand. I reluctantly stood there, leaning on the wall like a bad-ass when the door re-opened and in walked a civilian woman. Everybody jumped to their feet.

"Gentlemen. My name is Zoey Harris. Please be seat-ed."

Zoey.

She was stunning. She was only a couple years older than I was and had a body that I would kill for. I'm serious, if I had her body I would never pay for drinks ever again. She was an athletic brunette and it showed on every inch of her skin. Her body was *tight* and not just the damn *you be hot girl* kind of tight but the *damn your body is a lean mean piece of work* kind of tight. She reminded me of Michelle Rodriguez -- Vin Diesel's woman in *The Fast and the Furious*.

She looked at each of us with a single glance, one that took in every detail, and moved around the room handing out folders. She paused at me.

"We all have sunglasses, Mr. Thompson," she said smugly. "No need to show off yours indoors. Please remove them."

"Oh, we all have them," I said with a cocky grin as I removed them. "The only difference between you and I is that I make them look good."

She took a glance at my naked eyes and snickered.

"Oh, I am even happier with your codename choice." I glanced down at the folder.

Name:	Specialist Benedict Thompson
Codename:	Bright Eyes.

Well, crap.

The vision ended and reality returned. I glanced down at Jason's shades. I didn't use a pair like that in Iraq; I used *that* exact pair. Those were *my glasses* and they were found at a murder scene.

"What the hell, Jason?" I muttered. I felt it instantly, the quickening of my pulse, the shake in my arms, my fingers clamping together into a fist so tight that it sent waves of pain throughout my body and worst of all I felt my chest heaving, desperately trying to pull in air. I used to be a soldier supreme, a poster boy for the army, but soldiering and I parted on very poor terms. It was like leaving a job without giving two weeks notice except instead of a bad letter of recommendation I got a leg full of shrapnel, a medical pension and a horrifyingly strong case of the crazies. So seeing this aspect of my past, me stomping around like Chris Evans minus the shield, did little but bring up every fear, anxious feeling and throw me into a full-blown panic attack.

I gasped for air, any air, but found far less the recommended dose available. My leg throbbed, every pain I'd ever suffered through manifested as one violent phantom pain, and then buckled, taking me with it. I hit my hardwood floor with a thud, and the benefits of layering my floor with a carpet, or a trampoline, suddenly became clear.

"Ben!" Jason rushed over and grabbed my shoulder. He lifted me up slowly. "Breathe, man, breathe."

I pushed him away and fell back to the floor, landing on my ass with a thud. "What the hell, Jason?" I repeated, louder this time. "Seriously, what the hell?"

"What did you see, Ben?" he begged. "Tell me."

Then it hit me. He didn't know what I saw, the look

on his face, the concern and confusion, put it all into perspective. He had no clue what was going on.

"I saw Iraq!" I yelled. "I saw myself in a meeting planning for a mission. I saw myself use those shades to look good and block out the sun. Those shades are *my sunglasses*!"

Jason stared at me. I kept yelling, "How the hell did you get my shades?"

"It was at a crime scene."

"Bullshit! How do my glasses end up in a crime scene stateside?"

Silence filled my apartment. I'd hit my cursing quota for the day and needed to stop. If I cursed anymore, I'd lose PG-13 rating and end up with a hard R. Then again, if anybody was closely watching what I was doing in my bedroom I'd surely end up with a NC-17; a sad, depressing, crippled NC-17.

"I need your help, Ben," Jason explained. "Something weird's going on and I need your help. I need you to see -- visionize -- what I cannot."

I looked up at him with open eyes. Nobody likes war, nobody sane at least, and for those who go over all you can do is fight for your country and pray to god you come home more or less intact. Nobody comes home the same person they were, it just doesn't happen, but you try your best to come home looking and acting like somebody your friends and family recognize. I didn't.

I was king shit before I left, and worse of all I knew it. I came back a shell of what I once was. I didn't look the same -- I was less pretty and more haggard -- I didn't walk the same -- I barely walked at all -- and I didn't act the same. The docs called it posttraumatic stress disorder or PTSD for short. I called it broken.

Every soldier, sailor, airman or whatnot deals with PTSD differently. Some find solace and comfort by talking about it, other drink the pain away, some find salvation by turning to religion and others surrounded themselves with the love of friends and family. None of those cures worked for me. Talking about my past only made me anxious, drinking the pain away only made me drunk and sick the next morning, also my pension isn't big enough to support a drinking habit, religion seemed an unlikely route for a psychic and I was too ashamed of myself to find comfort in family. I chose another route. I found comfort in TV.

Dealing with PTSD is hard enough when you're a mundane person, one of the blessed normal populace, but when you're a psychic, when everything you touch brings up a horrific vision of your past, PTSD becomes worse. A psychic needs a method to withdraw from the world, both present and past, and TV became that method. I was never a big watcher of TV growing up, save for a western. It wasn't that I didn't like the medium, I loved the big screens and I adored the small, I just never had the time. I was too busy working and womanizing, hanging out and being active. I mean I'd always make time for a high-octane action film, what male wouldn't, but films and TV just weren't that important to me.

When everything I once had slipped through my grasp, and my fingers' touch became a personal torture device, I turned to TV. Life was so much simpler there. Everybody was handsome, everybody was funny and a grievous injury was only ever a flesh wound. You could be caught in an exploding car and in a week's time you'd be back to new, ready for some other adventure. A mystery could be solved in forty-five minutes, or, god forbid, an hour and half: without commercials, the good guys always won and life was interesting. In TV-Land a teacher with cancer can become a drug kingpin, a MLB pitcher can own a bar and fall in love with two women, a FBI agent can hunt aliens and an uncharted island could end up being purgatory and the source of all good in the world – or a time traveling, location hopping, confusing plot device.

I'll be honest: I loved *Lost*, but that show was bat-crap crazier than I am.

My problems never seemed that important compared to movies. Who really cares about a broken soldier when John

McClain has to save Washington, DC from hackers, or Stallone has to stop Van Damme from stealing nukes and revitalizing his acting career? Who wants to read about a cripple ex-soldier when they can watch Arnie defend a small town or Stallone prove he can still box at sixty? Who wants to listen to me suffer when they can see Ford battle Oldman in a plane or Stallone have an axe fight with Conan the Barbarian? I may have developed weird feelings for Mr. Stallone.

The only problem with using TV as an escape was I found myself retreating further and further from the world and deeper into my own imitation of depression-meet-hobo-hermit. The worst part of anybody's life is when they realize they hate what they've become, but can't do anything to change it. I was a sad sack of crap until I got a chance to look myself in the face, stare into the hollowed eyes I possessed, and literally murder myself. I changed that day, for the better I hoped, and had even given that *surround yourself with loving friends and family* method a go -- and it was helping -- but despite the progress I was making, anything that brought me back to Iraq still made me uneasy.

Jason stared down at me, not knowing what to say. I looked around my living room and pictured all the items that had once caused me grief: the boots with foreign sand still trapped within, the issued combat shirt that had seen more than I ever had and the expensive shades that earned their worth in the first thirteen seconds of touching down. Each of these items once caused great pain in their visions, showing me horrors of my deployment, but much like everything else in my apartment they too had become psychicly numb. I glanced at my bedroom door. There was still one remaining item in my home that I feared, one I dared not touch.

"Fine," I muttered, as I began the ungainly climb to my feet. "Let's do this thing. Where are we heading?"

"Thank you," Jason said as he stood up. "We're heading to a pair of upscale hotels, Wilmont Towers and Lyon Estates."

Chapter 05
I Used a Lot of Big Words

The drive to a crime scene is always unsettling. You never know what to expect. Will it be gruesome like something from *Hannibal* or will it be quirky and funny like from *Castle*? Will I stare down at the dead candy maker, slide on a pair of shades and say something dumb like *well at least he beat diabetes?* For clarification's sake, I wasn't going to ever say those words -- out loud. Add into the mix that I'd received a mysterious call predicting that I'd be coming here and that I was being driven there by the man I'd long thought as the deadbeat father of Robby, and it was very unsettling.

For ten years I hated this man for running out on Annie and unborn Robby, and rightfully so, but six months ago, when he showed out of the blue to save the day during an intense firefight, I learned more about him.

Jason Daggett worked for Croxallé and before that he worked for a company called KyroCorp. KyroCorp was a medical company that was working on a method to stimulate something called the Lycotta gene in order to produce superpowers. As it was explained to me, in very, very simple terms, genes are small things in each of us that effect what we will become.

You, however, probably already knew that. I thought jeans were pants. Who knew?

The Lycotta gene is a heredity gene that when properly treated, by natural means or external coercion, can alter a human body to produce meta-human abilities. The gene exists in nearly every human in varying amounts. Most people have so little that it does nothing but give you the occasional deja-vu. Other people have tons of it. My family apparently craps the stuff. Under the right condition, the gene can produce powers on its own, like surviving an IED detonating under your Humvee (I wouldn't suggest that method), but it can also be forced through experiments. The results were unpredictable at best and only one true fact was known, the more Lycotta gene you had in you, the better chances you had of pulling off the Clark Kent impression. KyroCorp, through experiments and controlled breeding, had been trying to produce powers for a decade. They called it Project: Canaan. So when they found out about my family, and our Lycotta filled defecation, they sent in their own fertilizer producing machine: Jason Daggett.

Jason admitted to me it was the hardest thing he ever had to do. He was ordered to take the name Greg Hazeltine, seduce Annie and produce a child. Apparently aside from crapping Lycotta, the Thompson line is also pretty damn good at shilling out the good stuff. I don't know what my sister did to him in bed, or let him do to her, but apparently Jason fell head over heels in love with her and didn't want to leave. I don't know much about KyroCorp, I do know *some* things about Croxallé, but whatever it was these companies really did, they scared and hurt Greg/Jason enough to ignore his emotions and run back to them like a Hallmark daytime movie.

I need to stop and point out a very heinous issue. In telling you all this, I just had to picture my sister doing really, *really* nasty sex stuff. That's not cool. That image will not go away. And when I say nasty, I mean *nasty*. We're talking *lonely-man-at-his-computer-all-day-long-while-pinning-for-his-physio-therapist-and-decides-to-explore-the-really-hidden-disturbing-stuff-on-the-internet* nasty. Thanks for that. Really.

I also like to point out that in that explanation I used a lot of big words, most of which I did not know the meaning of six month ago. Yay me!

There was only one thing that made this drive awesome and that was Jason's kick-ass car. It was a 1971 Chevy Chevelle SS. It was cherry red with black stripes down the hood. It had black and red leather seats, and every inch of this car just had me dripping. I felt like the girl that that Nickleback song *Animals*. That was a weird reference because of her actions in that song. Look it up. It'll put an *interesting* image in your mind.

Did I just create Ben/Jason slash fiction? Do people care enough about me to even *write* Ben/Jason slash fiction? Do I get royalty checks for slash fiction? Probably not.

"Robby's seems to be bouncing back," I said, slowly answering the question that Jason couldn't ask. I eyed Jason as I said this, catching the faintest hint of a smile forming as I did. "He's a tough kid."

"He gets that from Annie," Jason said as he slowed the car down to take a corner. "She always was the tougher of the two of us."

"I don't know if I really *should* ask this," I started, "but what was it like, dating my sister?"

Jason didn't answer. He just drove. I tried to read his face, to pull from it any details I could, but I didn't get much. There was, in my opinion, a hint of a forlorn look. The car came to a halt and Jason looked over at me. "We're here."

Climbing out of his car, I looked at our location and frowned. We were at a hotel. Crap.

Two men, dressed in black suits with shade covering their eyes, approached. They looked nearly identical, dark hair, built frame and the mile long stare.

"Building's secure," the first said quickly. I called him Humpty.

"We've got an hour tops before the law returns," the second finished. I nicknamed him Dumpty.

"Good." Jason tried to introduce them to me, but their names flew in one ear and out the other. My brain had already named them and nothing, not even their actual names, would replace that in my mind. "Where do you want to start, the victim's room or the killer's?"

I looked up at the fifteen story hotel and admired the building. It was art, a glass sculpture meant to be admired. This hotel, the Wilmont Towers, was the richest of the rich in the hotel world. Whoever died in here made a crap load more than I did. I looked across the street at its competition, the Lyon Estates, a building as epic as the one before it. If the Wilmont Towers was suppose to the be building equivalent of the David, penis and all, then the Lyon Estates was the Venus de Milo, with glimmering breast and no hand for to cover them with.

"Let's start with the dead guy," I reluctantly muttered as I carefully placed my Stetson upon my head. "Let's get this over with."

In my touchy-touchy world nothing has proven to be the bane of my existence more so then a hotel or a motel. Everything I touch tells a story. Some of them are nice, some are funny, some are naughty and others are disgusting. Rented rooms are disgusting.

People treat hotels like crap. When you don't have to clean up after yourself you lose all respect for the place. When my powers first kicked in, I expected bathrooms to be the worst. I was mistaken. The things I've seen people do in a washroom, from my visions -- I need to add that in -- are nothing compared to what I've envisioned people doing in a hotel room. Hell, in some motels I've seen people use the room *as a* washroom.

My powers, as I've learned, are heavily based around emotions. The stronger you feel about something, the more likely it is I'll see it. So if you feel really sad while you cook your pancakes in the morning, chances are when I break into your house and touch your frying pan, I'll see you cooking in your underwear moping around. A hotel room is filled with emotion, from the regret of being away from the ones you love, to the excitement of a vacation or even the lust/regret you feel as you cheat on your husband while sleeping with that hot guy from the band. It affects the universe, it affects the room and it affects my visions. So seriously, stop feeling stuff.

Jason, with Humpty and Dumpty close behind, escorted me into the hotel lobby and handed me his phone. I glanced at the screen and stared at an unfamiliar face. "The victim's name is Giuliani Continente. He was the CEO of Leti-Wind Pharmaceuticals. He's very rich, very powerful, a well-known womanizer and just ended marriage number four. While he's a successful business icon, he's also viewed as a modern-day Tony Stark."

"He's popular for being a drinker and womanizer."

"Exactly."

"What killed him?"

"Sniper shot to the heart." Oh great, the room was going to be messy. "The sniper fired a 7.62×54mmR from a Dragunov sniper rifle. The shot came from across the street from a suite in Lyon Estates."

Jason led me to the elevator, but I pulled away and hobbled to the lobby. The woman behind the counter was surprisingly composed. She dealt with the customers, the guests the hotel had, and reassured each that despite the recent *unpleasantness* that none of their services would be interrupted. I gave her a smile. She gave me a frown.

"Yes?" she asked coldly.

"Hi there," I replied, throwing as much false-cheer into my voice as I could. "I'm investigating the... unpleasantness... and I have a couple questions to ask you."

She gave me a look and scoffed. It was the suit thing. Everybody always wears a suit; I don't. I hate suits.

"I'm sorry, but there's nothing I can help you with." A stonewall; I expected as much. Someone hired to look after the richest people in the city was also hired to make sure people like me didn't go poking around. Too bad for her, I was dead set on poking around. I pulled off my gloves, exposing my flesh to the re-circulated air, and gave her a final smile before placing my hand on the counter.

A shiver and a twitch, and time seemed to freeze for a moment before moving backwards as time rewound before my very eyes. Thousands of people moved before my eyes, one blending into the other until they all became a blur. I gritted my teeth and tried to focus on the case, on the counter, and on the woman running the service desk. My vision went blank, leaving me in darkness, before the lobby faded into view once more. The woman behind the counter, Kathryn Crafer as my vision informed me, smiled as a large man approached. The gentleman was a sports star, some NBA player, and smiled as he approached her.

"How are you today, sir?" Kathryn asked with her trademark professional grin.

"I'm in the mood for some fun," the athlete said as he slipped her a pair of bills. "I want the usual, but I also want something different."

Kathryn pocketed the bills and pulled a small bag filled with a white substance from beneath the counter. She discreetly handed to him. "What else are you looking for, sir?"

"Someone to party with," he replied quickly.

"I can send one of our finest specialists up for you."

"Nah, not like that." He gave her a nervous look.

"We are perfectly discreet here, sir. Nothing will be held against you or leave these walls."

"I'm just looking for some young honeys to party with." He said, "And when I say young, I mean..."

Kathryn's just nodded. "I understand, sir. We have some young ladies on our roster that are big fans of yours," she assured him. "I'll make sure they drop in and say hello."

The vision faded, reality returned and my Swiss-cheese based memory kicked in. Holy statutory rape, Batman! I'd heard about this before. That athlete, whose name still escaped me, was accused of sleeping with a sixteen-year-old girl. The alleged story was that a few girls showed up at his hotel room to meet him, stayed for a bit, and eventually he slept with one of the underage minors. She also reported that she was fed drugs and booze in excessive amounts. Nobody was ever charged because there was no proof, which made it his word against hers, and eventually the story just faded away. It was rumoured that she was paid off by one camp or another.

"I know it's your duty to keep the secrets in this place a secret," I told Kathryn, who had begun to stare at me weirdly. "But it's also my duty to tell the cops and the media that not only do you deal drugs from this desk but that you also arranged for the sixteen year-old girl to be brought to Mr. Famous Athlete's room."

Her eyes went wide. "You have no proof."

"True," I said, using a tone that had far more bravado then actually warranted. "But if I slip this to the newspapers, not only will this hotel's image be ruined further, but you'll be dismissed out of principle. So you and I can both go on doing our duties or we can let things slide and keep everything between us."

She stared at me for another moment, partly out of worry for her position but mostly out of instant loathing for my guts, and eventually caved. "What do you want to know?"

I started with the basics. How often did Giuliani Continente attend this hotel?

"Mr. Continente is a favoured guest. He uses this hotel for business meetings, conferences, parties and even has a standard reservation for a once a week visit."

The more I poked, the more I learned. It turned out that once a week, every week, Giuliani Continente paid for a room, the same room, and spent the entire afternoon within its walls. Nobody came or went; he just enjoyed himself there. He was very paranoid about the entire event and paid to have several specific requirements met. He needed the room swept for listening bugs before hand, by hotel security, and required the room cleaned by a specific member of the cleaning staff, somebody he'd vetted and trusted.

I thanked Kathryn and hobbled over to rejoin Jason. He raised an eye, but I just shrugged. We all boarded the elevator and started our climb upwards. The elevator cabin was spacious, large enough for a dozen people but with mirrors to make the small space feel larger. It had a brass railing that ran alongside the inner-wall. As Jason, Humpty, Dumpty and I rode the device upwards I silently slid my hand back and grazed the brass railing. My back shivered, my eye twitched, and my world faded away. Again I was bombarded by an endless assault of images but as I focused, picturing only Giuliani Continente, eventually my plot-driven powers settled on a single scene. It was Giuliani Continente in the elevator cabin, riding it upwards to his penthouse suite, accompanied only by his personal assistant.

Holy Hell, Batman! She. Was. Hot.

This woman was everything I lusted after alone in my room. She was tall and well built, with bouncy blond hair, a stunning rack, firm lips, sultry eyes and stance that just demanded dominance. My favourite part was her legs. They went on for miles and miles, but I loved how they grew up and made an ass out of themselves.

I might have started drooling in the elevator.

With a hungry look, while gently biting her bottom lip, she glanced up at the elevator camera, installed purely for security purposes, reached back and started stroking her boss' crotch through his pants. Instantly his body reacted.

And so did mine.

I released the railing and breathed deep as I tried to compose myself. It turned out Mr. Giuliani Continente was sleeping with his personal assistant, and to be honest I didn't blame him one bit. In a world where people can be famous for drinking like an Irish fish and feasting on an endless parade of hot, beautiful women who want nothing more than meaningless sex, I find that I can't hate a guy for doing what he's known for. I can hate him for not sharing it with me and I can be insanely jealous, but I can't hold it against him. Too many women, it seemed, were willing to hold themselves against him for me to get even close.

The elevator reached the top floor and we all poured out. The three suited men seem to move in the same manner. Jason would step out first, and then Humpty and Dumpty would follow. Humpty would go left while Dumpty went right. Each of Jason's lackeys moved in the same way, short steps while their hands stayed close to their sides. I had guessed they each carried a handgun at their side and by keeping their right hands close, they kept their weapons at the ready. I hobbled out and moved for the door. I reached Giuliani's penthouse door and quietly grasped the doorknob. A shiver and a twitch, and I descended back into the past. Giuliani stood behind Ms. Sexy Personal Assistant as we were before his front door. He stood there, his arms wrapped around her mid-section, his fingers tickling her breasts, as she fiddled with the suite's doorknob with one hand and Giuliani's knob with her other. The door beeped and opened just as Ms. Sexy Personal Assistant heard a gasp. She looked to her left to see an unknown woman, a guest in another top-floor suite, covering her mouth in horror as she saw the lewd display unfold before her. Sexy PA released the door, blew a kiss to horrified woman, tightened her grip on Giuliani's crotch and then used it to pull him inwards.

The vision faded as did my breath. Damn, I needed a cold shower. I stepped into the room and looked around. The suite reminded me of the *Hangover*, before they trashed the room, and was just as nice. It was a massive room with three smaller rooms inside of it and by quick glance I could instantly tell it was nearly thirty-seven times larger than my apartment. While saying thirty-seven times suddenly seemed excessive, saying three times larger seemed right on the ball. I expected to see a body, but it had already been removed by the coroner, leaving in its place a weird smell, several blood stained carpets, and a room that was never going to be rented again. I hobbled to the wall made up almost entirely of glass windows. The snippy winter air poured in through a small bullet hole.

I glanced at the wall and reached for it. There is a saying that goes *if these walls could talk*. With psychometry they can, my problem is getting them to shut the hell up. That being said, I was excited to see what my powers showed me next. I had deduced that Giuliani Continente had been using this room for an affair (I am a detective after all) and had been so careful as to not let wife one through four, while they were still the wives, find out. I'd also just visionized Ms. Sexy PA actively groping and publically fondling her boss' no-no parts. I was excited, to say the least, to see what Ms. Sexy PA looked like naked and with her ankles behind her head.

With the eagerness of a fifteen year-old boy who realized that with his psychic powers he could see boobs, not the greatest metaphor I'll grant you, I pressed my palm against the wall and waited for boobs.

Boobs!

A shiver, a twitch, and I saw Ms. PA stepping into the suite. The moment her foot crossed the threshold, her entire demeanour changed. She slouched slightly, released her boss' crotch, and plopped herself down into the nearest chair and kicked off her heals. Seconds later, a phone appeared in her hand and tablet on her lap. Her fingers and lips moved like blurs as she fired off three emails and made one phone call. Ms. Sexy PA was actually a pretty damn good PA.

Giuliani Continente walked into the bedroom portion of the suite and found a young Latino man, in his mid twenties, putting the finishing touches on the bed. "Hello, Mr. Continente. I am just finishing the bed. Do you need anything else?"

"Yeah, you." Giuliani took the Latino cleaner into his arms and passionately kissed the man. The cleaner didn't pull away or act surprised, instead he pushed himself in closer and kissed the CEO back, harder. The made out for only seconds before their hands began to fumble with the others clothes and both fell to the bed in a passionate embrace.

With a gasp of surprise, which led to a choking cough, I pulled away from the wall in shock. Giuliani Continente wasn't boinking Ms. Sexy Personal Assistant; he was boinking Latino cleaner boy.

Didn't see that one coming.

I mean good for Giuliani Continente, expressing himself in whatever way he felt comfortable; I'm not judging, it just caught me by surprise. Yet the more I thought about it, the more I realized the hints were all there. He was a famous playboy-womanzier so being caught with a man would destroy his image. Any regular affair and he'd just be applauded for it. The demand for the same cleaning staff wasn't because he was paranoid, it was because that was who he was sticking it to -- or receiving it from. I didn't watch long enough to decipher the batting order.

Man, I am a horrible detective.

Without a body to touch, or the walls saying anything useful, I walked over to the window and gave it a gentle touch. My present faded away and the past returned. Giuliani and his Latino cleaning man had just finished, wrapping up their encore in the shower, and they chatted briefly as each dressed.

"You know I love spending time with you," Giuliani began, "but I'd like to see more of you."

The Latino man just shook his head. "Must we go over this again?"

Giuliani let out a loud sigh and climbed off the bed, rising to his feet. "I hate that we argue about this every time." He exited the bedroom and moved for the lounge, passing before the massive window. "Every single ti-"

Giuliani's body flew backward as a small hole formed in both the window and the man. Then there was silence.

Reality returned, accompanied by a wave of heartrending emotions. When you see the innermost moments of a person, or events that will be their last, you tend to get emotional. Visions are strong and by the very nature of the power they come with an empathic lining. Only the heartless could see what I saw and be dry in the eyes. That being said, I couldn't be seen shedding a tear or two. Crying showed that I had emotions and as we all know emotions are ovary dependent. So in order to disguise my random burst of tears, I relied on a subtle technique I had mastered years ago.

I faked a coughing fit.

A regular person coughs and it seems normal, watch a cane-bound gentlemen go into a coughing fit and people suddenly take notice. The best part is they notice you coughing, not you crying like a little girl. While I faked my sudden and repetitively occurring reflex, often used to clear the large breathing passages from secretions, irritants, foreign particles and microbes, I shot Jason a glance. He stood by Humpty and Dumpty and listened carefully as each whispered something to him. I wanted to believe that this was the corporate world's version of the telephone game but to be honest that seemed silly. What corporate company would play telephone when *duck, duck, goose* seemed the superior choice?

Did I trust Jason Daggett? Not really.

Did I trust Croxallé? Not as far as I could walk (which, by the way, isn't very far at all).

I knew Jason was keeping stuff from me, I'd be a big idiot to believe otherwise, but the questions were what exactly was he keeping from me and was it relevant to this case? I had the ability to find out, but did I really want to?

For most normal people a decision like this would end up in an internal debate that culminated in a pros and cons list. I, however, am Benedict Thompson. I am far from normal. My internal debate took place as an epic wrestling match between curiosity and reason.

Entering the ring was the most electrifying emotion in sports entertainment. Can you smeeeeeell what the Curiosity is cooking? Curiosity sauntered to the ring, dressed in black shorts with a raised eyebrow and waved his arm high into the air pulling with it the roar of the crowd.

He was followed by the challenger who was dressed in a bandana and with a kick-ass beard. The challenger climbed into the ring, walked to the center and ripped open his shirt to the deafening cheers proving that even to this day Reason-Mania was still running wild.

The two titans circled slowly, waiting for the go ahead, waiting for the bell. At the sound of the ding, they leapt at one another and locked arms in a grapple.

Jason came to me, he needs my help. If there was something important, he'd tell me.

Reason hoisted Curiosity into the air and tossed him back. Curiosity hit the mat hard and stumbled downwards. With a groan, he climbed back to his feet.

He wouldn't just come to you to lie to you. That'd be insane.

Reason charged forward and slammed his foot square into Curiosity's chest. The black-shorts wrestler doubled over in pain. Reason smirked as he grabbed Curiosity in a front face-lock and fell backwards, forcing the black-shorted wrestler's skull into the mat. Reason leapt to his feet and cheered. He had just pulled off the devastating DDT and the crowd loved it.

I have to trust Jason. He did show up when Robby and I needed him the most.

Reason pulled Curiosity to his feet and whipped him at the ropes. He watched as the black-shorts wrestler bounced off the ring's edge and stumbled back towards him, his arm extended and ready for a cloth-line strike.

But Jason lies for a living.

Curiosity ducked under the arm, regained his footing, and bolted full speed for the opposite end. He bounced off the other set of wires and, with his extra burst of speed, charged at a surprised Reason.

He lied to Annie and abandoned both her and Robby.

Reason turned around just as Curiosity struck, his elbow slamming into the bandanna-wearing wrestler's face. Reason collapsed to the ground. Curiosity stood over the fallen body, hunched slightly, and smirked as he put his hands on his waist. That was a signal. Curiosity's finisher was close at hand.

Jason Daggett worked for Croxallé. He was not to be trusted at all.

Reason climbed back to his feet and turned to fact his opponent, realizing at that moment, a breath too late, what was about to happen. Curiosity grabbed Reason and tucked his head under his opponent's arm. He then reached across Reason's chest and around his neck, and with a powerful fall, slammed the already stunned Reason back-first onto the mat.

It was the Curiosity-Bottom!

Curiosity rolled onto Reason and pinned him with ease. The referee slid beside them and slapped out the count. One, two, three; and it was over. The winner and still the people's champion: Curiosity.

My inner debate made me realize two things. One: that pun-based names like the *Rockbottom* don't work as well when you change your wrestler's name to Curiosity, and two: The Hulk Hogan v. Rock Match at WrestleMania X8 in Toronto, Canada was E.P.I.C.

I grew up on a farm; of course I loved wrestling. I also had that WrestleMania on DVD sitting on my shelf.

I needed Jason to come closer, I had to touch him, but I needed to do it subtly. So I relied on a classic trick I learned years ago. I faked a coughing fit, again. Only this time I dropped to one knee.

When a man forced to walk around with the assistance of a cane starts coughing, people take notice but when said man drops to one knee, and perhaps accidently drops his cane in the process, people suddenly get really concerned. A cane makes me look weak, I know this. I came to this realization a while back. I don't like to seem weak, I was raised to be a guy's guy, but occasionally, and I mean occasionally, it has its perks. So when I started coughing loudly and fell to one knee, my cane dramatically skipping across the floor, people took notice.

Jason was the first reach me. He crossed the floor in no time flat and caught me. "Ben! You okay?"

As his hands caught my arms, he suddenly clued into his mistake. He'd fell into my ruse and he knew it but there was nothing he could do to prevent it. I reached over and touched his suit jacket. It only took the faintest of touches to activate my power and with a shiver and a twitch I fell back into the past.

I was in an office, high up in a skyscraper, and I saw Jason sitting at a desk, feverously typing away on his computer. The door opened and Humpty and Dumpty entered. Jason looked up and frowned. "Anything?"

"No, sir."

"Then we go with Ben." Jason climbed from his chair and approached a metal cabinet. He keyed in a combination and waited as the electronic lock approved. With a beep and a click, the door swung open. Inside the metal cabinet was a small army of handguns. Jason removed two and handed one each to his suited lackeys. "Okay, we go get Ben and see what his visions can tell us."

"What do we tell him?" Humpty asked.

"Do we tell him the truth?" Dumpty finished.

Jason paused as he stared blankly into his cabinet. "No. This was our kill order. He won't believe us."

"What if he finds out?" Humpty asked. "He'll trust you less."

"He is psychic," Dumpty added. "They're good as finding things out."

"Then I'll deal with that as needed." Jason closed the metal door and re-armed the lock. "In the meantime, we are under strict protect orders."

Reality returned. Jason stared down at me but I avoided his gaze. I wasn't sure what to make of my visions. Like most things seen by my third eye, and I don't mean my penis, I was left with more questions than answers.

"Show me where the killer took the shot from."

Chapter 06
I Even Killers Turn Around in an Elevator

Walking in the Lyon Estates made me think I'd taken a wrong turn or that there'd just been a glitch in *The Matrix*. Lyon Estates looked almost identical to Wilmont Towers, an extravagant five star hotel built for the rich and famous. Both had the glimmering appearance of money, the sleek modern look, and the spacious design that screamed lavishness. Even the blonde woman manning the counter was a dead ringer for Ms. Crafer.

"Are you going to talk to the blonde in this hotel?" Jason asked.

I shook my head. "Let's just go to the room."

Humpty led the way, with Dumpty picking up the rear, to the elevator. Jason pulled free his phone and thumbed through the screen. "Reports say that a single male rented the room three days ago. He never checked out; he just vanished."

We paused at the elevator door. Jason held his phone up, instead of handing it to me, and showed me a short video. It showed a man in a suit wearing a black hat standing in the elevator as it climbed upwards. The man, who held a thick briefcase, rocked on the balls of his feet, his face hidden by the brim of his hat. The video told me two important facts. One: he knew where the cameras were and tilted his hat *just* enough to stay hidden. This meant he'd known the layout of the elevator. Two: he wore a trilby hat like it was a fedora.

This meant he was a douche.

For those who don't know the difference, the structures of the two hats are similar but the trilby has a sharper crown and, most importantly, a much narrower brim. To most folk, the distinction is so minor that it's viewed as unimportant, but in the hat-wearing world to call a trilby a fedora is blasphemy. It's like saying Arnold Schwarzenegger starred in *Rocky*, John Wayne starred in *The Good, the Bad and the Ugly,* or Harrison Ford starred in *Die Hard*: pure, unadulterated blasphemy. In the hat-wearing world, knowing what hat you're wearing is just as important as how it looks. Also all other hats are inferior to the Stetson.

I got Jason to replay the video. I squinted as I tried to get any detail I could, to catch what I had already missed. I was trying to pull a Sherlock Holmes moment out of thin air but the truth of the matter is, and always has been, I'm just a shitty detective.

"One more time," I asked. Jason hit the button and restarted it. I watched closely. The man stood in the elevator, alone, his face protected by his hat, and his briefcase in his gloved hands. He didn't speak or move, he just stood there rocking back and forth on the heels of his feet.

The elevator doors opened with a ding. I stepped on, shuffled to the left of the door and turned around. Why does everybody feel the need to face the door in an elevator? Why don't people face the mirrors? I stared at the door, now to my right, and waited for the other three to board. I looked around the spacious cabin, which looked identical to the one I rode in the Towers, and pulled off my glove. I reached back and discreetly touched the brass bar. Our killer could hide from the cameras but he couldn't hide from my visions.

A shiver and a twitch, and I fell back into the past. I found myself, or the omnipotent essence form I took in a vision, in the empty elevator. The door opened and I saw our killer standing on the other side, patiently waiting. I eagerly focused on his face, anticipating the first look that would reveal his identity but instead found… nothing.

As I focused on his face, as I stared through my third-eye, all I saw was a messy blur. It was like that woman who tried to restore a painting and totally botched it. It was like the cosmic paint that made up my killer's face had been smudged.

What the hell?

This wasn't supposed to be possible. While I'll admit I know jack shit about my visions in the grand schemes of things, like whom or what decides what I see, I did know a few things; the most important being that there was no filter or pixilation for faces in a vision. You couldn't be the whistle blower who asked to have his face blurred and his voice changed. If you appeared in a vision, you did so in the cosmic full-monty.

The killer stepped into the elevator alone, stepped to the left of the door and turned around. There he stood, silently rocking, as the cabin climbed the building's height. Part of me wanted to smirk, but it was overpowered by the insane amount of confusion I currently felt. Even killers turn around in an elevator.

Reality returned and I was left with sheer and utter confusion. Someone was able to hide from my vision. This was ground-breaking and frightening at the same time. Was I going to be useless from here on in? Was I going to see less nudity now? Seeing random nudity was one of the very few benefits of being a temporal voyeur. I was stuck in confusion when the most horrifying thought came to mind, more horrifying then the idea of *Stop! Or My Mom Will Shoot 2* (which would be weirder due to Estelle Getty's death). If I was done getting cosmic cheats from the universe, then I was going to have to rely on my skill as a detective to solve cases.

I was screwed; cosmically screwed.

By the way, while it's on my mind, who thought that teaming up Sylvester Stallone with one of the *Golden Girls* for an action movie was a good idea? I mean, what's next? Are we going to get a remake with The Rock and Betty White? Dwayne Johnson stars as Fighter McBad, a disgraced wrestler who wants to join UFC, but in order to do so he needs to train as an MMA fighter. Yet when no other coach will take him under their wing, he has no choice but to train under Betty White, the grandmother of UFC Hall of Famer Ken Shamrock (who we'll pay 10k just to get a cameo).

Actually that idea's not half bad. It's a nice fish out of water movie, very Steve-Martin-Queen-Latifah-You-Got-Me-Straight-Trippin'-Boo type of movie.

I CALL COPYRIGHT!!!

The elevator opened, bringing an end to the most awkward, self-doubt, and tangent-filled elevator ride I'd ever participated in, and the four of us stepped out. Just like in the Towers, Jason stepped out first, than Humpty and Dumpty emerged. Humpty went left while Dumpty went right, each moving in short steps while their hands hovered by their sides. Again I shifted to the left and stepped off the elevator, yet the moment my foot hit the floor, I froze. Something felt wrong. I spun around and stuck out my cane, catching the elevator's sensor, and stopped the doors from closing.

"Ben?" Jason called out my name but his voice fell on deaf ears as I stared into the cabin. Without saying a word, I stepped back on to the elevator, paused in the middle and turned around. I didn't shift or move; I just stood in the middle.

"Ben? You're spacing out," Jason said cautiously as he stepped into the cabin. The moment his foot crossed the elevator's threshold, stepping into the cabin, I instinctively shifted to my right, finding myself standing once again in the same position I did before I disembarked, the same position that my killer stood in. "Ben?"

"Holy crap," I said suddenly. "I'm not horrible at this."

Jason raised an eyebrow.

"Look at your video," I said, snapping my gloveless fingers. "Our trilby-wearing killer steps onto the elevator and shifts to his left and turns around to face the door. That would put him right where I'm standing, to the right of the door."

"So?"

"So," I said as I pushed Jason out, with my gloved hand for courtesy sake, and shifted to the center. "When you're alone in an elevator, you stand here. It's instinct or training or whatever. Whatever feeling inside of you that makes small decisions, like let's watch *Expendables 2* again or pizza would go great with *Expendables 2*, also tells your body to stand in the middle of an elevator. It doesn't even make much sense. You have to do that awkward leaning to hit the button, but you still have the urge, the need, to stand in the middle. Hell, I wouldn't be surprised if it goes back to days when we used to live in caves because apparently everything we do is because we used to live in caves."

"Actually, historians say that humans didn't live in caves," Humpty corrected from the hallway. "Bears lived in caves. We lived in huts."

"Not important!" I yelled back. "So where does our trilby-wearing killer stand when he's alone in an elevator?"

"Wasn't he wearing a fedora?" Dumpty asked.

"No, he was not," I snapped. "He stands to the side. Why? Because he wasn't alone."

Jason glanced down at his phone again and nodded his head slightly. He was thinking about what I'd just said and he was starting to see my way of thinking. My father used to do that same type of nod.

"In this crazy ass world of ours, I'm Anthony Michael Hall and you're Chris Evans. Our killer is Tom Berenger; I'm not too sure who Humpty and Dumpty are yet."

"Humpty and Dumpty?" Oh crap! Did I say that last part out loud? I ignored my blunder and pushed forward.

"But Tom Berenger isn't in that elevator alone," I declared triumphantly. "He's standing there beside Kevin Bacon!"

I exited the elevator with a smug look on my face. Maybe I wasn't such a bad detective at all. I looked up to their faces, expecting admiration and a congratulatory nod, but all I got was three confused faces staring at me.

"Kevin Bacon?" Humpty asked.

"An actor killed Giuliani Continente?" Dumpty asked.

"No, no. Bacon didn't kill him, Berenger did," Humpty corrected. He paused and looked at me once more. "Is Berenger still considered an actor? Why would Berenger kill a CEO?"

"Wait, who am I?" Jason asked.

I hate the moments when I remember, often too late, that not everybody speaks the same language I do. In truth, very few people speak *cripple-soldier-stuck-at-home-so-he-watches-TV-and-movies-all-day-ese*. It's a tough language to learn.

"You are Chris Evans," I began slowly, fully aware how this explanation would make me look. "From the movie *Push*; I'm Anthony Michael Hall from TV's *The Dead Zone*. Our sniper is Tom Berenger, from *Sniper*."

"Makes sense," Humpty added.

"Oh, now I get it." Dumpty interjected.

"And the man in the elevator with our killer, who bee tee dubs I am calling Tom Berenger until I find out who he is, is Kevin Bacon from the movie *Hollow Man*." Again all three stared at me. "Because in *Hollow Man*, Kevin Bacon was invisible."

I hate explaining things. Where was Dave when I needed him? Dave would understand. There's a reason he's my BFF.

"One question, Ben," Jason asked.

"If I have to explain the plot of *Hollow Man*, then I'm out. I quit."

"No, invisible *Footloose*. Got it." Actually that's not a bad movie idea at all. I CALL COPYRIGHT! "So there is an invisible man with our sniper-"

"Tom Berenger," I corrected.

"With Tom Berenger, and that's good and all, but my question is this." Jason paused for a second. "How is this relevant?"

I froze for a second. What a stupid question. Why

would he ask that? It was obviously relevant. I mean now we knew... I mean this gave us a lead to... it helped us find out...

Aw crap!

We entered the suite, one that looked nearly identical to Towers' save for the bloodied carpet and dozens of medical personal, and I looked around. For two competing hotels, they sure looked a great deal alike. This room was posh, hella posh, and cost a crap load to rent. Somebody paid a crap load of money to rent a room so he could kill a man paying another crap load of money to rent another room to secretly guy-bang a member of the cleaner staff. This was the most expensive assassination of all time, period. That ruled out a government kill job. I used to work for the government and they were stingy stooges. There was no way they'd pay for an expense budget this big just to kill a guy.

One suspect down, trillions more to go.

I walked towards the windows and looked at the table and chair that had been set-up in front of it. The killer would have set his rifle on the table, the barrel aimed through the glass and across the street, and sat at the chair, waiting. "Where was my glasses found?"

Jason pointed to the table. "It was lying on the table beside the spent round. The cops got the round before I could get a look at it."

I look back at Jason and frowned. "The cops got here first, right?" He nodded. "So how did you get the glasses?" Jason just shrugged. He wasn't going to tell me. I should have seen that coming.

"Fine." I shook my head. "What did the report say about this room?"

"Not much," Jason said, fishing his phone back out from his pocket. "He ordered room service a couple times, nothing special -- burger and fries -- but aside from that, he never left. He didn't even order any movies or porn or nothing."

I snickered. "What about internet usage?"

"If he used any internet, he didn't do it from the hotel."

I walked to the table and rapped it with my knuckle. All it takes for my powers to activate is my skin touching an object. It doesn't have to be my fingers. It can be any part of my body from my head to my toes. I've learned this several times in different ways. The worst one was when I stepped into a shower at a gym. Elaine suggested I try working out in a gym and I listened to her -- never again. Now you ladies may not have the same problem that us gentlemen do in gyms, I've learned that you have entirely different issues, but a typical men's changing room is filled with naked old men who feel the need to stand like Captain Morgan and show off their wrinkly privates.

You can help the Cap'n make it happen.

So my feet hit the tiles and my powers trigger. So I go from a world of naked old men letting their junk fly like a pirate's black flag to an endless vision of naked old men letting their junks fly. Welcome to hell, thy name is Benedict.

So when I rapped my knuckle against the table, the simple touch was all it took to send me falling back down the rabbit hole. This vision was different. Instead of a single scene or a bombardment of psychic screams what I got was an organized montage of the three days sped up into one two-minute video. If Rocky Balboa can get a montage, why can't my visions?

The montage was boring. My killer, Tom Berenger, just turned on the TV to the basic channels, used his phone a lot, and sat in the chair staring through the Dragunov's scope. He slept on the bed, briefly, and waited. The only change was when he got up to take a dump or when he covered up the gun to answer the door for food.

The montage slowed down when he finally squeezed the trigger. The rifle jerked, a small hole appeared in the glass, and Berenger jumped into action. He dismantled the rifle, returned it to the briefcase, and moved to clean the room. He retrieved the spent cartridge and carefully placed it on the table. Before he pulled closed the briefcase, he withdrew the glasses, *my* glasses, and held it up in the air. It was like he was presenting it to the world or making sure somebody saw him put there. But there was nobody watching him, I should I know because I was watching… holy crap he was making sure *I saw* him put it there.

Now I was really confused; I mean, more so then normal. He closed the briefcase, withdrew a phone, and started dialling. "It's me; job's done. Make sure your men are the CSI on scene. I'm moving for my exit."

My vision ended and I looked around. There were nearly a dozen CSI agents walking around, none of which were Ted Danson or David Caruso, but each seemed intently busy doing their jobs; each of them save for two. I almost didn't notice them, they were swabbing fibres, but the one that did catch my attention did so by suddenly looking up at me and making eye contact. His expression, a wide-eyed look, meant he'd recognized me, or he was really drunk. He nudged his partner, said something quietly, and both men started closing up their supplies.

I glanced at Jason. I still didn't trust him. I knew he wasn't going to kill me, or at least Humpty and Dumpty weren't, but I didn't know what the true story behind them coming to me was. I needed a few moments alone. I needed to ditch him, at least temporarily.

I hobbled over to Jason and leaned in close. "How well do you know Humpty and Dumpty over there?" Jason glanced at his two lackeys and repeated their real names. I forgot them immediately. "Yeah, those guys. Look, I know they're your guys and all, but I just had a vision and our Berenger was talking to some guy on the phone. He said to make sure his two moles were part of your investigation team."

"My men?"

"Yeah," I lied. "He said his two moles were in the

Croxallé security team."

Jason pulled back and gave me a glare. "I'll look into it."

Jason walked off and called Humpty and Dumpty over, and immediately I forgot their names. While the three talked, I looked for the two crooked, allegedly -- don't want to get sued now -- CSI dudes. I caught sight of the pair just as they exited the room. I hobbled after them. I move much slower than two able-bodied men do, so by the time I hit the hallway, they were climbing into an elevator. I watched the floor indicator blink as they descended, hoping to catch what floor they got off on. The elevator light blinked and paused at every floor. Those douches did the most nine year-old-est trick ever, they hit every floor button on the damn panel. Jerks!

Since I had time, I grabbed my phone and hit redial. Mia's voice popped up on my phone a few moments later. "Hello again, Benedict. You know a girl needs time to do her work. You could do to learn some patience."

"This is something different, Mia," I said quickly. "What do you know about Leti-Wind Pharmaceuticals?" I got nothing but silence. "Mia?"

"Where are you, Benedict?"

"Why?"

"Leti-Wind Pharmaceuticals just came across my desk. Its stock is dropping. What's going on?" Again silence, from my end this time. "You're there, aren't you? Benedict, listen, I can't ask the question. I cannot lead you on this, but I need this answer. So I'm asking again. Where are you?"

I knew what she was looking for and honestly I had no problem helping her. "I'm at a crime scene that occurred in both Wilmont Towers and Lyon Estates."

"Who was the victim?" Her voice was tingling with eagerness, like a 17 year-old boy about to see his girlfriend naked for the first time or -- well, Christmas. I guess using Christmas as a metaphor would have worked just as well, but I went to boobs first. How male am I?

"Giuliani Continente."

"I got confirmation! Run with it!" Mia yelled to someone at her office. In polite circles, if you were to yell to someone in your office, you'd put your hand on the phone and cover the talky part in order not to deafen the unlucky guy on the other end. In her excitement, Mia forgot to do that. I understood and could easily forgive her; I might not ever be able to hear again from that ear, but I'd still forgive her. "Benedict, thank you very much. I love you right now. Sex? You want sex? I'll give you sex. You literally just made my career."

"How about answering my question," I laughed. I was kicking myself, I would love sex with Mia Roan, she was gorgeous, but I was...well... I wasn't taken, technically, but somehow the thought of sleeping with Mia, while appealing, made me feel guilty. Truth was, Mia wasn't a *just jump into bed* type of girl - as far as I knew - that was just the way her and others in their field talked. "Leti-Wind Pharmaceuticals: what type of company are they?"

"Oh right," she laughed. "They're a pharmaceutical company. They're trying to fight the good fight, while making a shit-ton of money. They're researching cancer treatments, AIDS cures, Parkinson's treatments, and every other major ailment. They've released numerous major drug and medical discoveries."

"Are they in competition with Croxallé?"

"Sure, as well as every other evil medical company in the world." She said evil sarcastically, but she didn't know how right she actually was. "But neither of them have any major competing products right now. They have minor stuff, but they're not Microsoft/Sony or Apple/Google at the moment."

"So Croxallé is going to benefit from Continente's death then?" I asked. "Like they planned it or something?"

"Sure, stock prices will go up, but if somebody was *planning* a death, this wouldn't be the time to do it. If I were *that* rich and evil, I'd wait until Leti-Wind and I were about to release the same product, like say… the cure for the common cold, and *then* I'd kill them. It would be devastating." Mia went silent again. "How did Continente die?"

"He was assassinated in his room in the Wilmont Towers. His killer camped out in the Lyon Estates and shot him with a sniper rifle."

"Holy shit, Benedict." She has a way with words.

The elevator dinged and the doors opened. I said my goodbyes, with a promise to send her proof, and climbed into the elevator. I pressed my bare finger across the panel and felt the shiver and twitch take over.

The two CSI agents, whom I'm calling Bob and Doug until I learn their real names, stood in the elevator's cabin. Bob started pressed all the buttons. "We've got to lose him."

"We'll get off on the third floor and take the stairs to parking garage," Doug ordered. "We can't take our CSI vehicle, so we'll wait there for our extraction."

"We could steal a car?"

"Too high a risk."

Reality returned and I smirked as I returned my hand into its glovey-home. Their hit-all-the-buttons trick, accompanied by their get-off-on-the-wrong-floor trick, would have been enough to lose anybody normal. I'm not normal. I cheat. I thumbed the button and started the descent down.

There is that moment where adrenalin and common sense seem to disagree on your current choice and start to debate. Common Sense says something like, *what are you doing? You're going to be outnumbered and you're unarmed. Stop!* These are good points, but suddenly adrenalin will says something very persuasive like, *yeah but they're lab geeks. You can take on a couple lab geeks.* Adrenalin has a habit of being the stronger influence because before long you find yourself going, *yeah, who cares if I can barely walk, fight, or take a piss without a cane. I can take on two lab geeks. Hell, I feel great. I could take on two and a half lab geeks.* So when the elevator came to a halt and I stepped out into the parking garage only to find both lab geeks standing by the door waiting, each with a pistol pointed at me, I was left with only one thought:

Screw you, Adrenalin. Screw you.

Chapter 07
You Needed Your Sister to Get Laid

Bob and Doug led away from the elevator and towards a rear corner, their pistols never pointing anywhere but my head. There was no doubt about it, following them into the garage was a dumb idea and I was wrong for doing so. I'm a guy and therefore I have a natural dislike of admitting I'm wrong, I think that's how World War II started (I never really studied history), but as I felt those pistols looking at me, I somehow knew I'd made a mistake.

I was wrong.

Now that I think about it, if I had said those words to a now-ex back in my early twenties, I would probably be married by now.

"It's the dumb-ass cripple with a cane and a dumb-ass cowboy hat," Bob said with a smirk.

"Hey!" I defended. My hat wasn't stupid.

"He's the one we were warned about. The one that got Moore pinched on the ship."

It took three seconds for me to realize what they were talking about. I didn't know anybody named Moore, nobody I got arrested at least, but I did know what ship he was talking about. "You're WhiteStar?"

"Maybe he's not as dumb as we thought he was," Doug laughed.

"Hey!" These two were jerks. In fact, I'd go as far as

to say that Bob and Doug were hosers.

"You know bringing him in could make up for the shit you're in for smashing up that car last week."

"You know I smashed a jeep up once," I interrupted. I slowly turned around to face the pair, and their barrels, and put up a cheerful smile. "Back when I was in the army, I was assigned to go pick up my major's jeep and drive it back. Now I was really drunk the night before, so I was hung-over. So I'm driving this jeep and BAM!"

That's when I struck.

In the past year I've had too many guns pointed at me. It's rather unsettling. In the older days, the working legs days, I could disarm both of them relatively easily and quickly, but since my accident even just standing without my cane can prove difficult. Elaine says my leg is getting better and that one day I won't need the cane, but until then I have to make use with what I've got. So if I was going to be forced to carry a cane with me all the time, I was going to learn how to fight with it. That's why I hired Jack.

My first strike, swinging my cane quickly, knocked Bob's gun from his hand and sent it sliding across the floor in classic action movie style. My second swing put the horse handle of my cane into Doug's neck. I grabbed my cane with both hands, holding it horizontally, and slammed it, and my-self, into Bob, checking him to the floor like a hockey player.

Disarming a person doesn't require the Jett Li style moves from Lethal Weapon 4 (although it was so cool to see him disassemble that gun), most of it just requires quick sur-prising movements. It's about catching just a hint of hesitation or distraction and acting upon it.

So with Bob on the floor and Doug desperately try-ing to remove his Adam's apple from the back of his throat, I did the only sensible thing and dove for the abandoned gun. I couldn't outrun, or out-hobble, the two men, and Bob would be back on his feet in seconds; I could, however, get his gun and start shooting.

I hit the concrete in the most ill-advise belly flop and

grabbed the gun. I rolled on my back and fire two rounds. Bob, back on his feet, tackled Doug to the floor safely behind the nearest car as my two rounds flew by. I scrambled to my knees and rapidly crawled away, taking cover behind a very expensive BMW. I looked at my stolen pistol, thankful that my hand was gloved again, and gave it a quick one-over. It was a SIG Sauer P226 with an attached suppressor. I ejected the mag and did a quick count. They had a ten round magazine, plus one in the chamber, and I'd wasted two. That gave me nine shots to either drop them both or cover myself as I hobbled away.

The BMW's metal doors dinged loudly as a pair of 9mm rounds bounced against it. I raised my SIG and returned fire, snapping off two rounds -- seven remaining. There wasn't a loud bang from their side or mine, due to the silencers. When a SIG is fired with a silencer, or a suppressor as it's professionally known, in lieu of a bang it makes a gust sound that always reminded me the sound Robby, or any kid, made when trying to spit watermelon seeds out from their mouth using their tongue.

It was suddenly very apparent that I wasn't getting away or winning this battle, at least not with the ammo I had, so what I had to do was get help. This was a crime scene, there had to be cops everywhere. I just had to get their attention. The BMW pinged twice more as I crouched down. I tried to ignore the sound as I unscrewed the suppressor, but as the pings continued my heartbeat raced and my breathing became laboured. I wasn't the same man I was six months ago, I wasn't this weak guy shutting out the world. I was somebody new, somebody trying to better himself, but as I was caught in another firefight I felt the old symptoms rising. I don't want to be broken, I want to be whole again, I want to be a real boy, but PTSD is not something you could just wish away, especially when the fairy was as blue as you were.

With the suppressor removed, I popped up my arm and fired two rounds, followed by an identical pair immediately after -- three left. To me, I've always found the SIG

Sauer to have a hollow-echo sound when it fired, an effect amplified by the sound bouncing off the numerous cars and wall in the parking garage.

Somebody had to have heard that.

I nearly crapped myself when a thunderous bang filled the garage and the pings against the BMW suddenly doubled. It wasn't just Doug who was shooting anymore; Bob had joined in as well. He obviously had a back-up gun, a revolver of some sort. He probably held off firing because it wasn't a silenced weapon, but since I let the cat out of the bag he was going Rambo.

At that moment I wanted nothing more than to return fire and go all Rambo on their asses but with only three shots I couldn't, it was impossible. Going Rambo required at least fifty rounds fed together through a belt system. With three rounds the only options left to me were to go Jackie Chan (my leg twitched in pain at the mere through of being that acrobatic) or to go Bruce Willis. I needed a John McClain moment, a Yippie-Kai-Yay light the plane on fire or shoot myself through the chest to kill the bad guy moment.

Then I saw it. Doug was creeping out from behind cover. He was trying to flank me. I popped up and squeezed off a round. The bullet slammed through the windshield and shattered the glass. I fired another, the bullet whizzing by his head, taking with it a hair or two, as he dropped back down, and squeezed off a third, one that found a home in the car's hood. Doug popped back up with a gun in each hand, a silence SIG in one hand and a revolver in the other, and I suddenly realized my mistake.

It wasn't Bob who had a back-up gun, they both did. That meant it wasn't Doug who was trying to flank me: it was Bob. I spun around to find Bob behind me. I levelled my gun him and squeezed the trigger. I heard nothing but a click. I was out of ammo. Bob smirked as he levelled his gun to my forehead. "Say good night, Cowboy."

So much for my Yippie-Kai-Yay moment.

Like an invisible truck suddenly hit him, Bob abruptly flew to the left, crashing into a car almost thirty feet away. I spun to the parking garage stairs and saw my saviour waving his hand in the air. Jason stood there with Humpty and Dumpty behind him, a pissed off look on his face and an extreme eagerness to hurt someone. Doug turned both weapons on Jason and snapped off several rounds. My telekinetic saviour turned his hand slightly, moving it from Bob's direction to Doug's, and squinted. The bullets bounced off an invisible shield and ricocheted off in random directions.

There is something you may not know about Jason Daggett. He's Neo. Yes, that Neo. Jason will free each and every one of us from The Matrix and he'll do it by stopping bullets while industrial music plays in the background. If you have to pick someone for your baseball team when you're little, do yourself a favour and pick Neo. It pays off.

Humpty and Dumpty emerged from behind Jason, each holding a gun in their hands, and quickly snapped off a trio of rounds each. Doug dropped behind cover and bolted for the exit; Bob followed behind, moving with an obvious limp.

"Do we pursue?" Humpty asked.

"Secure the room," Jason ordered.

"Radioing surveillance," Dumpty added. The two split up, their weapons up, as the searched for potential threats.

"How the hell did you find me?" I asked happily.

"I followed you. I knew you were up to something. Food for thought: those two don't work for Croxallé." Well damn. He caught me in a lie. Well played, Jason. "What did you find out?"

"Berenger had people in the CSI team," I explained. "WhiteStar people."

"Why didn't you come get me? I could have help."

"Because you're lying to me. You want my help, but you won't tell me the truth. What am I suppose to do with that?" I yelled. "This was Croxallé's kill order. So what am I doing? Helping you cover it up?"

Jason just frowned.

"Look until you want to tell me the truth, I'm out," I declared while turning away. "I'm done with the lies." I hobbled to the exit, slipping past the onslaught of cops dashing for the garage -- I did not want to have to deal with that -- and waved for a cab. My phone buzzed as I climbed in. It was a text.

Annie: Hey Ben, we need to talk. Meet me for coffee?

Crap. I was about to get the older sister treatment. Suddenly the firefight seemed easier.

Coffee with my sister never actually meant coffee. It meant a beer and some nachos at some downtown pub. I actually loved this tradition and would normally be looking forward to it if it weren't for the upcoming sister-tone I was about to get. I entered the pub and found her sitting at a table, the nachos already before her and a beer and a coke waiting patiently to be consumed. I waved to her as I hobbled over. I gave her a cheek kiss and slid into the chair across from her. She was alone at the table, no Dave, no Robby, and no Alice, and that was a rarity. Annie just got an evening off and she decided to spend it with me, all to guilt me.

"Hey," she smiled. "This one's yours." She looked at my hand and saw it twitching slightly, an aftermath of the shoot-out. "You okay?"

"Yeah; just a rough day."

"There's always Dad's solution." I laughed. Dad's solution to a hard day on the farm was a nice drink. It was never in a bad way, but in a relaxing way. His solution to a really rough day was a shot of tequila, then a nice drink.

"So what's up?" I asked.

"Special Agent Rachael Puzo." And it began. "She's

living with you?"

So I explained. I told her about hooking up after our first meeting; I told her how a week later, after Robby was safely home, she called me up and wanted to have a drink. I told her how after that drink we ended up back in bed. I told her how it happened again the following week and the week after that, and then a couple days after that. I told her how we started hanging out more, spending the night and how she even left things at my place. While Annie didn't like the idea of me having sex while Robby was missing, she was happy for me. Then I explained the rules: I explained how this wasn't serious, it was just for fun, and how we weren't in an R-Word.

"Are you exclusive?"

I shook my head. "No. We agreed that it wasn't."

"That's not what I asked, Benny." There are only two people in this world allowed to call me Benny: one was my Grandmother; the other was Annie. My own mother didn't call me Benny. She didn't even call me Ben. My mother called me Benedict. She didn't like short forms of certain names. "I asked if you were exclusive; you as in you, not you as in you and Rachael. Since you and her stared this relationsh--."

"I'm not allowed to say that word," I interrupted.

"Well, I am. Since you stated this quasi-relationship, have you slept or dated anybody else?"

We Thompsons are tough people. We don't scare easily and we aren't big on talking it out, we're independent folk, but when something is needed to be said we'll ask it and Annie was amazing at it. "No. I haven't been."

"You feel guilty at the thought?" I nodded. "One of the best parts of being an older sister, Benny, is being able to tell you what to do."

"And one of the best parts of being younger is ignoring you." She leaned over and smacked my shoulder.

"I get to give you advice, so listen up, jerk. You need to make a decision. She's said she doesn't have the time for a relation -- for an R-Word." I laughed. "And you're broken enough and dumb enough to say no to one right now."

"Hey!" Why was everybody calling me, or my hat, dumb? Was this a meme or something? If it was, I disliked it greatly and I was going to bring back grumpy cat.

"But she has stuff at your place and you haven't stopped her. Also, it seems like she has a key. So it's up to you. If you want this to happen, then you have to make a move. You have to make this happen. Sometimes, Ben, you have to man up and figure out what you want."

Now I was torn. I could see myself with Puzo and it seemed nice, but if I went to her, and listened to Annie, then neither woman would ever let me live it down. I could hear it already, Annie dancing in circles singing, *you needed your sister to get laid; you needed your sister to get laid.* Then to make thing worse Rachael would show up, hold hands with my sister and join her in the dance; both of them singing, *you needed your sister to get laid; you needed your sister to get laid.* Those who have siblings know how it works; you can never let them to be right because you'll never hear the end of it.

Annie and I laughed and ate. I teased her about not drinking until she reminded me that breast-feeding meant she couldn't drink. I replied with a joke about how Alice was born of Thompson blood. She was going to start drinking eventually. So why not start her off now? Annie disliked that joke entirely. As the evening progressed, I found her suddenly getting quiet.

"Ben," she spoke softly for the first time that night. "I need to ask you about the shoot-out."

I sat there, frozen. I didn't know how to respond. I knew this was coming, that it had to happen eventually. When a gunfight breaks out in your own living room as your brother and husband fight off evil mercenaries trying to kidnap you and your son, you eventually want to talk about it.

"Benny," she whispered. "You shot people on my front lawn; you killed people to save Robby. Benny..." she trailed off.

"Push comes to shove, killing's as easy as breathing."

"No," she snapped. "You're not getting out of this with some crappy Stallone line. Ben, people kidnapped Robby and they tried to kidnap me. The cops said it involved Greg."

We sat there in quiet for a moment that seemed to just drag on. "Why, Benny?" she whispered. "What was it all for?"

"I don't know." I hated lying to her but there was no way in hell I could tell her the truth. "I don't know."

We finished up our food and drink, in relative silence, and exited the pub. Annie perked up slightly as we walked towards her car.

"Want to see what Dave's getting me for my anniversary?" she asked as we approached a jewellery store.

"How do you know what he's getting you?"

"Because I told him that if he doesn't get me this pendant then he's getting my wedding band back." We laughed together as we stopped at a display window. Through the bars, and in the light of the streetlights, she pointed to the emerald pendent that shown in the night-light. "That one."

It was pretty pendent. Hell, it was gorgeous. It was also hella expensive. I knew what Dave made, roughly, and if it weren't for the WhiteStar hush money they still had, he'd never be able to afford it. I looked at the rest of the display, the emerald earrings and the jade earrings, and then I moved downwards to the rings. My eyes fell on it almost immediately and my heart nearly stopped. Sitting in the center was a black ring with dark green inner circle.

That was my lucky ring.

Chapter 08
You Detectives are a Sad, Sad Lot

With my powers I only ever see the past, I mentioned that already, but that's not exactly true. 99.999999% of the time I only ever see the past. Twice, I've seen the future. I can tell right away that it's a future vision; a shiver runs up my left leg instead of my back, and my right hand twitches instead of my eye. The first time it happened, I was touching a business card from a man named Joseph Price, the secret agent with a thousand names. My vision was of me standing by my phone, holding said business card, and calling him for help.

That hasn't happened, yet. That's not the one that worries me.

The second time I saw the future, I was standing over Alice's newborn body, rubbing my thumb over the horse pendent I bought her. When a WhiteStar goon tried to kidnap Annie, a gunfight broke out with Dave and me acting as Sly and Arnie. We won the battle, thanks in part to our own personal Neo showing up and then vanishing, but the stress put Annie into labor. Alice was born prematurely and spent the first little while in one of those incubation tubes. I was staring down at her, making the same promise to her that I did to Robby when he was born, when my thumb touched her necklace and shot me into the future.

In the future, I was dead.

It wasn't the far, far future or even something reasonable like fifty years, it was sixteen years from now, and I was dead and had been for a few years. I learned some good news in that vision: Alice survived the incubation and grew up into a healthy teenager, who was wearing clothes her Dad would hate. Robby grew up into a strapping young man and I had a fifteen year-old son named Clint.

Clint Barclay Thompson.

I've tried to recall that vision dozens of times, for little else then to look at my boy and stare at his eyes, but it never worked. There was something about his eyes that drew me in. It wasn't Rachael's eyes or Elaine's; it was somebody else's, somebody who was dead. That made Clint the boy with the impossible eyes.

The saddest part of that vision, aside from me giving up my life to save them all, was Annie giving Clint my lucky ring, a ring I wore all the time and was never without. It was a ring that meant the world to me, that I apparently stared at for hours while deep in thought. It was a ring I'd never seen before.

Until now.

The band was a hardwood ring with jade inlay in polished black zirconium. It was also hella expensive, so much so that I could never afford it. Thank god for small blessings.

"Benny?" I looked over at her and smiled. I was zoned out there, lost in first signs of a horrific future-vision. "You okay?"

"Sorry. I was looking at that ring," I said, pointing to it with my gloved finger. "Just a cool ring."

It wasn't a lie, but it wasn't the truth. How do I tell my sister, who doesn't know I'm psychic, about a future vision in which I die, and how that ring that I'd just stumbled across is the first hint of that vision coming true? Does Hallmark even make a card for that?

The two of us smiled and walked on. I made a promised as we walked, a promise to myself, that any future vision I saw would not define me. Nobody could tell the future, it was always in motion. According to Robby, and one of his many geek shows, time was always flowing and time could always be rewritten.

Time can be rewritten.

I hope his show didn't copyright that saying.

I woke up the next morning to my phone all but exploding. The smart phone screamed that someone was calling, that I had missed emails and even a text I'd ignored and on top of that, it was time to get my lazy ass out of bed. I grabbed the phone and answered it.

"'lo?"

"Ben, it's Jason; get dressed. I'm coming to get you. I'll be there in an hour." He hung up before I could tell him to shove it.

I grumbled and sat up in bed. Waking up alone was something I was used to, but more and more I was starting to dislike it. I thumbed through my phone and pulled up my emails. The first one was from Jason. It held copies of the unreleased police files for Giuliani Continente's investigation. I gave it a quick scan, not really reading it, before I forwarded it to Mia. The next was from Mia herself.

Benedict;

I'm still looking into your case. Sorry it's taking so long but there seems to be a lot here. You may have stumbled onto a bigger story then Continente's death. If it is, and I can run with it, then you will not be able to turn down the sex I offer this time. :P

Seriously; you turned down this. You detectives are a sad, sad lot.

Mia.

PS. When I wrote *this* I was making a motion towards my body with emphasis on my fantastic rear.

Chances are that woman will be the death of me, future visions be damned. With the emails out of the way I pulled up my texts.

Hotwire: No weird money trail. Everything's legit.
Hotwire: We need to talk. I got a lead on a cold case.

Hotwire's first text was disheartening. I was hoping a money trail would prove to be an easy answer to that case, but it looked like I was going to have to wait on Mia information before I could proceed.
I thumbed down my list of texts.

Puzo: I know I was supposed to be there last night but I got caught up in a case. Some idiot started a firefight. Sorry. Talk tonight?

I quickly typed in a reply.

Me: You okay? And I sound like a worried woman again.
Puzo: I'm fine. Wasn't in the fight. Some jack-ass started a gunfight in a parking garage.

I reread the message twice. What were the odds that her gun battle in a parking garage was a completely different gun battle in a parking garage than mine? I didn't love the math; I didn't love math in general, but this equation seemed to garner less affection. Rachael worked on missing children cases, she worked on Robby's, and she didn't work on murder cases. So what in the blue blazes was she doing there?

Me: Another missing child case turns into a gunfight? And I thought it was just me.

Puzo: Classified Ben. Behave.
Me: Sorry. See you later.
Me: Bonus points if your nekkid.
Puzo: Nekkid? Really? You're such a redneck.
Me: That's OUR word. We earned that word.

I smirked and went to place my phone on the night-stand. I never got the chance. It rang in my hand. I flipped it over and glanced at the words unknown caller.

"'lo?"

"Round Two, Mr. Thompson," the familiarly un-known voice taunted. "Let's see how you do it with this round. Why did Ford replace Willis?"

Expendables 3 Questions: too easy. "Willis wanted way too much money for three days worth of shooting. If you're trying to stump me, stop using Stallone films. Why did you kill Giuliani Continente?"

"It was your fault he died, Ben. I pulled the trigger, but it is your fault. Because of you, I've had to watch people die all around me and I was unable to stop it from happening. Now it's your turn. You will be forced to watch people die around you and there will be nothing you can do about it," he explained. "Which actor almost became Indiana Jones but couldn't because of TV?"

Another easy one, this guy wasn't trying to stump me at all. "Tom Selleck. What's with the movie trivia?"

"I love movies. Ever since I got here, I have been fas-cinated with your movies. The action, the silly plots, the ma-chismo and the tag lines, it's all glorious. I am the Haig. Such cheese."

"Them be fighting words," I defended, realizing how silly that sounded. How could I give a shit about him bad-mouthing movies when he was killing people? "What did Giuliani do to deserve death?"

"This is what I will do, Ben," he continued, ignoring me. "I will push you to your limits. I will make you suffer un-til you beg me for death, until you break. You and I are living in our own action film, Benedict Thompson, and here is the truth: You are about to be punished for your sins."

"Oh, come on," I snapped. "I saw that film and guess what? Bond killed him in the end. If this is a movie, Mr. Jerk-Face," I couldn't actually see his face, it was a phone, but I assumed it held jerk-like properties, "then you need to understand that you are not the hero. You are the villain and the villain *never* wins."

"I don't have to win, Ben," he taunted. "I just have to make sure you don't. See you at the restaurant."

It didn't take a detective to deduce that whatever the hell Jason wanted me for it probably involved a restaurant. I dropped my phone on the bed and glanced at the clock. I had forty-seven minutes until Jason showed up. As much as I didn't want to see him, I really wanted to just watch TV, I did need to shower. I climbed out of bed, pulled on a shirt and pants, and limped for my living room.

Limping: I hate the word. I hate it almost as much as I hate the world hobble, but limping and hobbling is all I do. I can walk without a cane, with a limp, but only just. I can walk from the TV to the kitchen, the kitchen to the bed, and the bed to the booze cabinet and back. Anything beyond that and I'm boned. So I hobble with a cane. Hobbling is that one word that perfectly describes what it is I do. It's a weird word, with awkward spelling, weird sounding syllables, and even that last 'B' sound that makes your cheeks puff up and your lips purse like you're a five year-old trying to raspberry the world.

I made it to the living room before my door opened and I heard the cry of a familiar voice. "Ben? You in?" I looked to the door to see Elaine walking in.

How is it I go days without speaking to anyone, and start to go a little stir crazy to the point that I picture myself fighting side-by-side Sly in a weird *Expendables/Rocky* crossover, and other days, when I want to be left alone, I get bombarded by everybody.

"Hey," I replied curiously. "Um... what's up?"

One look was all it took and I knew something was up.

Elaine was normally the epitome of smiles. In fact, the Greek goddess of smiles, Grin-o-ditee, once came down from that ant-hill they call Olympus and felt threatened by her smile. So she punished Elaine by putting her in my life. It seemed excessive. I'll be honest; I never studied Greek mythology, but I stand by my facts. Whether my story be true or false, Elaine was always a smiling woman, except for today.

"Can I ask your opinion on something?" I nodded. "It's about Steve."

Crap. The last thing I wanted to do was chat to my crush about her current boyfriend. "Sure, but I have to be honest, I'm expecting someone here in about forty minutes or so."

"I'll be quick." She hummed and hawed for a few minutes as she desperately tried to find the right words to phrase her question. I covertly took a quick look at my watch. I was not going to get a shower. She plopped down on my couch and finally spoke, "You've dated a lot of girls, haven't you?"

"In the past, yeah."

"How did you know when things were coming to an end?"

"Most times she threw something at me."

Elaine laughed. "I'm being serious."

Sadly, so was I. When I was younger, I was a very good looking guy, still am I guess, and I knew women found me attractive. It led me to get into trouble with women every once in a while. While I always thought myself a good person, I was fully aware of my susceptibility for poor decision making. When your girlfriend finds you in bed with one of her female friends, there are only two paths the future can take. There is a bad path, that involves anger and break-ups, and there is a good path, that involves fun. Almost every time this happened, and sadly it happened more times than I care to admit, the future would take the bad path. I'm not that guy anymore. It's amazing what effect a near death experience can have on a man.

On a side note: The one time the future took the good

path, the relationship *still* ended in break-up. I was dating this girl, Carol, and after a few months I went to this party and made a *really* bad decision to hook up with this brunette named Jennifer (I make bad decisions). Carol showed up at my place and walked in on Jennifer and me *enjoying* each other. Carol surprised me by deciding to join in. The three of us spent the night together, and I remember thinking that I'd found someone wonderful and how I was *really* glad this didn't end up in a break-up. Two weeks later, Carol left me for Jennifer. The two of them got married a year ago; I attended the wedding. I bought them a toaster.

"I've always thought that a relationship reaches its end when things stop being easy," I offered. "No relationship is *easy*, they're a lot of work, but when they become more trouble than their worth, when they provide more heartache then happiness."

She curled up on herself, wrapping her arms around her body. I continued speaking, "When you start drifting apart, when love isn't the first thing on your mind, then that's sign it may be over." Or if she leaves you for the woman you both slept with. That is also a subtle hint.

She glanced at me and suddenly smiled. "Have you eaten breakfast yet? Of course not, it's you." She unravelled her arms and stood up. "Let me fry you up something to eat."

Elaine was the type of girl who always cared about people, she seemed the happiest when she was helping or was playing homemaker. So as she was talking to me, looking to the cripple-man with serious mental issues for advice, she wanted to cook. She moved to my kitchen and pulled open the door. "Wow, you actually have food. Getting laid suits you, Mr. Detective."

I've always thought so.

"How about you get dressed," she snickered. "In something better than your torn battered shirt, and I'll fry us up some eggs and we can finish talking."

I looked down at my Rolling Stones t-shirt and shrugged. "This is my Stones shirt from when I saw them at

Madison Square Garden. I got this when I was nineteen years old. I waited in line for days to get tickets for this show. I had to use leave time."

"Stones? Really? How cliché," Elaine laughed. "Now if it was The Spice Girls, I'd understand."

I limped to my bedroom, grumbling to myself. Who doesn't like the Stones? I pulled off my clothes and quickly changed into a pair of dark blue jeans and pulled on another Stones concert T-Shirt. This one I got when Dave surprised me with tickets for the *50 & Counting* tour. We saw them in the Barclay Center in early December. Nothing beats ending with *Sympathy for the Devil* and coming back to do the encore and singing *You Can't Always Get What you Want, Jumping Jack Flash,* and ending the entire concert with *Satisfaction.* Pure. Rock. Bliss.

I emerged to hear the sizzling sound of my frying pan. Elaine looked at me and frowned. "Another Stones T-Shirt? Really?"

"What?" I defended as I pulled on a denim shirt over it. "This one isn't tattered or ripped." Elaine rolled her eyes. I limped to the kitchen island and slid onto a stool.

I don't cook much, but I love my kitchen. It had two sinks, an island counter in the middle, and nice window that looked out into my backyard. The only thing that my kitchen missed to achieve perfection was:

a) A better set of appliances -- my stove was old as sin, my radio-clock was broken, and my fridge was just all levels of crappy

b) A nice woman to properly use it.

Now before I go further, I have to explain and clarify my last statement. I'm not trying to be sexist or say something like a women's place is in the kitchen, I don't believe that and I have way too many women in my life who could, and would, kick my ass if I started speaking like that. That being said, I grew up on a farm, a hard working farm in which my mom cooked dozens of meals while making sure our farm stayed afloat. So when I think of the perfect kitchen, it's always accompanied with the smell of a home cooked meal and the sight of my Mom cooking a meal while wrangling in Annie and I and answering the phone for some business related aspect of the farm. The kitchen was the hub of my childhood home. If the farmhouse was the White House, and my Dad the President, then my mom was the Secretary of Defense and the kitchen was her War Room.

"So what's wrong between you and Steve?"

Elaine just shrugged. "I don't know how to put it in words. He seems distant these days. He seems focused on other things, like friends and work. Work..." She trailed off for a moment. "Then there is how he treats my work."

I raised a silent eyebrow. Steve was a male nurse and Elaine was a physiotherapist. Elaine continued, "When we discuss work, things get tense. It's almost as if he thinks his work is more important than mine." Elaine paused. "I mean, it obviously is, he helps saves lives and I just help people walk again. Then there's the topic of you?"

"Me?"

"You, Rich, and Jaina," she quickly corrected. "My three patients; he thinks I get too close to my clients. He says I should be more like him, where you care about the people but you move on as soon as possible because there is *always* going to be someone else needing your help."

Elaine turned off the stove and slid an omelette before me with a fork and glasses, and a glass of OJ to wash it all down. I glanced up at her. "Okay, I don't mean to be ungrateful but I thought you were frying up eggs? I was looking forward to that. When did it become an omelette?" I asked as I squeezed on some ketchup and cut myself a piece. I took a bite and smiled. "Correction: when did it become a *great* omelette?"

"How does your song go? You don't always get what you need, but if you try real hard you'll get what I want?" I thought she was joking, but sadly she wasn't. The look on her face said she was completely serious. This was as bad as the guy who though the Purple Haze lyric was *'Scuse me while I kiss this guy.*

I decide not to correct her. "The truth is you need to decide, for yourself, whether or not it's worth it. You need to talk to him about all of this. Your jobs are so similar, but so different. A nurse and a doctor saved my life: fact. But they had nothing to do with the aftermath. They had nothing to do with getting me walking again or making sure my leg didn't become a shrivelled up prune. Your job is important and you need to tell him that.

"Are you too close with your patients? No. A nurse has to let his patients come and go because there is a massive line up behind them. You have to get people's trust before you can help them. You have to dig deep into a person, find out what makes them tick and use that to push them forward. You can't do that without getting close." I paused to let my words sink in, and more importantly, for me to feast on this omelette before it got cold.

She shrugged and took a sip of my OJ. For the next few moments, all we did was eat and drink in silence, glancing up at each other momentarily. Finally she broke the silence. "So how's it going with Lady FBI? She pull jurisdiction yet?"

I smirked. Cop show talk; I loved it. "Things are good, a little weird but good."

"Have they gotten serious yet?" I wanted to answer, to say yes/no and to click the it's complicated button on Facebook, but I decided against it. Truth was, I didn't know how to answer her question. Did I hint to Elaine that there was room for her with the hopes that she took me up on it or did I say things were going great and see how she reacted? Instead I just shrugged and kept eating.

"Do you like Steve?"

Well, crap. That was a landmine if I'd ever seen one, and an ache in my leg reminded me that I didn't see the last one I came across. My crush had just asked me what I thought of her boyfriend, the man that stood between her and I, and the man she was currently having issues with. How does a man answer that? Do we go all serious and tell her the truth or do

I take this chance to get in between the two of them in hopes that somewhere, in the future, I could be with her? There was no right answer to this question. It was right up there with *do I look fat?* and *what do you think of my mother?* These were the dreaded questions, the question where it was easier to teach a shark to be a vegetarian than to answer them.

"He's seems okay." Looks like I was going serious route. I'm a decent guy and, now, I'm too honest for my own good. "He seems like he takes care of you." I shrugged. "I really don't know him that well."

I was being half truthful. The first time I met Steve, I thought he was a little douche. He was the stereotypical male nurse, well, he was straight so he was the other stereotype, and seemed to be pulled directly from a male-nurse-hunk-calendar. Now while my first impression could have being *slightly* biased since shortly after I met him, he pulled a major faux pas. He asked me about Iraq.

There is an unwritten rule about the men and women who see combat and/or go overseas. You don't ask about what happened to them. You don't ask about the friends they've lost and you *never* asked about the lives they've taken. You just don't do it -- ever. If your friend or family member ever wants to talk about it, they will; until then you leave it alone. Those of us who go over there, or anywhere, and fight never come back the same. The nurse, the male nurse, had the nerve to ask me about it. This man, this man I'd *just* met, asked me to talk about the experience I had around dead bodies. Dave asked me about my experiences in Iraq, but Dave was my best friend and I'd known him for years. He'd spent thousands of hours doing BFF duties: looking after me during hangovers, bringing me to stripers after break-ups, bringing me to other strippers after I decided to fall in love with, date and then break up with said stripper. Dave had earned the right to ask. Steve did not. So needless to say, I wasn't Steve's biggest fan.

My door opened and Jason walked in without as much as a knock. Seriously, people need to start knocking or I'll have to start locking my door. "Ben, I need you to kno-"

Jason stopped as he saw Elaine sitting in my kitchen. "I'm sorry. I didn't know you had company."

I gave him a glance. The man looked like a mafia goon: black jacket, black suit, black shirt, black tie and black shades. I was half expecting him to pause, look at me and say those all-powerful words: "It's 106 miles to Chicago. We have a full tank of gas, half a pack of smokes, it's dark and we're wearing sunglasses."

I would have replied with two words: "Hit it."

When, God, when, when will I get my *Blues Brother* adventure?

"Jason, this is Elaine," I introduced, reluctantly. "Elaine, Jason."

"The physiotherapist?"

Elaine glanced at me. "How does he know that?"

"I thought you were with Puzo?"

"It's not like that," I corrected. Elaine looked at me with a weird expression. "What do you want?"

"I need your help and I have the answers you're looking for." I didn't expect that.

"Another case, Ben?" Elaine asked with hopeful eyes. Elaine loved cop shows as long as they were light hearted and she always was intrigued by my work. Sadly, the first time she joined me things didn't go well and she ended up in the same room as a dead body. "You don't need help, do you?"

"Sorry, Elaine, I can't. This is the wrong channel."

"AMC cop show?"

"AMC at least." Jason raised his eyebrow at me.

"Okay," she said as she scooped up her things and grabbed her jacket. "I'll head out. Talk later?" I nodded. She let herself out. I glanced at Jason.

"Okay. Talk."

Jason took a seat at the island and watched as I finished my omelette. "There's been another murder, same type of round, similar circumstances and a random object let at the crime scene."

"And?"

"And it has same *special* circumstances as the last."

"So this is where you tell me everything," I declared. "You've been holding back, you've been keeping secrets. Continente was your kill order and you know it. So if you want my help, you better tell me the truth and nothing but it. If I ask a question, you answer it and if I even think you're lying, then I'm out."

"You are the most difficult detective I've ever hired, Ben. You better be worth the money." I was getting paid? Oh shit. Sweet.

"Okay. Tell me about the kill order."

"Giuliani Continente's murder was our plan," Jason explained. "Croxallé has... contingency plans for our competition. If things get too good or too bad we can... even out the playing field. We've never used them, nor would we, but they're there." I frowned. I didn't know how much I believe that. "The Giuliani Continente murder was based completely off the plan Croxallé had set-up for him. From the twin hotels to the sniper shot to the head. We planned every detail. All you had to do was open the file, find out when his next sex visit was and wait. But we didn't order this kill. Someone went rogue."

"So which guy of yours killed him?"

"We don't know." He frowned. "This is my responsibility, Ben. This is my division and things have gone shitty."

Suddenly I felt sorry for Jason. He was there when I needed him, when Robby truly needed him. While I didn't accept his excuse for not being there for Robby's life, I understood it. I knew what it's like to have somebody else dictate what you can and cannot do with your life. The military was like that.

"And this second murder?"

"It's another of our contingency plans," he explained. "Another kill we planned but didn't order."

I finished my omelette and downed the last of my OJ. "Okay. Let me grab my coat."

"Ben," Jason said. "Get your gun."

I dumped my dishes into the sink and limped to my bedroom and over to the nightstand. I pulled open the top drawer. In a small dish sat two ball-chain necklaces. One held two oval tags, my army dog tags, and the other held three keys. With the conveniently placed pencil I shoved the first chain aside. I don't like to touch my dog tags anymore. Unlike everything else in this apartment, they still hold with them the worst of the worst of my life, the most emotional and devastating moments of my past. Touching them is like reliving my own personal hell. I grabbed the keys and closed the drawer. I limped to my liquor cabinet. I pulled out the bottles one by one and laid them on the floor. I pulled free a metal lockbox. The black box was roughly the same size as a case of pop, twelve cans. I moved to the island and placed it on the counter. I quickly unlocked the box and removed my weapon of choice, my Beretta M9 pistol. I gave the weapon a check, refilled the magazine, and slid it into a holster. I clipped the leather holster to my belt and pocketed the extra mags. Last, but legally not least, I grabbed my firearm license and slipped it into my wallet.

The M9 was the army's sidearm of choice for decades. I had trained with a M9 and spent many nights in the field sleeping with one by my pillow. When I went into battle, I had a M9 by my side and in Iraq when my rifle jammed and the Elite Guard came over the wall, I reached for my M9 to save my life. The closest thing I'd ever had to a long-term monogamous relationship was with a M9. Puzo may not like this, but I may love my M9 more than I have any woman.

Warning: Incoming Bad Joke.

I *may* love my M9 more than any woman, but trust when I say it's all emotional. If you try and take your relationship with your sidearm to a physical level, make sure it's ready first, otherwise the entire relationship ends in a bang.

I warned you that joke was bad.

"Now I'm ready."

"What was it like dating Annie?"

I sat in Jason kick-ass car as he drove us to the crime scene and just like before it was too quiet -- awkward quiet. I had two options while we drove. One was to stare at Jason's dashboard and steering wheel and wonder if any of the buttons did James Bond things, and the other was to ask questions. Jason shut me down last time but what was I if I wasn't persistent?

Please don't say crippled. That would just be low.

"Pass."

"There's no passing Jason," I explained. "You agreed to answer all my questions."

"Not this one," Jason declared. "Ask anything else."

"Fine," I grumbled. "Tell me about Project: Canaan."

Jason looked at me. For nearly fifteen seconds, all he did was stare at me. It was terrifying, mainly because he was driving and wasn't watching the road, and also the longest fifteen seconds of my life. "What do you know about Canaan?"

"I know a little bit," I began. "KyroCorp started it, Croxallé picked it up. It's about trying to make the Lycotta Gene spit out Supermen. They made you hook up with Annie because of it to make Robby."

Jason nodded as he drove, his eyes, thankfully, back on the road. I decided to continue. "We came across a report by Annie's doctor. He talked about how the children were in Choirs and that Robby was a 1st Choir child. Dr. Caine was worried about 1st Choir. He said some would be dangerous."

"Caine was right," Jason finally said. "There are some dangerous children out there; luckily Robby wasn't one of them.

"Project: Canaan was so vast. They used control breeding, scientific experiments, gene therapy and a crap load of methods that I can't understand or even say properly but they got it. They got their super-powers. They also got trouble."

Jason just shook his head. "They got so much trouble. Nothing went like they wanted it to. Did you know that the man who discovered the Lycotta gene, Dr. Ashley Lycotta, experimented on his own child?"

"Who would do that?"

"He was told to," Jason said. "Damn it, this company just rips so much of humanity away from us."

"But that was KyroCorp, you work for Croxallé," I asked.

"KyroCorp is Croxallé," Jason admitted. "When KyroCorp looked like it was going bad our bosses closed it down and opened Croxallé. New company, new name, same mission; they could continue their work without the public baggage from the last company. One day Croxallé will get too public and it will close down. Then they'll re-open as a new company, a new name but continue to do all the work the last one did."

The car got quiet again.

"Why do you stay with them?" I asked, finally piercing the silence.

"Another time, Ben," Jason said as he steered the car to a halt. "We're here."

I looked out. We were at a high-end restaurant, one of those places that only catered to the rich. For me to eat here I'd have to cash in my military medical pension and probably start selling my body for money.

Benedict
You don't have to put on the red light
Those days are over
You don't have to sell your body to the night
Benedict
You don't have to wear that dress tonight
Walk the streets for money
You don't care if it's wrong or if it's right

Sorry, Sting, the song wasn't working; we should all just stick with Roxanne.

Jason reached into his jacket pocket and pulled out a couple business cards. He handed them to me. I gave them a look. Benedict Thompson: Insurance Claims Investigator.

"Um... what the hell?" I asked.

"Last crime scene we were able to buy access from some FBI lackey," Jason explained. "After the shoot-out, he got caught and been re-assigned to a different aspect of this investigation. So we're going to have to lie our way in."

"But corporate insurance investigator? Really? Can't we pretend to be somebody cool?" They did it on TV all the time. The moment I heard those words in my head I was glad I didn't say them out loud.

"Our victim is Richard Rayner. He's the CEO of Claymont Development," Jason explained. "They buy property, build it up, and then sell it or rent it for absorbent fees. They also have numerous insurance claims and protection on their higher-echelon men. We're talking millions in claims. So you are the insurance guy and I'll be your security."

Jason tried to exit the car, but I stopped him. "I may have a lead." He eyed me for a second. "Somebody called me yesterday and told me how I ruined his life and now he's going to ruin mine."

"I take it this isn't common for you."

"Aside from ex-girlfriends, not in particular. He told me about the estates. He called today as well and made more threats and mentioned the restaurant."

"Any other details?" His face was still.

"He had an accent," I added. I scrunched up my face and tried to sound like my mysterious caller. "I'm a bad guy and I think threatening Ben is a good idea. La di da. Also I'm pretty sure I have ED and I'm taking the frustration of that out on an innocent cripple. How big of a jerk am I?"

He just stared at me. "That sounded like an Irish man trying to impersonate a sick German, but instead you sound like a Scotsman with a scarf on."

I'm really bad at accents.

Jason climbed out of his kick-ass car and I followed. Humpty and Dumpty stood by the car waiting for us. I pull my jacket tight, making sure my pistol remained hidden beneath it, and carefully placed my hat atop my head. I hobbled to the door. Jason did the talking, flashing cards and throwing names out faster than I could keep track. There is an art to being a liar like Jason and it was one I had little talent in. Sadly, I was gaining practise.

The uniformed police officer waved Jason and I in. The restaurant was a mess. Tables were over-turned, chairs knocked down and broken, and shattered plates and glasses littered the floor amongst discarded floor. Then, sitting in his chair with his body slumped forward over the table, was a dead man.

"You must be Richard Rayner," I whispered as I approached him. "Sorry to intrude."

I pulled off my gloves and touched his jacket. A shiver and twitch pulled me into the past. Richard sat at the table, joined by other in his company, and each chatted as they ate their meal. "So we're looking at a nine percent increase in cost for the Chicago skyscraper."

Richard rolled his eyes. The Chicago plan was a crappy one to begin with. It had looked good on paper but so much had gotten in the way between then and now. "Fine; I'll approve it. Just get it done and start getting *some* money from that hunk of junk."

The woman at the table took a sip of her coffee before talking. "Did you hear that the parent got *another* offer to buy some of the subsidiaries?"

"Won't happen," Rayner laughed. "The parent is solid. It would take a lot for them to sell anything under them right now. You've seen the reports. This will be a monumental year for them. There is nothing that can sto-."

The sniper round snapped through Rayner's body. At first nobody knew what had happened, nobody save for the people at the table, but as Richard's co-workers started screaming so too did others when they saw the dead body that sat not feet away. Two more shots, the bangs unmistakeable this time, ripped into the restaurant and caused panic. People screamed, people bolted for the door, and people trampled anyone in their way.

Reality returned. I hobbled back to Jason. "What was the object? What was out of place this time?"

"It was S.O.G. Seal Pup." I felt my body tense up. It was the knife I used Iraq. I used it in Afghanistan. If this was anything like the glasses, then this knife was mine.
"Let me see it."

Jason waved over a man and got him to hand me the knife. I touched it and vanished back into the past. My hearing kicked in first as sounds of explosions and gunfire filled the air; next I noticed the temperature. Gone was the ridiculous cold that plagued the land in the final days of winter, before the gentle touch of spring took hold, and in its place was an unbearable heat. Finally I noticed the sun, that unrelenting burning beast that acted as the source of the miserable warmth. No longer was I safely stateside, instead my vision had taken me to a warzone.

"We have reinforcements incoming!" Command screamed over the comms. "All team take defensive positions." As my vision came into focus, I spotted four other soldiers hunched together, and I recognized them all.

Sometimes a vision would give me information in a method not dissimilar to VH1's Pop-Up Video and other times it left me in the dark to figure things out on my own. For this vision I knew the date, I knew the place and I knew the name of every US soldier fighting and none of it was because of my vision. This was Odin Squad and we were on a mission.

Yet in my current vision, I was crouched by a door, a M4A1 rifle hanging from its sling, as I searched my vest for my C4. A burst of weapon's fire forced the four of us to the ground.

"Odin, this is Zero: disregard that order," a female voice ordered over the comms. "Complete your objective."

Zoey.

"Thompson: prep the charge. We're breaching the room," Blaine yelled as we each popped back up, weapons in hand. "Everybody else: return fire!" Our rifles roared to life as we opened fire at the hallways below.

The date was March 28th and I was in western Iraq. This was the first airborne assault into Iraq, led by the Rangers, in order to seize several airstrips. I didn't need the vision to tell me that the Iraq's Republic Guard were currently firing upon us and that they had us pinned down; my memory was doing so on its own.

"Screw the breach. Thompson: kick it down."

"With pleasure."

My three friends popped up, moving as one, and wildly began opening fire, spraying round after round down the hallway. It was called suppression fire and they were trying to keep me from getting my ass shot. With a solid kick, I booted open the door and stepped in, my rifle barrel leading the way. The room held a single guardsman, crouched by a desk, who opened fire the moment he saw me. I already knew he was there and dove into a roll. The bullets whizzed by my head as I rolled to my knees and snapped off two rounds with such speed that they made only a single bang. Both rounds found themselves a new home in the guardsmen's shoulder, forcing him back to the floor in a foreign cry that I could only assume was a curse or a prayer.

I, or more accurately Younger Me, stormed the room and kicked away the gun. He called out clear and flipped over the hostile, securing his hand behind his back with a zip-tie. Fifteen seconds to kick-open a door, do a dramatic roll, shoot a bad-guy and hog-tie him like a farm animal. Damn, I was kick-ass when I was younger.

I'll be honest; I was also damn good looking.

The rest of my team pulled back into the room and secured the door. I pulled out a USB key and popped it into the laptop that sat on the desk. It took the flash-key thirteen seconds to search the computer and make a happy beep. While the rest of my Ranger brothers were tasked with securing the airfield, for which we helped, us four were given a side mission to find which computer held some unknown files the CIA were looking for.

I clicked on the radio. "Zero, this is Bright Eyes: Room secure. Target found. We have the intel."

"Confirm, Bright Eyes," a female voice came over the comms. "Take the computer with you."

Zoey.

The laptop, secure in a large case, had its cords strapped down. It wasn't meant to be the type of laptop you move easily from Starbucks to Starbuck on your endless mission to look like a douche; it was a military grade one that could endure a warzone. The cords couldn't easily pop-out from the laptop, they had to be removed when the protective case was off and I, or Younger Me, didn't have that amount of time. I pulled free my knife, a S.O.G. Seal Pup, cut the cord in two and shoved the entire device in my bag.

I returned to the present. Jason looked for an answer; I shook my head and waved him off. I needed a moment. I hobbled around the restaurant touching thing, sticking my fingers in food, and brushing table and chairs. With each stroke, I learned more about the personal lives of the people who ate there, accountants nervous about their tax dodging, waitresses desperate to make rent this month, and even the final detail of a massive joint-venture in the work that I really should invest in. I'm not sure about the laws surrounding insider trading, but I'm pretty sure that you don't get more insider then psychic visions. But despite my temporal prodding, I found nothing else of interest to the case.

I pulled out my phone and gave Mia a call.

"Hello, Benedict," she replied with a laugh in her voice. "Any more insider-murder-intel for me today."

"Um..." I trailed off. She was joking, obviously, but she was dead on. Ha! Unintentional pun!

"Holy crap, you're there, aren't you? You're there, again. Say it, Benedict. Tell me where you are."

"I'm at the crime scene of Richard Rayner's murder." I pulled the phone away as she screamed in her office.

"When whatever it is you're doing is done, I'm taking you out to dinner. You are going to make my career, Benedict. So it will be a fancy dinner; dinner and sex and wine and... and... hell, Benedict. You give me the story and I will just give you my body. Lock, stock and barrel. You will own my body. I mean, I'll need it for work and stuff, but aside from that you'll own it."

"God, I hope you never say any of those things on the air after your promotion." Although deep down having her say *Benedict Thompson can do whatever he wants to my body* on live network TV would be kind of a reputation booster, even if she didn't mean it. No more pity sex from Army Bunnies! "Does Claymont Development have anything to do with Croxallé?"

"I'll do a search." I thanked her and hung up only to have the phone ring almost immediately. I glanced down at the unfamiliar number and answered it. "Twice in one day."

"It's time we change the game up a little bit. Ben, if you could look down, you'll notice a spot on your shirt." I glanced down, thinking I'd spilt something and some anonymous do-gooder had called to tell me about it -- yeah right -- but instead all I saw was a glowing red dot. I instinctively tried to brush it away. It didn't move. This was a laser-pointer. Somebody had a weapon, a Dragunov sniper rifle if I had to guess, aimed directly at my chest.

I was really scared which meant I was about to get really sarcastic.

"Oh damn, I always stain my good shirts. This is why I can't have nice things."

"Make a sound, draw any attention to yourself or try to escape and I put a bullet through your spine. I need you alive, Ben, but remember that screaming is still alive."

"You're the sniper," I whispered. "Why are you doing all of this?"

"I can't help it, Ben," my mysterious caller answered.

"I've got all sort of dark thoughts in my head. They just rattle around, telling me to do evil things. I need to listen to them, Ben. I need to let them out."

"Bullshit," I spat, louder then I had hoped. Jason raised an eyebrow at me from across the room. I lowered my voice. "Bullshit. You're not pulling the Michael C. Hall routine on me, Dexter. You're an Croxallé security douche gone rogue."

The caller chuckled. "True, true; but imagine if my story had been true. You'd be the private detective battling a dark serial killer, a race against the clock until he killed again. Each murder scene he taunts you, leaving you clues and riddles. Then we meet at an epic conclusion where only one of us walks away. How exciting would that be, Ben? I'm seeing 30 million plus on opening Saturday."

The sad part was it sounded like a pretty kick ass movie. I'd probably get Matthew McConaughey as me, I think he could do bumbling, and in a surprise out-of-character casting I'd put my man Sly as the tortured sniper. I could make a buttload of cash.

"Damn it, Tom Berenger," I snapped. "What does WhiteStar have to do with this? What does WhiteStar and a dumb-ass rogue sniper want with a pharmaceutical company and a property development company? What is the connection between the two?"

"The two? Oh, Ben," he chuckled again. "You really need to think bigger."

He was teasing me; the sniper was teasing me on the phone. It had finally happened: my life had turned into a movie. I'd always wanted this, I always thought it would be awesome but it wasn't. It just involved a crap ton of guns pointed at me. I needed a script re-write.

"Who you talking to, Ben?" Jason asked as he approached.

"Nobody," I lied. "Just a buddy of mine who wants his Tom Berenger DVD back." Jason shrugged and walked off, heading towards Humpty and Dumpty.

Damn it.

"Good work getting rid of my former boss," the caller said. "Now if you look out the window, you should see two blue cars and a white van showing up. Exit the building and make your way to the van."

"And if I say no?"

"Then I pull the trigger."

"Who let corporate security in?" a female voice yelled from the kitchen. This voice I recognized, I'd heard it scream enough. This voice meant I was really screwed. I prayed it wasn't her. I prayed it was just her easily mistakable doppelganger. Sadly it wasn't; it was her.

Puzo emerged from the back and marched with a pair of FBI suits behind her. She froze as she saw me. Her eyes narrowed and she shook her head, just slightly, in disbelief. I put a stupid grin on my face and waved with my cane. She marched over to me and scowled.

"Ben. What the hell are you doing here?" she demanded. "Did you break our deal? Did you... read my phone?" Read my phone was code for visonize her.

"I didn't -- touch your phone, I promise," I stammered. "It's complicated."

"That's your woman, Ben?" the voice taunted. "How very unfortunate."

"What's going on?" Puzo ordered.

"I can't," I sheepishly replied.

"Last chance, Ben," the sniper warned. "Ditch her and move to the van, now."

"Are you working a case, Ben?" Puzo asked. "Are you working this murder?"

"No!" I snapped, answering both at once. "No! No! No!"

"Bad answer, Ben." The red dot moved off my body and crawled onto hers. "Now I have to take something from you."

Chapter 09
Synchronized Killing: New Olympic Sport

I panicked and sidestepped, putting my back between Puzo and the red dot. Here is a free lesson to all the future baddies in the world: If you need to take somebody alive -- if you're not allowed to kill the person -- don't let them know that. It means they know your limits.

"Well played, Ben. Looks like she lives," my mysterious caller taunted. "I can't say the same for everybody else though."

I froze when I heard the bang. I knew he couldn't kill me, but for some reason I still expected the pain. Instead the nearest FBI agent flew back as a sniper put a bullet through his chest. Puzo grabbed my shoulder, tossed me behind the nearest overturned table, and took cover herself as her hand quickly pulled her Glock 22 from its holster. Throughout the restaurant, the cries of sniper rippled from front to back.

A second bang echoed as the restaurant owner dropped to the floor, blood pouring out from his body via a new hole. The restaurant went silent for a moment, a brief second, as all the cops and FBI tried to remain covered.

"It's all on you, Ben," he repeated. "It's all on you." I hung up the phone. His voice was irritating.

Jason dashed across the restaurant and slid in beside me. He looked up and noticed Puzo. She glared at me. "You're here with him?"

Jason opened his mouth to argue, or to defend himself, but I interrupted with, "Now's not the time!"

"I think I know where he is," Jason said between pants of air. He pointed to Humpty and Dumpty and said their names. I instantly forgot them. "They've narrowed down which perch the sniper is using, or at least the two best options. They're going to try and sneak out and-"

"No," Puzo snapped. "We lay down covering fire, and try and get the civilians out."

"Your rounds will barely reach him, let alone hit him," Jason snapped back.

"They'll keep him pinned down while the rest of us make for the side door," she explained. Puzo listened as Humpty and Dumpty pointed out their best guesses. She told her FBI lackeys to get the civis out once she started firing.

The four of us, Puzo, Humpty, Dumpty and I (Jason was unarmed) popped up and opened fire. My M9 snapped off in a familiar bang, and I shot across the street and aimed at the roof of some clothing store with a ridiculously large neon sign on the top. The others aimed at the office building. My rounds dug deep into the sign, or ricocheted off its metal, but never actually touched the sniper. The killer popped out from behind the sign, finally revealing his position and snapped off another round, one that went wide to our left.

The remainder of the cops and feds bolted for the door to the right, crossing the floor in a crouched run. A uniformed cop kicked open the restaurant door and marched out first, his issued pistol carefully held before him. He paused mid-stride as he saw the rear doors of the white van pop open and four men armed with assault rifles emerge. The cop didn't hesitate or flinch; instead he followed his training and tried to snap off a shot, but the armed men were faster. The four assault rifles cackled loudly as a wave of high calibre rounds tore through the cop and two waitresses. The sniper was mowing down innocent bystanders and using the attack to force us directly into the path of his rifles.

I screamed loudly as I snapped off another twin rounds

only to have them, much like the others, come up short. "He's just out of range!" I yelled.

"If we drop him, we can flank the maniacs with the rifles," Puzo replied.

"Gun!" Jason ordered. Humpty slid his pistol across the floor into Jason's waiting hands. He spun upwards and aimed across the street. With a loud grunt, he squeezed off three rounds. The bullets zipped across the street, moving at a speed reserved for a round twice their size and tore clean through the sign, into the sniper and out through the back. Jason dropped back down behind cover. I stared at him in disbelief. His shot wasn't possible.

"I gave it boost," Jason answered, as if he plucked the question from my mind. "My own special boost."

It took me days to figure out what he did (truth was somebody else explained it to me), but when Jason grunted as he shot he was summoning all of his telekinetic energy and shoving each round with the full strength of his powers. The result was a massive boost to the speed and power of the bullet.

The sniper fire stopped, but the rifle fire continued.

"There." Puzo pointed to her SUV. "I have a rifle in the back and more ammo. I'll cover you two as you bolt for the car."

"We are to protect Jason," Humpty said.

"And Ben," Dumpty finished. "You will be our collateral protection."

"We'll cover you as you and Ben make for the SUV," Humpty finished.

Puzo opened her mouth to argue but Jason shushed her. "It's impossible arguing with them. Just do it."

Humpty and Dumpty quickly rose to their feet and opened fire. They moved as one, like a well-choreographed dance of murder. Synchronized killing: New Olympic sport. They advanced slowly, their pistols roaring to life, but despite bombarding the murderous men with 9mm bullets, none of the bad-guys even seemed to look their way. One of the assault rifle wielding jerks did glance in their direction, but he suddenly developed a pained look and instantly ignored them.

"Go!" Puzo and I ran out through the broken window and across the parking lot. When I said *Puzo and I ran*, what I really meant was Puzo ran and I -- let's say it all together now -- *hobbled*. A sudden flash, like that from a camera, stunned Puzo and halted her in her tracks, but before I could say or do anything, I felt the, sadly, familiar feeling of a boot to my bum leg. The gimp limb buckled and I dropped to the ground. I swung out with my cane but watched as it froze mid-swing and an unseen force tried to pull it from my grasp. Somebody was trying to pull my cane from my hand from a distance. I was fighting a Jedi -- wait: that's name was owned by Disney -- I was fighting a futuristic space samurai wielding a magic laser sword from the past.

This unlicensed dollar-store version of a Jedi pulled my cane free from my grasp and suddenly made it vanish. Seconds later it returned to me via a strike to my back and a jab into my neck. I gasped for air and tried to scramble away but when you're fighting the invisible man, crawling away can quickly become crawling towards. A boot slammed against my forehead and the world became dizzy.

I heard the screeching halt of a vehicle and felt several strong hands grab me and toss me into the back of the van. I felt Puzo falling on top of me shortly after. I tried to call out for help but found my voice falling on nobody's ears but Rachael's. The van sped away just as I tried to stand up.

Have you ever tried standing up in a moving van? Don't. All that happens is you get torn up and thrown around like a condom wrapper in a frat house. I collided with the side of the van, felt my face smack against the steel, and found myself pulled into the past.

This wasn't a normal vision; my initial disorientation during a vision was pretty bad but when you added in dizziness then things get thrown around. My vision felt like I was watching TV but with someone changing the channel every three seconds. It was like dating that girl who can't stand commercials, so she changes channels to watch two minutes of another show so she doesn't have to suffer through them. If that wasn't bad enough, picture said girl changing the channel to avoid commercials only to find out that her back-up channel is also airing commercials. She panics and starts flipping randomly in an effort to avoid all commercials and eventually just causes an epileptic seizure for everybody else in the room.

This vision felt like that.

I saw two men standing by the van, one watching the parking lot as the other hotwired it. The engine turned over and roared to life and both men climbed in.

Then the channel changed.

I saw a gaggle of men standing around the van and three blue cars, one talking as the others listened. They were reviewing their attack plan one last time before they attacked.

Then the channel changed.

I saw the van doors being kicked open and the men pouring out, their assault rifles spraying a hail of death down upon the innocent civilians and surprised police officers.

Then the channel changed.

I saw the van roar to life once more, the wheels spinning and the van driving with nobody behind the wheel.

Then the channel changed.

I saw another vision begin to form, but reality interfered. The van flipped over and just like before, I got tossed around. I slammed into the roof, which somehow had become the wall, and collapsed to the floor, which looked suspiciously like the former wall. It took a second for me to click in, but I realized the van had somehow been flipped over on its side. I hadn't felt a crash or a smash or even a sudden swerve; instead it was like the van had suddenly just been flipped.

Puzo was back on her feet first. Both her Glock and my M9 were gone, left wherever they had fallen, but Puzo was far from unarmed. She reached for her ankle holster and pulled free her back-up pistol. "Ben: let's go."

I looked for my cane and found it missing alongside

my weapon. I grunted and limped for the door.

Puzo kicked the van door open and carefully looked out. She kept crouched as she exited, her pistol drawn and held before her, and dashed for the nearest cover. I crept out of the van and looked out over the street. We were blocks away from the restaurant, the sounds of the shooting still echoing in the distance. Puzo's gun snapped off as the third blue car approached. The car suddenly flipped, much like the van, and crashed downward into the street front first. I glanced across the street to see Jason approaching, his hands waving like Bugs Bunny in that sketch where he was a symphony conductor.

Jason was more than just *a* telekinetic. He was *the* telekinetic. This man could lift cars, he could stop bullets, and he could throw boxes and stones like they were baseballs. The man was the unholy offspring of Neo and Luke Skywalker. Picture Keanu Reeves and Mark Hamill having sex, now -- actually you shouldn't do that at all. Seriously, please stop. It's stuck in your head now, isn't it? Meh, not even sorry.

Suddenly it all made sense: the van didn't flip by an accident; Jason had flipped it with the power of his mind. I started to move, wanting to leave the van and limp to cover, but the stunning blow of a boot stopped me mid-stride. I crumbled to the ground, hard, and watched as two men shimmered into view. One was a lanky brown-haired man while the other was a Middle-Eastern solider with a weapon drawn. I looked to my own personal Neo for help, but found him busy as a squad of men that crawled free of the wrecked car. I tried to crawl away but the Middle-Eastern man put his boot to my head and forced me to the ground. I fought to stay awake, to keep conscious and to fight against the oncoming darkness, but the more I fought, the stronger the darkness got. The Middle-Eastern man lowered his weapon at me, pointing the barrel at my head, and smirked.

A bang echoed and the side of the Middle-Eastern's skull exploded outwards, spewing blood and grey matter onto the dirt below. He crumpled to the ground, the lanky brown haired man shimmering out of sight, as I sighed in relief. I glanced over to my right and saw a crouched Puzo holding her smoking pistol pointed in my direction. There is something to be said about the feelings you develop after a woman lets you sleep with her. There is something else to be said about the feelings you develop when that same woman saves your life. I smirked at that thought and fell back as the darkness took hold and I passed out.

When you wake up after a fight, assuming you in fact do, you don't wake up eyes first or brain first -- you wake up pain first. This wasn't the first time I'd woken up in pain; it wasn't even the first time I'd woken up surprised that I survived. Back in the military, back in my all or nothing days, waking up in pain was a daily occurrence. Most times, it was the pain that came from a rough workout or a tough day at work, but there were times when I woke up bruised and broken from fights and battles. That was then; this was now. Now was supposed to be different, but it wasn't. I kept finding myself waking up after firefights and super-man attacks. Although every drop of common sense in my body told me that I needed to change my life style -- and trust me, I had tried -- I knew it wouldn't be the last time I woke up like this. Fate kept finding a way to throw hell at me.

So when I woke up after that van crash, surprised I'd even woken up, I was at least familiar with the process. What I wasn't expecting was to find myself in a bed and in one of those Johnny gowns that covered my front but left my ass exposed to the elements. I winced as I sat up and looked around. The room had white walls, lame art and beeping equipment on either side of me. It was obvious I was in a hospital, but this room was far nicer than anything my health care or Obama-Care could provide.

I had no sweet clue where the crap I was. This feeling… this was new. While I felt like I was hung-over, I knew I wasn't. I'd never woken up sober and not known where I was. It just didn't happen -- mainly because I never go anywhere. To my right was a small end table with my hat, my gun, my gloves, my jacket and my cane. Beside it sat a new pair of jeans and a black collared shirt neatly folded. I climbed out of bed and moved to the table. I grabbed my pistol and pulled it from its leather home. I gave it a quick check, confirmed it was loaded and eventually cocked it. I levelled it at the door and breathed quietly. My heart was racing, I could feel it, but I knew I needed to calm down. I gently placed the pistol back on the table, keeping it in arm's reach, and pulled on the new pants.

Normally I *love* a new pair of jeans. I love how they feel on my legs, I love how they feel when I rub my hands down them, I love how blue they look, and I love the smell a new pair of jeans has. These jeans had all of those characteristics, but I couldn't enjoy them. I just yanked them on and pulled on the black shirt after it. I fumbled with some socks and pulled on my boots. With the end of each step, I reached for my pistol, just in case. I had no clue what could walk through that door and honestly, knowing my luck, the odds were fairly high that whoever it was would be trying to kill me. Actually the odds were higher that whoever it was would be trying to kill the person *nearest* to me and I just got caught in the crossfire.

I pulled on my jacket, and felt the familiar weight of my keys, wallet, and phone in the pocket and topped off my entire ensemble with my trademark hat. Then I grabbed my cane. With my walking aid in one hand, and my killing aid in the other, I hobbled to the door and quietly opened it. I glanced into the hall and found it bustling with activity. With my gun hidden by my jacket, I exited the room and moved to the nearest door.

"Ben!" I spun around with my gun up pointed outwards. I found Puzo looking down the barrel. "Whoa!" Her hands shot upwards and I pulled my gun down. She stepped closer and gave me a hug. "We've been waiting for you to wake up."

"Where are we?" I asked, finding my voice very dry and in need of water.

She scowled. Wherever we were, she wasn't very happy about it. "We're in Croxallé head-quarters."

Whoa. I didn't see that coming.

Chapter 10
Taking Life Advice From Fictional Characters

I was in Croxallé Headquarters; this was intense. I looked around and found myself in complete disbelief of that fact. This building couldn't be the HQ of the evil medical company I'd grown to despise, it was too bright and clean. Nobody was getting tortured, nobody was getting killed or experimented on; in fact people were walking around with smiles. They looked happy and content. Nobody looked evil. There wasn't even a single henchman or evil assassin ninja lurking around. Once again, TV had lied to me. I hate it when it does that to me.

Puzo led me down a hallway and I found myself coming to very frightening, and yet somewhat reassuring, realization. I had assumed that there wasn't a ninja nearby because I couldn't see one, but any ninja worth its salt would never let the good guy see them, especially not a hobbling cane-wielding good guy. So that being said, there could still be a ninja in the shadows with a sword out ready to kill me at a moment's notice. I suddenly felt very relieved.

Let's never fight again, TV!

Puzo escorted me to a security office and held the door open after we were buzzed in. The security office had numerous desks and computers, with active screens nearly everywhere. There were a couple offices attached to the side, but mostly this was a cubical zone. Puzo tensed up as she walked in, and I could see her eyes darting all over. The main difference between Puzo and I -- aside from the genitals -- is that she's a real detective and I am not. My first reaction in a room is to look at the gorgeous female who I'd like to see naked. Her first reaction is to scan the room and take in as many details as possible. There used to be a time where the first thing I'd look for were weapons and an exit, but times had changed just like I had.

Amongst the numerous people actively working sat Humpty and Dumpty. They sat by a laptop and carefully examined the screen. Humpty looked up at me and waved us over. Jason exited his office and ushered us all into a conference room.

"How are you feeling, Ben?" Jason inquired.

"Been better," I replied. "How long have I been out?"

"Couple hours," Puzo said.

"So did you get who did this?"

Jason shook his head. "Nothing yet. We downed a couple, so did Rachael, but they were mostly goons; nobody who had any connection to us."

I glanced at Puzo, but she kept her face still. She wasn't happy, but she wasn't angry. She was just standing there, absorbing everything she could. Jason continued, "We've informed Special Agent Puzo here that we suspect that the sniper is a former member of Croxallé's security staff."

"So how many former staff do you have?" Puzo asked.

"Our security staff is quite large," he began. "And we draw from former military and intelligence agencies. We have highly talented people all across this country."

I slid into the nearest chair and watched as Jason, Croxallé's head of security, and Puzo debated. She lashed out at him over the ethics of hiring disgruntled ex-soldiers and Jason defended his company. Their voices started to fade as I zoned out. I glanced across the room, my eyes landing on Humpty and Dumpty. I found myself snickering. If I was going to keep working with them, eventually I'd have to learn their names. The more I stared at Humpty and Dumpty, the more I began to wonder where they were hired from. Were they intelligence or military? If they were military, then which branch were they from and what rank did they hold?

Rank.

The world suddenly snapped back as I sat up in my chair. Rank; my mysterious caller had called me Specialist Thompson. "Who do you have that was in the Iraq War?"

Puzo and Jason both looked stunned at my sudden outburst, but they both quickly recovered. "Most of them. It's why many of these soldiers are getting out."

"How many of them participated in the initial invasion?" Jason pointed and Dumpty quickly started typing on the laptop. "The killer called me on the phone, right before he put a hole into your agent."

"We'll track his number," Puzo reached for her phone and started frantically typing. I gave her the number.

"He called me Specialist Thompson," I explained. "I only held that rank for just over a year. I got promoted to Specialist, like, four months before the war, and got promoted to Corporal by the end of the year."

"That's almost unheard of," Jason said.

"I know. It was part of a PR campaign after the invasion. They rewarded a lot of soldier and made a public deal of it. Add in some *can't say* stuff and I got a quick bump." I paused. "Then there's my knife." Puzo paused on her phone and turned to me. That got her attention. "The knife at the second scene was my knife. I used it in the invasion. I used it when the Rangers took an airfield. I was in my own vision."

I paused before throwing out my trump card.

"I think he wasn't one of the good guys either. He had an accent." I suddenly sounded like a horrible person. He had an accent, so he *had* to be a bad guy. I mean, what was next? He was required to wear all black, have a twisty moustache, and carry a big bag with dollar signs on it?

Jason stood there quietly as Dumpty tapped away

on the laptop. Puzo returned to her phone call, and Humpty just stood there, quiet and stoic. I slouched down and began to question myself. When I became a detective, I started by doing a great deal of research in to the trade; as you might have guessed, the term 'research' actually meant watching TV and movies. I watched T*he Maltese Falcon, Remington Steel, Psych, The Mentalist, Murder She Wrote, Magnum PI, Sherlock, Elementary*, and even *Columbo* and studied how each solved crimes. What I learned was three things:

a) TV crimes are much simpler than real life;

b) I would make a very lame Thomas Mangum; and

c) The case is much easier to solve when they show you who did it in the beginning. Thanks for that Columbo.

Oh, how we miss you, Peter Falk.

One thing that did stick with me was a famous quote from Sherlock Holmes and all its infinite remakes: "One begins to twist facts to fit theories rather than theories to fit facts." It was a warning on making a theory too early into an investigation. So as I sat there, I began to question my theory.

I knew I caught an accent on the phone, but I couldn't place it. Was it a leap to claim it as a Middle-Eastern accent? What about my rank? There were literally millions of people who could have come across that rank. Entire support staff members and upper military members would have seen my name and rank pass before their eyes dozens of times before they chose me to be promoted. Anybody could have seen that. I also couldn't ignore that people got ranks wrong all the time. My theory had more holes in it then Peter Weller did in the opening of *Robocop*.

"We have a name that may fit," Jason said aloud. He spun the laptop around so I could screen. "His name is Nouri Allawi. Do you recognize him?"

I glanced at the screen and stared at the face of the Middle-Eastern solider. I recognized that face immediately. It was that of the man who kidnapped me, threw me into the van, and then pressed his boot to my head and threatened to put a bullet in it. It was the face of the man Puzo shot.

Take that, Sherlock Holmes. My theories are amazing. That would teach me about taking life advice from fictional characters.

"I put a bullet in his head," Puzo said as she leaned in for a look. She looked down and frowned. "This can't be right. His date of birth is 1976. That man does not look forty."

She was right. The face looking back at me was a man entering his thirties, not one looking to exit them. His face still looked fresh -- all except for his eyes. His eyes looked old, much older than the rest of him. They looked like he had grown up decades ago. Everybody, no matter how old they are, have a hint of the child they once were glimmering in their eyes. Allawi didn't.

"What's his power?" Puzo asked.

And there it was: the elephant in the room. It was big, grey, and massive enough that if we wanted to harvest his metaphorical tusks that we'd make enough off the metaphorical ivory to never have to metaphorically work again. But I would never do that, harvesting ivory is wrong, hella wrong -- even in a metaphor.

I'd been beating around the subject, Jason had been beating around the subject, and whatever the hell Humpty and Dumpty were they were also beating around the subject. Six months ago, I'd learned that the world was filled with more powers then psychic visions and fiery eyebeams. The world had far freakier things, but it was a big secret and somewhere, deep down in it, was Croxallé and something called The Visegar Company. Everybody who knew about this secret fought to keep it that way. Some say the world's not ready for the big reveal, others say it will rip the world apart. I don't know much about either of these statements, but I decided not to say anything to anybody about it. I look crazy enough as it is without spouting crap about a real-life Spider-Man, Hulk, Batman, and Superman walking around the world. Also, chances are if the truth about a real-life Spider-Man or Batman showed up, Disney and Warner Brothers would hold hands and sue the living daylights out of them.

Jason moved to speak, to refute her statement, but Puzo never gave him a chance. "I'm not an idiot. I'm a cop. I figure things out."

"Rachael..." I started. I didn't know how to reply. I knew sooner or later she would find out, and while I'm not surprised that she deduced it on her own, somehow I thought she'd come to me first.

"I'm not sure how much I believe, but I've seen evidence that points to a psychic, a man who can shoot lasers from his eyes, a telekinetic, and a shapeshifter assassin." Lt. Hugo Chapman. He was a former Navy SEAL who developed the ability to look however he chose. When I ran into him, he was killing people while looking like Burt Reynolds, Mark Wahlberg and Heather Graham. His last days on earth were spent looking exactly like me while trying to kill me. I looked him dead in his eyes -- my eyes -- then put a bullet in his brain.

It was very symbolic. It was like a figurehead for my recovery.

"And none of that is even taking into account the cab driver I ran into who, I'm pretty sure, could duplicate himself." I glanced at Puzo in confusion. I hadn't heard that story. She shrugged me off. "Powers are real and somehow Croxallé seems tied into it. So I'm running the odds here and asking again: what is his power?"

Jason glanced at Humpty and shook his head. "He can heal."

"Like Hugh Jackman?" Robby loves those films. Jason nodded.

Puzo glanced at the screen. "So that date is correct then? He was really born in 1976?"

Jason nodded again. "Born 1976, recruited into Hussain boot camp in 1986, and fought for two years in the Iran-Iraq war as a child soldier. He served until he was an adult, then he was recruited into the Republic Guard and eventually promoted into the Elite Guard."

"Jesus. A child soldier?"

"He was reported killed-in-action during the Battle of Baghdad..."

"But his powers kicked in." Jason nodded at my statement. I knew the feeling. Mine kicked in after the horrifying explosion that, rudely, ended my army career. There was something about high-danger or life-threatening situations that could kick-start your career as a super-hero or super-villain.

"So he's still alive?" Puzo asked. Crap, I hadn't thought of that. "He survived my bullet to his brain?"

Jason nodded. "We never found his body."

"Great," I said loudly. "Now on top of worrying about a sniper, I have to worry about being stabbed by claws."

All four of them just stared at me. Each of them held the most confused look ever to exist on a human face since that one I wore while trying to watch *White House Down*. I mean, who thought that pairing Channing Tatum and Jaime Foxx together in an action film was a good idea.

"Claws?" Jason asked slowly.

"Yeah." Why were they confused? This was simple math. "Healers come with claws. Like Hugh Jackman. Why else would they have healing abilities if it weren't for claws?"

Puzo just sighed as she returned to her phone. "I'm not even dignifying that with an answer."

"Healers don't need to have claws," Jason explained. "It's not a prerequisite."

"I'm pretty sure it is," I defended. "I mean, why else would nature or science give you superior healing if it weren't for the ejection of battle-ready claws?"

"If claws were an issue, then why wouldn't nature just give you a built-in corridor in your hand so that when the claws eject they don't tear any flesh or skin?" Dumpty asked. Humpty spun his head around and glared at his partner.

"Obviously that would be an opening for infection. I mean, look at the penis," I defended in a tone that showed that information should have been obvious. "Look, let's drop this. We all need to agree that he'll have claws."

"The trace is a no go," Puzo interrupted, much to Jason's undying thanks. "The phone was a burner."

"So what do you guys do now?" I asked.

Puzo rubbed her forehead with her thumb. "I'll go back to the FBI and see what I can dig up from them."

I looked at Jason. "We'll do..." Jason paused. "Similar things."

"Sir." Jason looked up at Humpty. "We have a visitor approaching. *He* is almost here."

Jason's eyes shot up at the word *he*. Jason straightened his clothes and adjusted his tie. He glimpsed at the door just as *he* walked in. I didn't know who *he* was, but *he* was definitely important. Any man who entered a room with three assistants following behind him, two of which were on smart phones doing what I could only assume was either business or sexting, had to be important. Any man who wore a three-piece suit and walked like his shit didn't stink had to be to be important. I knew little about suits, jeans or nothing baby, but I could assume that suit cost more than my monthly military medical pension checks.

"Benedict Thompson," he smirked. "It's a pleasure to finally meet you."

He offered me a hand. I took it and gave it a firm squeeze. He looked down at my gloved hand and nodded in approval.

"That right there," he said enthusiastically, "is a nice firm handshake."

I tried to break the handshake, but this man wouldn't let me. He kept shaking it as he looked around the room. "This boy did everything right. He approached me while maintaining eye contact. Notice the web grip, none of this spread finger crap, and that's not even talking about the grip. It's firm. I get so much of this crush-your-hand-death-grip bullshit from work that this is refreshing." I tried to pull away yet again, but had no luck. "I now think you are a strong and trustworthy man, someone who demands respect and loyalty and yet I can revere. I like this."

"I'm glad you approve, sir, but I'm going to need this hand back very soon."

He chuckled. "Of course you are, son. Of course you are. It's a pleasure to meet you, son, I'm Thaddeus Clay."

Ever feel like a moment should be super dramatic, like some big reveal had just been made? Ever think that a moment you are currently experiencing should be that WTF moment before a commercial break or the end of a chapter? The type of moment that made you keep your eyes glued to the TV for the commercials to end or that made you rapidly flip the page and forgo sleep just to find out what happens next?

This wasn't one of those moments.

Chapter 11
That's it, Brain, You're on Your Own

With my hand finally free, I looked around. Jason was standing firm, Puzo's eyes were narrowed as she glared at Mr. Clay, and even Humpty and Dumpty seemed more -- proper. Could robots be programmed to be more robotic? I, however, was standing around looking like a dumbass.

I was missing something, something important. I could just feel it. But how did you ask what it was that you were missing without seeming like a dumbass? You had to be subtle; you had to be smooth.

"Okay, I'm missing something here and I feel like a dumbass," I blurted out. "Why is the room awkward?"

Way to go brain. Smooth one. That's it, brain, you're on your own; we're breaking up. I wrote you a poem:

Roses are red,
Violets are blue
Welcome to Splits-ville,
Population: You.

Disclaimer: When the above cowboy mentioned the word wrote he actually meant *stole it from 90's sitcoms*.

"Ben," Rachael said firmly. "Thaddeus Clay is the CEO of Croxallé."

Oh damn. I just shook hands with the devil.

"Special Agent Puzo," Clay smirked. "We've been seeing a lot of each other these days. Maybe we should make it official and let me take you out for dinner." He glanced at me. "You're not in a relationship with anyone these days, are you?"

That's just dirty.

"Senior Special Agent," Rachael corrected. Then she smirked. "A date? Perhaps. But warning time, I like to hand-cuff. You still in?"

I quickly pulled out my phone and started typing a memo, my excitement tingling with each letter I punched in.

Note to self: Rachael likes handcuffs.

I paused and suddenly came to a realization. She was a cop. She probably meant to arrest him or something. I glanced down at my reminder -- which suddenly seemed stupid -- and realized that I needed to delete it or edit it. Reluctantly, I tapped a couple more keys.

Note to self: Rachael likes handcuffs -- maybe.

"I think you and I like different type of ice-cream, Special Agent," he said, putting a slight mockery on the last two words. "I prefer vanilla."

He turned to Jason and raised an eyebrow. Jason, like a soldier, jumped to attention and started talking. "We believe that the sniper *may* be a former employee of my security division."

I frowned and glanced back at Mr. Clay. Jason wasn't lying, he wasn't hiding anything. Despite the fact that Jason came to me to protect himself from Croxallé, to cover and protect his own ass, he just opened up and revealed everything with no hesitation. I needed to know more, but was it safe to do so?

Like most of my internal debates, I found a lack of a mental list of pros and cons, instead I found myself at Fenway Park during the ninth inning of a Red Sox/Yankee's game. It was the top of the 9th inning, and the Red Sox were up by three. The bases were loaded and stepping up to the plate for the Yankees, with an average of .375, was the slugger Curiosity! The red-blooded crowd booed loudly.

The Sox coach stepped out of the dugout and marched to the mound. He patted the pitcher on the back, told him he did a good job, and sent him to the shower. He waved in the relief pitcher. The red-crowd roared, this time in cheers, as the pitcher Reason, takes the mound. The coach handed him the ball and whispered, "Don't screw this up."

The pitcher glared down the field and took his position. My mind started to race. He waved off the first pitch and nodded for the second. Reason kicked and fired the ball forward.

I needed to know more, but this wasn't the place to risk my life.

Curiosity swung, the bat missing the ball by inches as it suddenly sunk downwards. A slider -- strike one. The pitcher smirked, reset and nodded when the proper pitch came up. With another kick and a windup, Reason fired a second throw.

This isn't involved with the case; this is Jason's petty shit. This is Croxallé politics.

Curiosity narrowed his eye; it was an inside pitch. He just ignored it as it came in, cringing as it curved at the last moment and passed over the plate. A curveball -- strike two. The catcher fired back the ball and crouched back down. He gave only one sign this time, and Reason didn't shake it off. He wound up, kicked out his foot, and fired.

Jason wasn't family; he gave up that right years ago.

The ball was coming down fast; it was a center pitch and perfect aligned. Curiosity tightened his grip on the bat and started to swing, putting all of his strength behind this one slice.

But I needed to know. I owed Jason.

The air went quiet and people waited for the next sound, hanging onto its echo. The slap of hide on hide filled the air and the Red Sox fans exploded in cheers. Fast ball -- strike three. Red Sox won.

The internal debate came to a hasty halt like a screeching record. Did Reason just win? What the crap? Reason never wins; like absolutely positively never. My past relationships were proof of that. If Reason had ever won, like even once, I wouldn't have a string of angry exes.

I glanced at Clay and found him smirking. His lips moved, and for a moment I swore I could make out the words *maybe next time*. I had shaken hands with the devil and somehow he seemed to affect my mind. Was that possible? Was I just making it up? Or was it the massive headache speaking? I needed a drink.

"Mr. Daggett, offer our help to the FBI," he instructed. "But do not grant her access to our systems. She'll need a warrant for that."

"Refusing to help the FBI clean up your disgruntled employee mess?" Puzo said snidely.

"Not at all," he replied. "I just can't have this investigation conflict with your *other* investigation."

He gave me a glance. "Good day, Ben, it was a pleasure."

We watched him turn and leave, and I found myself thinking WTF? Seriously: WTF? I'm not normally the fourteen-year-old-teenage-girl who tweets with net speak, but it was all that came to mind. This man was bad guy. He was the type of man Jack Bauer would finally reach on Day Two after twenty-three long episodes only to find that he's actually Tobin Bell.

Tobin Bell played Peter Kingsley -- a rich guy trying to run up oil prices with war -- in the second season of *24*. He did a great job, but after I saw the *Saw* movies I couldn't help but wonder how that season would have been different if instead of playing Kingsley, Bell played his character from *Saw* instead.

"Give me the real recordings, Kingsley! The President cannot go to war over this nuke," Jack would say in his grisly tone while holding a gun to Bell's head.

"You want the recording? Well then," Kingsley would say with a smirk and a grin while pulling on his white mask. "I want to play a game."

Jack shoots him in the head.

BAM! The US goes to war and all of 24's history changes.

God, I love *24*. I may have squealed like a little girl -- a manly little girl -- when it came back on the air. Jack was back, baby!

Puzo clasped my shoulder and brought me back to the present. She looked me in the eyes and forced a smile. We had stuff to talk about. Stuff like her other case and why she was at my murder scene.

"I'll drop by tonight," she said, pausing before asking, "if that's okay?"

I nodded at her and she left, rubbing the side of her head with her hand. There was a time in my life when I'd beg to have a hot woman to come over, and here was one asking for permission. Inside I giggled and cheered like a thirty-year-old woman seeing a Backstreet Boys concert almost fifteen years later.

Jason walked into his office, rubbing his forehead while giving out a small wince. My head was hurting as well; it hadn't stopped since I got thrown around that van. I hobbled after Jason, wondering if headaches were contagious since mine seemed to be spreading to Jason and Rachael. Jason's office was classy, not Jack-Bauer-glass-office classy but still up there. He had several shelves full of books, a big screen television mounted on the wall, two computer screens on his expensive desk and several leather chairs strewn about.

"Take a seat, Ben." I'm a man bound to a cane; I don't need to be told twice. I plopped into the chair nearest to the desk as Jason took a seat behind it. The chair was made from real leather and seemed to swallow me whole. It was like what I could only assume sitting on a cloud felt like. One thing I do miss about being powerless is the ability to run my fingers across a good leather chair or over a smooth silk sheet without seeing a vision of some salesmen caressing it like a woman he just paid for, or your mother sprawled out on the sheets beckoning your father forward.

No level of therapy helps you with that.

I pulled off my glove and decided to risk it. I'd missed the feel of expensive leather. Besides, this was an evil medical corporation. Chances were I was going to see sexy assassins, hulk-like abominations, and witty banter reserved for spies and Bond-villains. I ran both hands across the armrest, and for a moment, a brief moment, I just bathed in the feel of good, expensive leather. It was heavenly; then came the shiver and a twitch.

The world rewound and my vision plunked me into this exact office at an unknown earlier date. Jason sat behind his desk while three other employees, two men and woman, sat in the remaining chairs.

"Sir, I don't see how we can continue our bid to upgrade our computers with this 14% deduction. It's just not possible. If we cut hours," the first guy said.

"You are not cutting my men's hours. We can't maintain our coverage-" the woman defended.

"And I'm sure as hell not eliminating vehicle repairs. Those cars are stretched thin as it is. As it stands we could use at least another fifteen cars, and not even armoured ones."

My vision faded away and I was left dumbstruck. A budget meeting? My vision decided to show me a budget meeting? The more I thought about it, the more it made sense. Times were tough all around, you just never know how tough until your local evil medical corporation has to cut costs.

As I looked around Jason's office, all from the comfort of this heaven chair, and spotted a baseball resting on a stand that stood firmly on the edge of his desk. "Hey, where did you get this?" I asked as I absentmindedly reached for it.

"Ben, no!"

I barely heard the words as my finger brushed the

baseball. Sport equipment normally wasn't too bad; you got to see a passionate strike out, a heroic homerun or that big goal shot on net. This was different.

Normally a vision comes with a shiver up my back and eyes begin to twitch; this time I felt something different. My entire body began to shiver and twitch and some force, some strong force, sent my body flying backwards like the time Annie fired me from a massive elastic she tied to a tree. I grew up on a farm; you had to make your own entertainment.

My body shook violently as each spasm ripped through my body; my eyes didn't twitch, they just rolled back in the back of my head and the world faded away. For the briefest moment, I saw Jason sitting in his chair, in this very office, holding the baseball and gently caressing it in his finger, but that image was quickly replaced as my powers bombarded me with vision after vision like the nerd in gym class being hit with red rubber ball after red rubber ball.

I saw Jason and my sister at a fair, each holding a pellet gun at one of those shooting gallery booths. Jason shot first, hitting ten out of fifteen targets, intentionally missing two to not make Annie feel bad and missing three because the damn game was rigged. Annie stood up next and dropped fourteen.

"Oh, the hell with that," Jason cried out. "Rematch: I was going easy on you last time."

"Bring it on, Greg," Annie snapped back with a grin, using the fake name Jason had given her. "You just got into a shooting match with a Thompson. You're in over you league, city boy."

I watched as they went round after round, spending nearly an hour, and an obscene amount of money, trying to prove whom the better shot was.

My vision shifted and I was at a Shea Stadium, home to the New York Mets. Annie and Jason sat in the seats that ran along the first base foul line, her cuddled up into his arms, as they watched the Mets loose. The Mets always lost. Annie was a Yankees fan; her blood was blue, which meant Jason was the Mets fan; as if I didn't have enough reason to hate him. They giggled and laughed and whispered sweet nothings to each other when a foul ball caught their attention. It was flying their way, high in the sky, but was set to pass them. In my vision, I could feel Jason reaching out with his telekinetic powers, grasping the ball with his mind and gently nudging it down towards her. She raised her gloved hand up and with a whoop of glee caught it. She was brimming with excitement, and she turned and kissed Jason. It wasn't a peck; it was a full-blown passionate love kiss. It was the kind of kiss that ended with a *to be continued later* look from here and a *I'm going to be sick if I have to watch my sister having sex with this dude* look from me.

My vision shifted.

Jason and Annie sat on the couch, cuddled together as some rom-com movie played on TV. She was smiling. Jason looked down at her and raised an eyebrow. "What is it?"

"I love you, city boy," she said. "You know that?"

"I do," he replied. He wasn't lying; I could feel it. "And I love you too, Desert Lily."

Annie bolted up. "What did you call me? Did you call me a flower? I'll have you know I'm a country girl, not some delicate-flower-city-girl."

"Hey, hey, I know," Jason defended. "That's not what I meant. A desert lily is a very beautiful flower that grows in some of Earth's roughest conditions. What I'm saying is just because you're a crazy rough and tough redneck woman-" She jabbed him with her elbow. "-Doesn't mean you can't be beautiful."

Annie stared at him for a moment, carefully mulling over his words. She eventually nodded and returned to his cuddling grasp. "Nice save, city boy, nice save."

My vision shifted again and again as every date played out before my eyes. I saw the time they went to the beach and Jason got caught checking out a drop dead, gorgeous woman wearing what could be a bikini designed for a mouse or a Barbie doll. I watched as she called him out on it and bitched at him for it, using that Thompson flair, only to have her words trail off into nothingness as her eyes fell upon the perfectly sculpted abs of some beach hunk walking past.

I watched as the two of them went Go-Karting, Annie driving like a maniac and running Jason off the road, stopping only to point and laugh before speeding off to win the race. I saw Jason give her something Robby would call the Luigi Death Stare. I saw Jason take her to a fancy restaurant only to find out that Annie enjoyed a good steak and some fries far more than any fancy food. I even saw their fights, their spats about the future and money. I saw their fights about marriage and the way they kissed to make up afterwards. I saw it all.

My vision shifted again, only this time it wasn't a date. I was in my sister's bedroom, the room dark but I could still clearly make out her sleeping form and Jason standing over her, fully dressed and bag in his hand.

"I'm sorry, Desert Lily," he apologised softly. "I can't believe I'm doing this. I don't want to, but I'm not strong enough to say no, not to them."

This was the night Jason left, the night he abandoned his pregnant girlfriend and vanished from our lives completely. Earlier that night was the last time Annie had ever seen Jason, the father to her child, and now I had to watch him say goodbye.

"When it comes to both of us, you were the stronger one. You always were. So much of this was supposed to be fake, but my love wasn't, not anymore. I love you with all my heart and I always will. I know you can't hear me, but I need a favour," Jason pleaded to the sleeping form. "Never forgive me. Never, ever forgive me for what I'm about to do -- ever. Hate me for the rest of my life. It's what I deserve."

He reached down and kissed her forehead. "I love you. Goodbye."

And with that he was gone.

It suddenly made sense to me what I was watching, why that baseball had so much power in it. Jason loved my sister, honestly and truly, and leaving her was the hardest thing he ever had to do. So Jason would spend hours in his chair, holding that baseball, caressing it, thinking back to the days gone past and the love he'd given up on.

I had just experienced a vision of a man reliving his memories, each more emotionally powerful then the last. That baseball held within it the combined emotional power of a life of regret, of love lost and opportunity missed. That baseball also had stored within it more memories and recollection then the fifteen year reunion for that redneck high school football team that won state that one year. Combined together, that baseball became of the second most dangerous artifact for a psychic like me to touch.

Chapter 12
A Young Man Walks into a
Cougar Bar for a Reason

"Ben," a voice yelled. "Ben!"

I came to and found myself lying on the floor of Jason's office with a nurse and a doctor standing over me while Jason, Humpty, and Dumpty stood back and watched. If this was a movie, I'd open my eyes, say something funny, and start flirting with the buxomly nurse, but my body was sore, my head was killing me, and every little noise and light send a massive wave of excruciating pain pulsating though my head. At that exact moment, the only possible words that would be able to come from my lips would be nothing short of a guhhh.

"Guhhh?" I moaned. Yeah, I nailed it. Cut. Print. I'll be in my trailer.

"Jesus, Ben," Jason said as he approached. "Are you alright? You scared us."

"Guhhh?"

"Is he okay?"

"Well, in a normal case we'd say he had a seizure," the doctor said. "But for him, I'd say it was psychic backlash."

I allowed my eyes to come into some sort of focus and stared up at the female nurse standing over me. I tried to wink and follow that up with witty banter and sexual flirting, but got little more than a scrunched up face and my new catchphrase.

"Guhhh?" Yeah. She totally wanted to jump my bones now.

"Put him in the chair and get him some water," the nurse explained. "He'll regain control in a second."

I found myself floating upwards and for a moment I thought I had died. My vision had come true and I had died. Man, that would be a shitty ending: killed by a baseball. It took me a moment to realize that Jason was lifting me into the air using his Keanu Reeves powers. Thinking I'd died seemed ridiculous the more I thought about. I couldn't be dead; I wasn't burning in hell.

It wasn't something I thought of often, I tried not to, but back in my soldiering days I'd taken a life or two. Sure, it was all in the defense of my nation. I was killing bad men who were doing worse things, but in the dark of the night, when I was alone with no one but my deliberations, I thought about it. It wasn't pretty.

Jason lowered me into the chair, and the nurse handed me a glass of water. The doctor stopped her. "Mr. Dagget, could you fetch Ben a real drink?"

Jason nodded, opened up his desk and withdrew a glass and some whiskey. He poured me two fingers and handed it to me. I took a sip. For a moment, it felt like my senses were heightened, everything was stronger. Water felt wetter, glass felt grainier, voices were louder and lights were brighter. Everybody smelled like they hadn't showered in days or were bathing in cologne or perfume. Yet the moment the whiskey hit my mouth, everything changed. Remember when you were young and you downed your first shot of whiskey neat? You wanted to be a real man, like your Dad, and drink whiskey like a tough guy. Yet the moment it hit, it started burning like a bitch and you started hacking and coughing like an idiot while everybody laughed. Then some guy, some *friend*, gave you a way-too-strong slap on the shoulder and it sent you into a deeper coughing fit. This whiskey was like that.

I hadn't hacked at whiskey in years. I had become

that real man -- ish -- but with one gulp, I was back to being a seventeen-year-old kid, under-age drinking at party while my Dad watched and laughed. The whiskey overwhelmed my senses, it attacked all of them and not in the right order. I could see the whiskey's taste, I could hear its smell, I could feel what it looked like, and I could touch what it smelled like. I hacked for a few moments more, Jason thankfully taking the glass back, and then I abruptly stopped. I looked around and found everything was back to normal. My senses were at their normal level, not cranked to eleven like some cult favourite mockumentary, and I could speak again.

"Guhh?" Damn it!

I shook the cobwebs out of my head and pulled my gloves over my hand. There was no way in hell I was touching anything for the next little while. I stood up and glanced at the nurse and the doctor. The nurse was cute, not cartoon-super-hot but still way above my league.

"Hello, Nurse," I said calmly, despite every urge to yell those exact words in an excited cartoon fashion not seen since vaudeville or the 90s. I glanced at the doctor. "Hello, Doctor."

"You're going to want to take it easy, Benedict," she said as she stepped forward. She pulled out a pen light and shined it into my eyes. I blinked rapidly. Then she flicked my forehead.

"Ow!"

"Yep, he's fine," she concluded as she pocketed the penlight. She offered her hand. "Dr. Madison Harper."

I shook her hand and gave the traditional once-over look that guys are infamous for. She was a head shorter then I was, older too, but still had her looks. She was a black woman with a firm face and strong eyes. I was surprised that for me the eyes stood out, because normally it's totally the breasts or the rear (I'm so male, I know), but somehow her eyes were dominating my attention. They were firm, strong and com-manding. They had experience, they had respect, and they had my attention. She was gorgeous in the strong-commanding-female way.

Spoiler Alert: I have a type.

I'm not saying I hadn't been with older women before, a young man walks into a cougar bar for a reason, but it wasn't what I normally went for. Yet somehow I could easily see myself engaging in some mutual form of carnal entertainment with her. Well, if she wasn't so very far out of my league, but a man can dream.

I'd like to point out that before my injury, before I changed, my gaze would never make it high enough to even notice the eyes on a woman. Now they do; that's character development right there. High five for personal growth.

"Why whiskey?" I asked. "Why not water?"

"Water doesn't have a strong enough taste or kick," she explained, almost bored with the subject. "You needed a reboot for your senses, a pallet cleanser, something with enough kick to get noticed. It's called psychic backlash. It happens to telepathics, telekinetics and your type of psychics."

Well, you learn something new every day. You know, for an evil doctor, she wasn't that bad. "So what do you do here?" I asked.

"I'm one of the senior medical physicians here," she explained. "I excel in meta-human physiology and paranormal abilities."

She was a high-ranking, evil doctor. Regardless, she was still nice in an I'll-flick-you-when-you're-down type of way.

She looked at Jason. "I'm going to get Dr. Hammett to look him over, give him a quick physical and then I'm sending him home."

"I nee--"

"I do not care, Mr. Dagget. I'm sending him home," she said as she escorted me out of the security offices, not giving Jason a second thought.

Strong, commanding, and brilliant; yeah, I had a type.

One of the most awkward things in the world is sitting naked on a doctor's table. The only thing more awkward then that is when the doctor walks in, takes a look at you with her wide eyes and then sheepishly says that you didn't have to naked at all, informing you that it wasn't *that* type of check-up.

Doc Hammett, Doctor Christine Hammett, was a younger woman, roughly my age, with skin that I could only describe as mocha coloured. She had bouncy brown hair, with blond highlights, and brown eyes. She had the standard white doctor coat over a blue set of scrubs and a stethoscope around her neck. She even held the standard doctor metal clipboard that had the mystical *chart*. I've spent a lot of time in hospitals -- having more metal in your leg than a fridge arranges that for you -- and no matter what hospital I was in, I never could see my chart. It was like the chart held dark secrets and when it wasn't being used it was required to be put in wooden crate, stored in a warehouse far, far away and then have suited individuals reassure me that it was being inspected by *top men*.

I quickly pulled on my pants and did up my belt. As I reached for my shirt, I found Dr. Hammett's eyes locked on my bare chest. Any normal guy would be complimented by such a firmly locked gaze from a woman, but I knew the real reason and it wasn't pretty. Dr. Hammett was staring at the scars that adorned my chest like a Rorschach test. When my Humvee ran over an IED, my leg took the full brunt of the attack, but my entire body was assaulted by shrapnel -- not to mention the damage I sustained when the IED, inconsiderate as it was, decided to pitch the vehicle off the road in a rolling faction. IEDs are jerks. Since then, most of my body healed nicely, my leg being the only bum -- aside from my actual bum -- but my chest was left with dozens of battle scars. It was unsightly and instantly killed any hope I had of being a male model. I mean if Ben Stiller could do it, then so could I. There is also the fact that I used to be really, really ridiculously good looking.

"Yeah, I know," I said, breaking the silence. "They suck. It'll teach me to fry bacon in the buff." She snickered.

"Do your war scars ever hurt?" she asked, regaining her doctor-y composure.

"Only up here," I said, tapping my forehead.

Hammett opened her chart and gave a quick re-read. The she close it with a snap and stood before me. "So I see when we brought you in, we checked you for serious injuries, but you seem fine now. You were beat up, but you're bouncing back."

"I'll be up and hobbling in no time." She raised an eyebrow and nodded towards the cane. "I don't run, I hobble," I explained.

"Well, what I really want to ask you about is your powers," she said with a nod. "Do you still get headaches from your powers?"

"Minor ones," I explained. "They used to be worse but with practise they've mostly gone away."

"Have you ever suffered psychic backlash like you did earlier?" I shook my head. "Nose bleeds? Temporary paralysis? Erectile dysfunction?" I shook my head at all three. Why is it I feared ED more than paralysis? It must be a man thing.

She continued to ask me questions, inquiring about my abilities and its side effects. As weird as it was to have evil Croxallé ask me personal questions, it was still brought me a sense of relief to openly talk about my abilities. I had nobody I could talk to about my powers, nobody that didn't require a mile and a half of explanations and questions to which I rarely knew the answers to, anyways.

"So, what's it like working for evil Croxallé?" I asked in a jovial tone. That was my tactic, dive into their creepy evil organization while using jokes and jests to find the answer. The fool detective -- who had done that before?

Psych, Castle, Columbo - need I go on?

Shut up, Brain! We broke up, remember?

"It's okay. We get evil benefits, just not evil dental." She was clever, this one. "We're not evil, Mr. Thompson."

"Ben, please," I offered. "I mean, you've already seen me naked."

She laughed. "We are progressive. We take leaps that others miss. It comes with failures, every aspect of science does, but mankind will benefit from what we do here."

She kept working, jotting notes down in her chart. "Besides, Croxallé isn't bad or mean. They recruited me right out of medical school and helped me take a massive leap up in my career. On the track they've put me on, when I'm Dr. Harper's age, I will be twice as far in my career then she is in hers; that's no small feat."

I gave her an impressed look as I dug into my wallet and withdrew a business card for SRG Security. I handed it to her.

"You seem nice, less corrupted," I said with a joking tone, a jest to cover the fact that I meant exactly what I'd just said, "So if you ever need anything, help, a hand, or something, give your local psychic a call."

She thanked me and handed a different card back. "I know you're not on best terms with my company," she admitted, pointing to her chart. "It says so right here -- 'does not play well with Croxallé' -- but if you ever run into a medical problem with your powers, something you think regular doctors cannot handle... Give us a call."

I pushed the card back and opened my mouth to object, there was no way in hell I was coming to Croxallé for help, but she flipped over the card and handed it back. "My personal number is on the back. If it's serious, I'll help you. Not Croxallé; me."

Oh, well, that was different. I took the card and thanked her. As I hobbled out the door, I found myself thinking about the entire situation. Was she flirting with me? Was she being nice because she wanted to ride the Ben-o-matic

Roller Coaster © 2014? Was she just genuinely a nice person? Yet as all those questions flew by two things remained: one was a small feeling of guilt and the other was the million-dollar question...

Did I have to apologise to Puzo for what just happened?

Chapter 13
Was My Brain Stalking Me?

I jumped in a cab and told the driver my home address. He sped off and I sat in the back quietly until we were a couple blocks away from the Croxallé offices. Then I leaned forward and gave him a new address. I needed to see a good friend about an old case. I needed to see Hotwire.

The first time I met him, he lived in the loft above a nightclub. Two weeks after Robby was home safe and sound, he sold it and moved. It took him a full month to tell me his new location. The club used to be a perfect hideout for my hacker friend; he'd run the legitimate business downstairs and run his slightly illegal one upstairs. The industrial sized AC unit installed in the club masked the intense heat signature from his massive computer system and kept him hidden away from prying police eyes. And yet for some reason, he gave all that up.

The cab came to a halt on the edge of the warehouse district of the city. The warehouse district is a weird one. It's on the edge of the business sector, it straddles the industrial sector and it's filled with desperate men cursing at the auto-correct function on their phone. Yet here I was, as desperate as them, but for something else all together different. I was standing in front of a cold-storage locker rental lot. It was like those storage wars lockers you see on A&E except it was colder and a front for an illegal business. Also, if someone didn't pay their rental fees then nobody wanted your expired meat.

I hobbled to the building and clumsily climbed the stairs to the office on the top. This new business had some advantage that the old one didn't. It was a cold storage locker. It was a place full of massive fridges; this place was going to have massive electricity bills on top of his super computer system, not to mention the heat signature that would mask his servers from any prying law enforcement with a thermal camera. The place was remote, off the beaten path so to speak, so anybody who approached it wasn't doing so by accident. And with an elevated office, and a scattering of cameras that I couldn't help but notice, Hotwire could spot anyone long before they reached him.

It was a genius set-up but not a new one. Criminals had been using this for decades and law enforcement had begun to catch on. Places like these often found prying eyes from cops, feds and even homeland. Hell, I wouldn't bat an eye if I saw Congressmen Brody bolt by with Carrie Matheson chasing after him.

Actually, the day TV starts to come to life before my eyes is the day I may need to accept the fact that I may need to cut down on my TV watching. Truth is, I should do that already but a healthy dose of a miracle drug known as *denial* made it very easy to avoid that.

As I reached the top I saw that I was smack dab in the sight of two different cameras that I could see, and probably at least one more I couldn't; I glanced at each and gave a dumbass wave. Amongst the silence, with little else but the echoing honking of a car horn in the distance, I swore I could hear the exasperated sigh of Hotwire from inside. The office door opened automatically and I hobbled inwards. A large hand clamped down on my left shoulder and booming voice told me to freeze.

I reacted.

Jack's training kicked in, supplementing my old tutelage, and I reacted. My plan was to twist to my right side, breaking his grip on my left, while elbowing my attacker with my right arm. While he was doubled over, I'd use my cane to sweep his legs out from underneath him and send him crashing to the floor. And finally, as he lay on the floor crying like a little girl and claiming I was the battle god, I would stand over him triumphantly and laugh while randomly appearing woman rushed to my side to congratulate me. Things did not go as planned -- big surprise.

Murphy's Law: No plan ever survives contact with the enemy.

Things started going wrong almost instantly. My elbow strike was off, the joint bouncing off his side instead of slamming into his gut, and he didn't double over. So when my cane tried to sweep him off his feet, I had as much success as I would if I tried to knock down a tree with a pencil. My attacker -- who turned out to be a large white guy with muscles upon muscles -- grabbed me by my shirt, hoisted me into the air, and slammed me into the nearest wall. With my back pressed against it and my feet dangling, I had but one option. I smashed his balls with my cane.

I didn't feel proud about that move.

He let go of me, in order to cup his sore genitals, and I fell to the ground hard, gasping for air as I hit the floor. As he doubled over, and eventually dropped to one knee, I climbed to my feet, prepared to take my victory pose. I was interrupted when his hand snapped out and backhanded my balls. I let out a high pitch noise akin to a squirrel being punched in his nuts, nobody likes their winter food supply being punched, and toppled over like a Ben without a cane.

Did I just become my own metaphor?

That went well.

You're still here, Brain? I told you: we're through.

"What the hell?" a familiar voice called out. "You're supposed to be a highly trained security enforcer and the aftermath of your fight with a cripple using a cane is you both end up on the floor clutching your junk?"

I looked up and saw two identical men walking to

me. I recognized each of them instantly. These two men were Hotwires. I winced and squinted, the two Hotwires melding into one as my double vision reverted to singular.

"You okay, Kerner?" My attacker grunted. "Ben?"

"Guhhh?" Damn it!

"Both of you get up and follow me inside." I climbed back to my feet and followed Hotwire, walking bowlegged past reception and into the back room. The thug known as Kerner followed behind me, his legs mimicking my walk.

Hotwire was a man of contrasts. Hackers were supposed to look like Justin Long or Matthew Lillard, not like Daniel Craig or Jon Hamm. Hotwire firmly fit in the second category. Hotwire, or Jimmy Wilcox, looked more like a playboy dynasty then a techno-geek. He had stylized black hair, a goatee and Italian suit three-piece suit.

"You're indoors, cowboy," he reminded me. I removed my hat. "So how was the belly of the beast?"

"Are you tracking my phone again?" He shrugged as he slid into his chair. I looked around at his new place. "Nice digs."

Compared to the studio apartment he had above the club, this new place was a step down. It was essentially an entire top floor of the main building that had been converted into a four-bedroom apartment. In the main room was the holy grail of computer set-ups. Hotwire's desk was shaped like a C with a wall of six monitors, three towers and a massive cooling unit.

"It does the job." I stared at the hacker for a moment. Everything about his demeanour has changed since I'd seen him last. He seemed colder towards me, more reserved. "Here."

Hotwire handed me a brown folder. I opened it up and quickly scanned the few files on the inside. "What's this?"

"A lead on your case, Cowboy," he explained. "I found some irregularity in bank statements."

"I thought you said Skit-Tech was clean?"

"They are. This is for Richard Slott, an employee of

Lionhead Security."

"Lionhead?" Security companies had me on edge recently. "They a PMC?"

"Oh, god no," he laughed. "These are warehouse rent-a-cops. They guard buildings in the middle of the night. Mr. Slott there guards a warehouse full of unreleased phones and tablets belonging to Skit-Tech."

I flipped to his bank statements. "Wow, someone made 10k in two months. I'm in the wrong business." I flipped a couple more pages. "Because, if anybody's wondering, being a gimp on a medical pension is a really crappy profession."

Hotwire just sighed. I recognized that sigh, it was the one Annie, my mom, Rachael, police, random strangers, that homeless guy who begs for change and somehow makes more than I do, and just about everybody else gives me when they can no longer put up with my jokes. Hotwire turned to look at me, his eyes getting his first good look at me since I removed my hat.

"Holy shit, Ben." His face was filled with genuine concern. I just blinked at him. He grabbed a mirror and handed it to me. "What the hell happened?"

I glanced at my reflection and gasped. I looked like shit. Start with the fact that I was dead tired -- it had been a long day, okay? -- add in a fire-fight and a car crash, and you started to see the damage on my face. Bruises were forming on my face, and above my left eye was a cut with several stitches. I must have been really injured in that accident. I pulled off my glove and reached up and gently ran my fingers over the injury. Well, at least that explained the headache.

"Jesus." I suddenly felt very dizzy. Hotwire jumped from his chair, grabbed me by the air, and gently sat me down. "Kerner, get me a Blue Bull."

"Guhhh?" And it's official, that's my new catch-phrase.

"Is this over freaking stock prices?" I shook my head. "Then what the hell are you into?"

"A sniper killing business people," I explained. "He's killed a crap load of people."

"So what does this have to do with you?"

"Jason, my nephew's bio-dad, called in a favour," I explained. "But now, I don't know. Somehow I think he's after me."

"For fucks sake, Cowboy," he snapped. "Why the hell didn't you come to me for help?"

"Well, it literally just got bad this morning." I glanced at my watch. How could it only be 7pm? Would this day ever end? Kenser showed up with a blue can of Red Bull, it was apparently blueberry flavour. I nodded at him and cracked open the can and took a sip. "You've been busy, dude."

"My shit's been minor," he defended.

"Really? Cause you moved and now have a body guard," I said as I placed the can down on the desk, the bottom of my hand grazing the tabletop.

A shiver and a twitch and I flew back into the past. Hotwire sat at his desk, rapidly typing away. "Hey, Kenser, come here."

Ian Kenser, my vision told me, exited the main bedroom topless, doing up the belt on his pants as he walked. I read somewhere (read = watched on TV) that it takes a man fully secure in his sexuality to be able to compliment and admire the attractiveness of another guy. If that's true, then what level of security do you have to have in order to be jealous? Kenser was built like a Greek god or a Norse deity. The man had short-trimmed blond hair and was tall but what really set him apart was his abs. The man was perfect. I'm not sure it would be possible for a guy to reach that level of perfection, I'm pretty sure he was just made like that. One day a twenty-five- year-old perfect male blinked into existence and all the world's women wept in happiness.

Kenser walked over to Hotwire's desk and gently rubbed the hacker's shoulders. He leaned in, kissed him on the cheek, and spoke gently. "What's up?"

On the day Kenser blinked into existence all the

women wept, that is unavoidable, but it wasn't for joy.

I jerked my hand back and reality snapped into place. "A very close bodyguard."

Hotwire smacked my shoulder. "Stop doing that! The last thing I need is for you to see me having sex on my desk.

"Ahh!" I bolted up from the chair and backed away. I'm not a judging person, people can believe and boink who and what they want, I just don't want to see it. "Why the hell do you need a bodyguard? What happened?"

Hotwire just shook his head. "The day I pulled Robby and your broken ass from the fire, I got hacked. Me; my systems got raped. I was digging into Visegar and having little luck in the process when a message came across my system. I had suddenly appeared on their radar and that in order to stay alive, I had to run. So I did."

I just listened as he continued. "I closed up shop, moved, and disappeared. I sold Terri's, I killed my system and I vanished. I resurfaced with this place. It's owned by a man who doesn't exist, who is working for another man who doesn't exist, who works for a bird who works for me."

"The Mr. Burns approach," I said approvingly. "Go on."

"Then I got him to look after me, he's proved useful already -- aside from that -- taking care of a threat or two. But when all is said and done, I'm hiding. So now I work in a warehouse, guarding people's expiring meat for a cost that is way too high but they come to me because the other cold storage lockers keep having *accidental* power outages."

Somebody once told me that in order to be a good hacker you had to have a loose definition of the words *legal* and *morals*. Hotwire had that in spades.

"So if you run a warehouse, why are you in a suit?" I asked quizzically.

He glanced at me and raised an eyebrow. "It's after six. What am I, a farmer?"

"Watch it, Alec Baldwin," I snapped. Hotwire smiled. This was the hacker I knew, the man who could quip back and forth. It was good to see him, even for an instance. I smiled as I took a big swig of my drink.

"Now I have to rebuild all my old back-doors and all because of some stupid Thaddeus Clay." I did a spit-take, an honest to god spit-take. I turned my head to the left, to avoid expensive computer, and sprayed out every drop of Bull. It was all reflex. It was very unfortunate that to my immediate left stood Kenser. I choked back a laugh as I stared at him, blueberry flavour Red Bull dripping down his face.

"Oh crap, oh crap. I'm sorry, so sorry," I pleaded. I froze as a horrifying thought crossed my mind. "I'm going to get punched in the balls again aren't I?"

Kenser just nodded.

Amongst fits of laughter, and confusion, Hotwire bolted into the kitchen for a towel. He returned to see me backing away from the hulking form of perfection. I may not ever get abs or a body like his, but I was about to be beaten to death by one. That's almost as close, right?

"Why are we doing spit-takes?" he asked as he handed his bodyguard a towel.

"I met Thaddeus Clay today," I declared. "He's the head of Croxallé."

Hotwire froze, standing there stunned. "Okay, my turn to do a spit-take; hand me the Red Bull."

"Don't you dare," Kenser ordered. "I'll punch you in the dick."

Hotwire just smirked. "Yeah, I doubt that." I think that was a sex joke, I can never be certain.

"Christ," Hotwire said; his mind racing as he returned to the subject at hand. "I was digging into Visegar and he showed up. So when The Visegar Company went under and their assests were scooped, so were their men."

I listened to Hotwire trail on and on but only caught random words as my mind raced. I could figure this out. It was on the tip of my tongue.

"...I mean that's not even his real name..."

Need help?

No. I can do this without you, Brain. The last thing I need is to go crawling back to my ex. But seriously, was my brain stalking me?

"...Tier Management..."

Rrrright. You can do this without me. As if.

You're a jerk. What did I ever see in you?

"...called Mordecai..."

Oh, come on, we had good times.

No, you're mean.

"...that's what Keystone told me anyways. He's been through stuff...."

Oh just man up and make a decision. If you don't, you'll lose what's most important to you.

Are we still talking about us? "Damn it, brain, just shut up and leave me alone!" I screamed. "No means no!" I blinked and looked around the room. Kenser and Hotwire were staring at me, confused and scared.

Crap. That was out loud.

Dumbass.

"Hey; look over there. It's a distraction," I said with a forced laugh. "I'm just trying to trying to work this out, Visegar, Croxallé...."

"KyroCorp," Hotwire added.

"KyroCorp is Croxallé..." I trailed off. That was it. I did it and I didn't need my brain to do it either.

Meh. You'll come crawling back.

"KyroCorp got all of Visegar stuff, or so we're supposed to believe," I began. "Then Croxallé bought our Kyro, but what really happened is they are the same thing. Jason told me that. When one company gets too big or public, they shut it down, start a new one, hand everything over and continue where they left off. They've been doing it for decades."

I blinked and looked at Hotwire, our eyes lock and we held our gaze in silence for a time that eventually began to make Kenser uncomfortable. "If that's true, cowboy, then..." He didn't want to finish those words.

"Croxallé is Visegar," I finished.

"Then Visegar didn't vanish," the hacker declared. "They hid. But they wouldn't put all their eggs in one basket. That would be insane. They must have split up. It only makes sense. Visegar still exist, it's just hiding in shell corporations." I tried to speak but he waved me off. "When they were one company, they would have had different divisions, now each of those divisions pretends to be its own company while really they are still part of Visegar. I mean, what would you do if your military team got caught in a city and you all had to hide and escape?"

"We'd scatter." I said, finally fully understanding.

"Croxallé is one part of Visegar. Who knows how many more are out there? Who else could be Visegar?"

"Lepton Enterprises," Kenser added. I turned to look at him.

"Oh god," Hotwire whispered. "Oh god, I didn't even think of that."

"What's Lepton? Off brand soup? Sorry. Humour is a defense mechanism," I apologised. As if they *didn't* already know that.

"As if I *didn't* already know that, Cowboy." Hey! "Lepton is a tech company that is supposed to be making VR tech to help train soldiers," Hotwire explained. "Instead they use it to simulate some of the worse situations imaginable and see how our bodies react."

"Your body thought you were about to die and you changed," I finished, pointing at Kenser. "You're super strong and tough, aren't you?"

He nodded. It made sense. The ability to lift a man in the air was not easy. That shouldn't have been that hard to figure out. Maybe I do need my brain.

"I'm Project: Samson," he introduced. "Three months ago I was an overweight grad student studying for my PhD in theoretical physics. Now I look like this."

Ha! I knew those abs were too good to be true. Now I didn't feel as jealous anymore. I didn't feel inferior; I only felt-- "Wait. Did you say PhD in theoretical physics?"

"That's right, Cowboy, he's smarter than both of us combined."

Good looking and brilliant. The world wasn't fair. I quickly returned to feeling inferior.

"Ben, we may be in over our head," Hotwire said. "I've found like-minded people online, people who have been guiding my search. There are connections to the Prague riots, the Port Alexander explosion and the Clockwork Killer in Eureka, Nevada.

"If this is a bad as we think it is, and it's probably worse," Hotwire concluded, "then we are out-gunned, outnumbered and everything could literally be seconds away from closing in on us. We're boned."

"What do you do when you're outgunned and surrounded, Ben?" The question floated through my mind, traveling from my past to now.

Zoey.

"We live," I said sheepishly.

Chapter 14
We Were Adults, I Swear

Kenser dropped me off at home and we shook hands. I thanked him, and apologised again for the spit-take and the ball bust, and climbed out. I was fairly quiet the entire drive, a rarity for myself, but my mind was elsewhere, firmly in the past. I hobbled to my door and raised an eyebrow as I spotted a wrapped package sitting on my front step. I shrugged, tucked it under my elbow, unlocked my door and walked in. There is something about returning home that makes me instantly more comfortable. I used to think I had agoraphobia, I was self-diagnosed, but I don't believe that anymore. People like Rachael, Elaine, and Annie had made sure that I got out and lived.

"You live, Ben." Her words floated through my mind again. I couldn't avoid it.

I hung my hat, dropped my cane in cane-holder-bucket-thingy (I really need to name that), and peeled off my jacket. I limped into the living room, slid the package across the counter, and unclipped my M9. I dropped it on the counter and left it there.

Every bone in my body, every endless hour of firearm safety screamed at me to pick it back up, to clear it and to stow it. I fought every urge and went for the booze. I needed a drink; I needed a couple. Hell, I needed a damn bottle.

I screamed at myself not to, to just reach for the vodka or the rum instead, but as I opened up the liquor cabinet and reached in, I found my fingers circling around the tequila.

Don't do it. Look, let's talk about this.

Leave me alone, Brain.

I popped the cap, grabbed a shot glass, and limped back to the counter. I poured a shot, stared at it, and downed it. This was it; this was the turning point. I could put the cap back on, put the bottle back in the cabinet and just have a drink of something else and be fine, but if I poured another shot, I was gone.

I have a pattern, a series of events that lead me to what I call Destructive Ben Mode. Once I start it, there's no going back until it's done and by then I'm just a wreck, useless to both the world and myself. I hate Destructive Ben Mode; hate it, so why do I do it? Why would I bother? Because of her, because of Zoey; it's all because of her. I'd do it a thousand times for her, the consequences be damned, and it all started with a second shot of tequila.

I poured a second shot and just stared at it. I returned the bottle to the counter and grabbed my pistol. My fingers moved without hesitation, holding the weapon like I had umpteen times before, thinking about what I had to do, and building up the courage for the next step. I ejected the mag and cleared the chamber. I double-checked the safety and lay all the pieces of the gun on the counter each beside one another.

I stared at the tequila.

Please. Don't.

A couple more of these, Brain, and I won't have to deal with you.

Please.

I grabbed the shot glass and downed the second shot. Destructive Ben Mode was a go.

I took two more shots before pouring a real drink, rum and coke, and I limped to my hallway closet. The booze weren't the destructive part, they were the courage, the boost I needed to man up and touch that one dreaded item. I opened the linen closet and kneeled down to the bottom. There, in a cardboard box, was my cursed item. In the world of psychometry nothing is worse for a psychic PTSD victim to touch then his dog-tags -- they were not in this box -- but in the world of Destructive Ben Mode there was something far worse. I opened up the box and looked inside.

Alone at the bottom was a black webbed military belt with a gold-coloured buckle.

I grabbed it.

The desert is freaking hot.

Surprise, surprise, but nobody understands how unbelievably hot it truly is until you go there. Picture those days at home when it is so warm that breathing becomes difficult; those days are the good ones in Iraq. For the foreseeable future my home was here, in Camp Victory, and to be honest, for overseas deployment into hostile, war torn death-villes, it wasn't that bad. My mother always said that life was what you made of it, be it working a crappy job, a crappy apartment or a crappy deployment. If all you thought about were the crappy parts then it was never going to get better; you focus on what's good and things become better.

Camp Victory may not be perfect, what posting in a war zone was, but it had it pluses. I had a good group of guys to hang with, my *awesome* body was getting that *awesome* tan and for the next three weeks I got to hang with Belledin. David was my best friend in the entire world. We were hommies and had been for years. Having him here, which was rare since we were now in separate divisions, meant I got richer. David couldn't play cards for shit. I was kicking his ass at poker, a game we were playing with a couple random people from different platoons, when a knock came at my hooch door.

When a soldier is deployed in Iraq you don't live in tents (unless you're really unlucky), you live in buildings known as hooches. They were portable buildings that could hold a few as two people and upwards of uncomfortable. They reminded me of the portables that schools used to attach to their buildings; the portable buildings that were just legal child-torture room. The temperature was normally so high that you'd sweat off a dozen pounds a day while trying to learn about math or potatoes. I grew up in a farming community; potatoes were on the curriculum.

"Dave, get that," I said. "I'm busy counting up your money."

"Screw that; your hooch, your door, your responsibility," he snapped back with a smile. "So get."

I rolled my eyes and climbed to my feet. I scooted pasted the guys, we were jammed tightly in there, and moved for the door. Out of the corner of my eye I saw David grab several poker chips from my pile. "Hey!"

"Ben, how's your sister?" he asked, his tone mocking but for some odd reason mildly serious.

That was a sore subject right now. I was ready to kill the last guy who hooked up with my sister, if I could find him again. There was no way I would let David, my main man, get near my sister; David and my sister, as if. I paused at the door, my hand on the knob, and glanced back at him. You know, that's actually not that bad of an idea. I pulled open the door and was hit with a wave of heat. "Holy crap, make it quick."

A man stood outside, one of the military messenger boys, and he smirked. "Specialist Benedict Thompson?" I nodded at him. "Somebody wants you." He handed me a note. I thanked him and closed the door.

"So?" David asked. I opened the envelope and gave it a read.

"It's that girl Zoey Harris," I explained. "She wants to see me."

"Wasn't she the civi that gave us the briefing?" Anderson asked

"Why did you guys get a special briefing? The rest of us didn't."

Clement snapped his elbow into Anderson's side

and shook his head. I smirked. "It's 'cause we be special and you be, well, what's a word that really emphasizes the word 'scum'?"

"I've found *Benedict* works well," David snapped back with a smile. I raised my left fist before him and with my right hand begin to turn an invisible crank. With each rotation, my middle finger extended just a little bit more. David countered by raising his fist sideways with the thumb extended. He then feigned blowing into the thumb like he would a balloon. With each puff, his middle finger inflated a little more as well.

We were adults, I swear.

I reluctantly exited my air-conditioned hooch, this being one of exactly two days it had worked since I got here, and marched across the base. Zoey Harris gave us our special objective when we took the airfield and acted as our comms agent during the mission. I knew she wasn't real military, she didn't act like one, but she could be PMC. There was also a chance that she belonged to some intelligence agency like the CIA. Spies were a dime a dozen out here, guiding us left or right and telling us how to pee and when to wipe. They were a pain in the ass, but they came with helpful intelligence -- when it was right. Military intelligence is often an oxymoron.

I knocked on her door and it opened immediately. Zoey stood there smiling. "Specialist, come in."

"Ma'am," I said as I entered. I gave her a once over, and loved what I saw. "What can I do for you?" Or to you? 'Cause I have a list of suggestions.

"I've going over the reports for the airfield. You did very well," she smiled as she picked up a folder and opened it up. "Where did you learn to shoot?"

"Grew up on a farm," I admitted. "And when the work's done you only have two options for fun: shooting stuff or screwing stuff."

"I'm surprised a guy like you is any good with a rifle then." She smirked. "How do you feel about the invasion?"

"It seems a little ridiculous to me," I shrugged. "So we're kicking ass and taking names but there will be insurgents, people left over who hate us. There is so much to do. If you think about it, we are going to be outnumbered by the same assholes that attacked us, by people who don't want our help and people who are resenting us being here."

"What do you do when you're outgunned and surrounded, Ben?" she asked. "What do you do when everything seems lost and death seems inevitable?"

"You bunker down and hold position," I replied.

"You live, Ben," she countered. "You live."

She coughed slightly, something to break the tension, and flipped the page in her file. "So how do you feel about your career in the army? Are you a lifer? Are you open to opportunities?"

"This is bullshit," I declared. "I'd rather not go through this entire song and dance. You're here and I'm here," I moved closer to her. "So let's just enjoy ourselves."

She gave me a cocky look. "Excuse me?"

This was where I excelled in the world. Women wanted me and I couldn't blame them. I was gorgeous. Hell, I wanted me. I looked her in the eye and flashed my patented smirk. It was like half a smile that came with my baby blues and a look that seemed to say everything that I wasn't. It put everything I was thinking, every naughty detail, out there teasing you at the infinite possibility of carnal pleasure. I'd follow this up by gently touching her cheek and brushing her hair back behind her ear, the entire time keep my gaze locked with her until the tension was too much to bear, then I'd lean in for a kiss and it was all downhill from there. It worked every time without fail.

I moved in and flashed my smirk, its magic working almost immediately. I stepped closer and gently brushed her cheek, allowing my touch to pass a spark between her skin and mi-.

She grabbed my wrist and twisted, hard, and kicked out my right leg. I dropped to one knee, my wrist still in a death-lock. In an attempt to free myself, I pushed forward, hoping to throw all my weight against hers and hopefully stumble her, allowing me to free my wrist. It didn't go as planned. I pushed forward but she just pivoted sideways, sending me stumbling past her, then with lightning speed she shifted her grip on my wrist, spun my arm behind my back, then used my momentum and her better positioning to slam me against the wall of her hooch, my arm pinned between her and I.

"You could have just said no," I said sheepishly, trying to save what little pride remained, as the rest seemed to pour of me like a faucet. I wasn't telling a lie. No means no; I would never cross that line.

"Who said no?" she whispered into my ear. "I just want you to know who's in charge here." Strong, tough women; I hope that doesn't become my type.

She spun me around, freeing my arm, and pressed me back against the wall. She kissed me, hard and firmly. I could feel her lips, dried and torn from the heat, just like the rest of us, but they still tasted wonderful. We kissed again and again, our hands each roaming up the other's body, our fingers working to undo and unfasten any clasp or belts in our way. My fingers were faster, unclasping the bra from outside the shirt and peeling both off her beautiful skin. She let go of my belt, reluctantly, to allow her tank-top to fall off but immediately returned to it the moment she was free. I gazed at her topless form, hungrily enjoying what I saw. Her skin was smooth and unblemished, an enticing buffet waiting to be feasted upon. I leaned in, ready for a taste, when she pushed me back against the wall.

"Shirt," she ordered. "Now."

She pulled free my black webbed belt and tossed it aside, her hand quickly vanishing beneath my combat pants as I pulled off my shirt. She gripped me firmly and gave me her own smirk. "I guess this'll do."

"That'll do?" I asked in disbelief. Where I came from that was a challenge and one I intended to win. I reached around her body and gripped her firmly, hoisting her into the air. I carried her to the bed -- a full two and a half steps -- and gently placed her upon it. I grabbed her belt and quickly undid it, swiftly pulling off her pants and panties. "Hey, you're really a redhead."

She slapped the side of my head and forced it down, finally allowing me access to the buffet. We put the AC to the test with every inch of my skin that pressed against hers, rubbing and twitching, each of us sweating more as out body temperature rose at an astonishing rate.

I was unrelenting, pushing her to the edge over and over, holding her there as long as possible only to pull back at the last moment, leaving her both furious and famished. For a moment, I thanked the Rangers and their obsessive need to sculpt us into perfect warriors with seemingly unending stamina and endurance, and for a moment, a brief instant, I saw her making the exact same thanks. I eventually took pity on her, or her on me, and let her succumb. We had explored the limits of each other, and the small bed, and blown past them until there was little left to either of us but sweat, pleasure and soreness that we found delightful.

We lay in bed, panting and straddling dehydration, just looking at the ceiling as we waited for our hearts to slow. I looked over at her and smirked. "That'll... do," I boastfully said between gasps of air. "Yeah... that'll... do."

She chuckled, a laugh that I instant fell for, and sat up. "Not bad for a redneck-farm-boy." I stared at her again, my eyes wide. Not only was she not out of breath, recovering almost instantly, she was challenging me -- again. I was not loosing this one.

"Oh... that's it... it... is..." She leaned over and kissed me, cutting me off.

"Relax, Farmboy," she smiled, a smile that instant stole me, and reached up with her right hand. She gently brushed my cheek, her eyes locked with mine. "You were fantastic." Then she kissed me.

She was using my move! Oh, it was so on.

Reality returned. Zoey; my Zoey. What started off as simple carnal became so much more. We were stealing every moment we had, risking court marshal and our careers, but it seemed worth it. For a while, it was only whenever we were in Iraq, war lovers, and I thought I was fine with that until I returned home when my tour was done and everything was lacking. I was eager to get back to her, to be with her despite the risk. I even volunteered for extra tours, just on the chance her mission would coincide with mine, just for the chance to see her, talk to her, or be with her again.

Then she surprised me. I was home, in between my second and third tour, or something like that, and life sucked without her. I was safe, no war zone, with my family and nephew. Yet somehow, without her it all seemed empty. I tried sleeping around, that didn't work either. I tried dating; it didn't work. David found me after one of those *didn't work* relationships, thought me heartbroken and took me to see strippers. I ended up dating a striper for a month; it didn't work either. All I kept thinking about was getting back to war so I could get back to Zoey.

Then she suddenly showed up, out of the blue, and things were better. She wanted more, I wanted more. I'd been with many, many girls before her, been in many relationships. I mourned each when they ended, but there was always one more waiting in the wing. The old me -- which, ironically, is actually the young me -- never seemed to have to try that hard to find a girl. There always seemed to be a line; now serving woman #244 (things can change so much). Yet all those girls aside, Zoey was the first I ever loved.

I still remember the words she said when she showed up. She looked at me, her natural red-hair grown out, and said: "Sometimes, Ben, you have to man up and figure out what you want."

I was happy. She even went to Annie's and David's wedding with me. I gave her a dolphin necklace to celebrate. Jewellery is my go-to gift for women. They never seem to complain.

Then everything changed. Then she died.

I looked at my glass. I had been drinking it without realizing it, a true sign, and all that was left were ice and glass. I stared down at it, the ice slowing melting, withering away into nothing. Everything I'd seen had reminded me of her, the knife, the glasses, everything; and it was driving me mad. I didn't have her and I never could. Instead I was just like the ice in my glass, withering away into nothing.

This was Destructive Ben Mode. I'd get drunk, grab the belt and spend the briefest of moments with her again. Then I spend the next two days drunk off my ass, mourning and thinking of the worst stuff possible. Was it worth it? I don't know, most say no, but for a moment with her -- just one more… maybe.

I screamed at the belt, pivoted and whipped my glass against the far wall as hard as I could. It shattered. I leaned on the wall and slid down to the floor, my ass hitting the floor with a thud. I sat there, cold, angry and drunk and did something I hadn't done in a very long time.

I cried.

Chapter 15
FREAKING PROMOTED!!!

"Ben?" a voice cried out as my front door opened. It was Rachael. I heard the crunch of broken glass then the unmistakeable sound of a Glock 22 being pulled from a holster. "Ben?!?"

Rachael was a woman of contradictions. There was the loving and caring part of her, the part that saw me slouched on the floor and wanted to run over to make sure I was okay, but there was also the careful, meticulous part of her, the part that saw an unknown situation and immediately thought of the potential threat to her and me. So when her foot touched broken glass, and her eyes fell upon my sad sack of crap of a body, her gun flew to her hands, and she moved quickly, but carefully, up the long hallway that was my apartment.

She pushed open the first door, gave it a quick scan, and satisfied that it was empty -- minus my embarrassing crap I keep in the first room -- she pressed on. She paused at my side, checked my pulse, and once she was satisfied I was alive, stepped over me and cleared the rest of the apartment.

There were many differences between Rachael and I -- breasts, leg functionality, varying level of expertise in the ability to urinate while standing up -- but this was a major one. The last time I was in a situation like this, in a situation where I had to choose between being careful and smart, or rushing to the aid of someone I knew and cared about, I nearly got my ass shot off.

Asses, that was another difference; one of us had a far nicer ass then the other. Yes, it goes without question that hers was nicer. I needed to get my ass replaced: it had a crack in it.

I felt her hand gently touch my cheek. She pulled my face to look at her and I melted. I was a wreck. I was a mess over a woman I'd lost and was now looking like a sack of crap in front of the women I was currently in a not R-Word with. She slumped down beside me. "Ben? What's wrong?"

I didn't know how to answer.

"Why is your gun out on the table?" she asked, a little more firmly. "How drunk are you?" I tried to answer but couldn't say anything, not even my patented *guhhh*. "Ben, you know what this looks like. Talk to me, please."

She was pleading to me. So I spilled. I told her everything. I told her about Zoey. I told her about our time together, about the time apart, and about how I lost her. I told her how she laughed, how she fought, I even told her how I gave her dolphin necklace to wear for the wedding. Then I told her how she was taken from me, lost on a mission.

Rachael sat with me and listened, holding me, comforting me, and eventually brought me to bed. I fell asleep almost instantly; being one of those emotional people is exhausting. How do women do it?

A splash of water hit my face and jolted me up from my bed. My head screamed at the sudden movement. My eyes focused, water dripping from my face, and I saw Rachael standing by my bed, wearing one of my shits and little else, holding the now empty cup of water.

"Guhhh?"

"Up. Now!" she ordered. "You decided to get drunk last night, fine, but you have voodoo to work this morning. So, up."

"We had an emotional breakthrough last night," I muttered. "Doesn't that warrant me an extra hour of sleep?"

"Yes, we did," Puzo said as she leaned in. "And tomorrow we'll get you a pretty dress to match those girly emotions of yours, but until then: Get. Up." She splashed me with more water. Where the hell did that second cup come from?

She pulled me from bed and tossed me into a shower, a *cold* shower. Despite my pleading, she refused to get in with me. Damn, that woman was almost as cold as the shower. I quickly washed and climbed out, limping to my bedroom. Puzo was already in the kitchen. Placed on my bed was a fresh set of clothes laid out for me. I pulled on a pair of pants and black collared shirt. This woman was dressing me now and she had good taste. I got dressed and grabbed my emergency drunk-shades and limped to the kitchen.

"Nope," she said as she slid across a plate of food. "No douche shades indoors."

I pulled them off and looked down at the food before me: sausage patties and fried eggs with melted cheese all on an English muffin. Puzo had just made a homemade egg McMuffin like I used to have at home. I took a bite and my eyes went wide. It didn't taste anything like Mom used to cook them; it was better. It tasted just like how Dad used to cook them.

"So I've been thinking," Rachael began. "You and I have talked about your visions…"

It was true. We had, and in great length.

"From time to time your visions aren't as random as they seem." That was also true. They were rarely clear but they tended to drop hints towards me. "So what if they're doing that again? What if they're giving you hints and you keep missing them?"

That was very likely. "So what does Zoey have to do with this killer?" I asked.

"You tell me," Puzo asked as she slid over a FBI file. I opened it up and glanced down. Rachael had gotten Nouri Allawi's file. "He was part of the Elite Guard. He was a sniper, and a good one, and he was in the Battle of Baghdad. Does any of that cross over with Zoey?"

The Battle of Baghdad; holy crap.

"Operation: Rogue Gambit." God, that name sounded cheesy when you said it out loud. All military operations had codenames. The Normandy landing was Operation: Neptune, the Allied amphibious landing in Italy was called Operation: Shingle, and the joint movement of US troops and ARVN troops into A Shau Valley was called Operation: Delaware. That being said, they all sounded infinitely cooler then Operation: Rogue Gambit. Whoever gave the mission cool names had nothing to do with this mission.

"It was a confidential mission I took part of during the Battle of Baghdad," I explained. "My team, and two others, had separate objectives."

"And Zoey gave you those objectives?" I nodded. Puzo grabbed her bag from the chair and pulled free a plastic bag. She handed it to me. I glanced inside and saw a pair of black, fingerless, gloves. My blood went cold. First it was my glasses and then it was my knife. What were the odds that these were my gloves? The fact that looked exactly like the type of fingerless gloves I wore in combat kind of altered the odds. "These showed up at what we thought was an unrelated case about a month ago."

"Can I?" I asked. When she nodded, I pulled the bag open and shook out the gloves. I fought back the hesitation, reached in and touched them.

The desert is hot. It is always hot. It has no other switch then hot. When you look at the temperature dial in the desert it reads *hot, freaking hot,* and *I'm going to touch the active oven on a summer's day while living on the sun* kind of hot.

My thesis statement: living in the desert can prove to

be slightly uncomfortable.

You sweat a lot in the desert. The only thing that makes you sweat more than the heat is bullets whizzing by you with the intent of making your body their new home. It was April 4, 2003 and I was in a shit storm. This was the Battle of Bagdad and the Third Infantry Division was moving on Saddam International Airport -- a spot thought to be the best-defended Iraqi location -- and Odin Squad was running escort.

Truth was, Odin Squad was using the invasion as a diversion. As the division moved inwards, Blaine signalled us to a halt. We dropped to a crouch and let the other troops move past.

"Blue Cap?" he asked, looking at our fifth member. "You ready?"

Blue Cap, Zoey, nodded. She was dressed like us, and moved like us, but each of us knew she wasn't like us. She was a PMC grunt or government stooge. As much as it pained me to think, she'd leave each of them here to die if it meant finishing her mission.

"Red Gun," she ordered. "Take us in."

Civilians always have a hard time adjusting to code name, spies do not. Blaine was Red Gun, Clement was Twister, Anderson was Camo Cat, and I was Bright Eyes. The codenames sound silly on a radio, but they're put in place to protect us. If the baddies hear that Ben Thompson kills Saddam Hussein then they'll target me and my family. If they hear Bright Eyes kills him, then they are none the wiser and spend all their time laughing at my stupid code name.

Blaine ordered me on point and we took off down a Bagdad street, pulling away from the rest of the troops. We had a small palace building to infiltrate. This palace was home to one of Hussein's relatives, some cousin or brother or relative to his dog. Truth was, there was actually a lab inside filled with biological material. Our job was to break in, secure and/or destroy the bio-WMD, and get ourselves out.

We reached the palace -- almost tiny by palace standards -- and quickly breached the building with a simple lock pick. We took up defensive positions as Clement worked his magic.

"Anybody else think it's weird that there is no security outside this building?" Anderson asked.

"It's hidden," Zoey explained, clutching her M4A1. "We'll be in the shit the moment we enter."

"Zip it," Blaine snapped. "Get your head in the game."

"Clear." We stepped inside and quietly moved down the large, empty hallways. The palace was empty. There weren't any servants; there weren't any rich folk; the only people we saw were two kids looting. They froze when my sights fell on them.

"Take what you got and get lost," I whispered. They bolted for the door.

"All hands on me," Zoey spoke over the comms. "I have the stairwell."

We converged on Zoey and moved down a hidden stairwell. Part of me grinned as we did so: the stairs were hidden behind a bookcase, a legit hidden stairwell behind a bookcase. I was tingling on the inside.

As we entered the basement, the decor changed entirely. It went from a fancy palace upstairs to an evil medical lab down. We looked around, our guns up and ready. We hadn't met anyone yet and we weren't willing to be ambushed. We reached the center of the lab when I heard a noise. I spun around, crouched down, and levelled my weapon in its directions. "I heard some...."

Something slammed through the wall and sent me skidding across the floor. I recovered quickly, spinning myself on the floor, and opened fire. My M4A1 cracked to life as I put a burst of three rounds into the Iraqi man who'd just attacked me. "Contact!"

I watched as the man dropped to one knee. That alone surprised me. My burst should have put him on his ass and sent his blood spilling out in a stain causing fashion. What happened next scared the living crap out of me. The man, still breathing, looked up and started to climb back to his feet. I just stared in disbelief. A single snap of a rifle, and the side of his skull exploding, sent him toppling downwards. I looked up to see Blaine standing there, his rifle up. "Ben?"

"Five by Five," I muttered as I climbed to my feet.

"If they didn't know we were here, they do now," Blaine called out. "Blue Cap?"

"I'm on the computer," she called out. "Give me twenty minutes."

"Hey, Boss," Anderson called out. "I got security footage here. We have Elites incoming."

"Everybody out the back door," Blaine ordered.

"We need this intel," Zoey called out. "They have a WMD."

"Crap," Blaine cursed. "Clement: set the explosives. Everybody else: Take position, boys. We're holding the line."

Through sheer force of will, my vision began to pick up, like a movie on fast forward, as I watched myself in one of the worse firefights I had ever been in. Four Rangers and one not-civilian locked in a room as waves of Elite Republican Guards marched down on us.

In the world of soldiering, there is nobody more badass then a Ranger. The US Marines are going give you some bullshit about how they're better, but Marines don't lead the way, Rangers do. So if we're number one on the badass scale -- and we are -- then from my experience the Republican Elite Guard would be number two. These guys are scary mofos. They will shoot as fast, fight as hard, and be as tough as a Ranger. So to be outnumbered and outgunned was bad, to be outnumbered and outgunned by them was worse. The only thing that was saving us was positioning.

"Boss," Anderson cried out. "We're losing ground. We need to book it."

"No shit, Sherlock," Blaine called out. "Ben: check the dame."

Dame; Zoey would kill me if I called her that. I pulled from the line and dashed back to her. "Time to go."

"He was the WMD..." she muttered. She turned to me. "I'm not done. It needs like five more minutes."

She nodded to an external hard drive she had attached to the computers, massive by today's standards. She opened her mouth to speak but I didn't listen. I grabbed the hard drive and pulled it free. "We're out of time."

The wall bust opened and two more Iraqi soldiers burst through. My rifle snapped up and roared to life. Two rounds into the first one's skull, no messing around this time, and I turned on the third. My rifle didn't bang at the third; instead it just jammed.

Fuck.

I dropped the M4A1, letting my sling catch it, and immediately drew my trusty M9. I pulled it up and snapped off four shots, one in the chest, two in the neck, and a final one square between his eyes.

"Yippie Kai-"

"No time, Ben," Blaine snapped as he bolted for the back door. "Time to go."

We exited the lab and bolted up the back stairs. I holstered my M9 as we ran and quickly cleared the breach from my rifle. As he reached the top, I pushed open the door, my bare fingers touching the steel. My eye began to twitch, a shiver ran up my back, and my sight blurred. For a moment, I swore I saw a sniper, a block away, shooting Zoey through the shoulder as she tried to run.

I shook it off and my sight returned. I saw Zoey crouch as she prepared to run. I looked around at the surrounding street. I had just seen this. There was a sniper nearby and I knew where he was.

"Zoey, do-"

It was too late. She was already bolting across. I didn't think, I just reacted, I snapped up my riffle and opened fired. For all I knew I was firing at nothing, the mystery sniper could just have been a stress-induced vision, but I didn't care. A shot fired off. The bullet didn't go through Zoey's head; instead it slammed through her shoulder. The sniper did exist and he shot her. My bullets must have scared him because there was no way he could have missed her head. I moved without thinking, bolting across the street -- with nothing for cover -- and scooped her up. I carried her across the street and ducked behind the closest building. It's in a moment like this, when you have the choice between emotional and careful, that you find out which side of the fence you fall on. I didn't just fall onto the emotional side; I fell there, bought the land, built a house and put it in my will for my future children only to have it seized by the government when I forget to pay my taxes.

Crap! I forgot to do taxes this year.

"What are you doing?" she grunted between jolts of pain.

"Not sure," I smirked. "Being heroic?"

She shook her head. "That'll do."

I popped out from behind the corner and levelled my rifle. I knew where he was hiding. He shot Zoey and now I had him in my scope. For a brief heartbeat I saw his face in my scope and I pulled the trigger. Back then I didn't recognize the face, I'd never seen it before, but now I did. Old Ben recognized the face. It was Nouri Allawi.

Reality returned and Rachael looked at me. "I killed him," I muttered. "I killed Nouri Allawi."

Puzo smirked. "Join the club. Maybe one of these days, it'll stick."

Was that it? Was this all because of revenge? Was Allawi just pissed off because I shot him? The more I thought about it, the more I started to think of the possibilities. His powers kicked in during the Battle of Bagdad -- I shot him in the head at the Battle of Bagdad. I triggered his powers.

Endless healing; who knew what lay on the other side, that gap between death and life? Every time he got shot by Puzo and I -- or anyone -- and he passed between the two beacons, was it just endless darkness? Did he see heaven only to have it pulled away from him or was it a choice? Was it a conscious choice? Did he have to crawl away from the light? I won't deny that having healing would be helpful for a bum legged gimp like myself, but crawling back to the land of the living each and every time: that just sounded exhausting.

It suddenly made sense. With healing like that, and in a soldering profession that he was, he would have to watch everybody around him die while he stayed young and eternal. It was why he tried to kill Rachael in the restaurant; it was why he gunned down the innocents before me. He wanted to make me feel what he felt. He truly wanted me to suffer. He wanted to punish me for -- holy crap! This was season one of *24*. I had just become Jack Bauer. I was on a military mission, I killed a foreigner (god, that sounds bad), and now it turned out he wasn't dead and he was back to make my life a living hell. It'd be epic if it wasn't so frightening.

I explained to Rachael what I saw, leaving out the confidential information that I wasn't allowed to say, and watched her reaction. She just nodded. The fact that she brought these gloves here, to me, proved she suspected something. I just voodoo'd her a connection. My voodoo wouldn't hold up in court, but now she knew she was on the right path.

"Where was this from?"

"One of the senior financial officers of Langovo Financials committed suicide," she explained. "He took a swan-dive off a top building. This glove was found in his office."

"Not suicide?"

"Nope," Puzo explained. "Too much that doesn't add up, like Stallone and Getty in--" she paused. "Ok, I might have been hanging around you too much."

I disagreed.

"These killings aren't random," Puzo explained. "Al-lawi is obviously crazy, but he's not that crazy. He was Special Forces and he was good at it."

"Special Forces are taught to move and plan. You

never jump into anything," I added.

"Exactly; there's a reason behind each of these kill-ings. We just need to figure out what it is."

"I gotta call someone," I said as I grabbed my phone and tapped Mia's name. The phone barely rang once before I heard her cheerful voice greet me. "Hey, Mia, I need a favour. Truthfully, I need an addition to my previous favour."

"Oh, Benedict, how did I get you calling me at all hours?" she asked whimsically.

"Your number is on my phone. All I have to do is finger you and -- wait. That sounded bad." That sounded *really* bad. I knew that because of the stern look I was suddenly getting from Puzo.

"I owe you that, Benedict," Mia laughed. "And more. You got me *freaking promoted!* So you name it, place, time, position and I'm yours."

Damn this woman was tempting even if I knew she wasn't serious. "Man, if you reward all of your favours like this then you must have a line circling the block."

"No, Benedict, I do not," she explained. "Okay I do, I'm gorgeous -- you know this and I know this -- but I only offer this to those who get me freaking promoted! I'm the new on-air reporter."

"Holy crap! Congrats!" I cheered.

"So, here's the deal. A) I will finish that favour you asked of me and then B) I'm taking you out for dinner." She paused, and her voice turned sultry: "And dessert?"

"I need to know what the connection is between the names I already gave you and Langovo Financials." Every urge in my body longed to take Mia up on her offer. They all screamed out in something that could only be described as the child of begging and demanding. Even my leg, my bum leg, decided to speak up, making promises to work again if I took Mia up on her offer. The only part of my body *not* to agree with her was my heart. Go figure.

"I'll get right on it." I thanked her, hung up and looked over at Rachael. She had my file opened up and was flipping through it.

"Ben, what is this?" she asked. It wasn't an accusation, but it did have a small smidgen of a FBI-Lady tone.

I limped over. "It's a different case I'm working on. A company doesn't have the stock bump they should leading up to a major product release. They suspect foul play and got me to look into it. All my leads came up dry except for that."

"This man has had a major boost in his financial," Rachael read aloud. "Go on."

"He's not even part of the company. He belongs to a security firm that guards buildings." I explained. "I'm trying to figure out what to do next."

Puzo raised her eyebrow at me. She'd already figured it out. She slid the file across to me and smirked. "You can figure this out in three questions, Ben. You just have to use that brain of yours."

Crap.

"What are his duties within this company?" she was prompting me, testing me. Puzo had always said I could be a good detective, even without my powers; I just had to work at it.

"He is nothing. He is a low level grunt, a security guard." I paused. "Somebody is paying him to steal some of their devices so they can have a finished product."

"Possible, but if it's as time sensitive as you say then this is way too late in the tech world to be worth it. At this point they could just buy one in stores and tear it apart," she explained. "What's his home situation like?"

"Married and has two kids." I looked at the file again. "He has no record either. He's not going to risk losing his job over thievery."

"Exactly," Puzo confirmed. "People have been taught that thievery is bad, which it is. So here is the final question, Ben: What is worth a big income of money but isn't necessarily bad?"

Damn her. She was making me work for this one.

I could help.

To hell with that, Brain. I could do this on my own. I could; I wasn't just reassuring myself. What could a low-level security guard offer that wasn't illegal? Maybe it wasn't about what was illegal and what wasn't, maybe it was about what seems to be legal. But what did a security guard offer to the world of high-tech toys and gadgetry? This man did nothing all day but walk the perimeter, check all the doors, locks and camera, and review all of the security footage over and over until he could do this by memory.

Man, you are useless without me.

I really wa-- holy crap. Suddenly it hit me. I knew what he sold. "He sold the security layout." Puzo just nodded. "But how does he think that it's not illegal? Doesn't that fall under corporate espionage laws?"

"He may be actually ignorant," Puzo began. "He could know nothing about corporate laws, or..." She was baiting me again. I scrunched up my face and started thinking really hard.

"Or... he was asked round-about questions. He sold vague information and the buyer pieced the rest together with well placed questions."

Rachael winked. "You're probably looking at a major theft about to take place," she explained. "It would be almost impossible to wipe them out completely, eggs and baskets and all that, but if you steal *enough*, you start to effect stock prices."

I stared at her for a second. She was good. She was very good. Despite the black flags that existed on her record, she'd still go far. She was too good of an agent not to.

"I'd turn this into your client right away and then call the cops."

I sat there quite for a moment and finished my breakfast. This was going to be a big paycheck. It's not that I needed the money, I really didn't have that many expenses, but with the extra income I could do something nice with it, maybe something nice for Rachael. In the last couple of months, she'd been there the most for me. If you promised not to tell

Annie, I might even go as far as to say in my entire life she had been there for me more frequently than any other woman.

A dark feeling grew in my stomach.

If I followed this train of thought, if I chose to actually peruse something with Rachael then that meant I was over *her*, that I was over Zoey. I didn't know if I was or not. While I was considering this new train, Rachael's phone rang and she stepped into the bedroom. Then my front door opened.

"Ben?" Elaine's voice called out. Oh crap, not again. "Ben?"

"Hey! In here," I called out as I limped to my feet. "Did we have an appointment today, Elaine?" She shook her head.

"I need to talk to you, Ben." She rubbed her arm nervously and glanced at me. "I... I..."

"What is it? You know I?ll help if I possib--."

Then she kissed me. It wasn't one of those romantic kisses where the world slows down and music plays in the background, and it wasn't the type of kiss that happens while rain falls down all around you; it wasn't even a great kiss, it was just an awkward kiss. It wasn't her fault, it was just a surprising kiss, the kind where you stand there, blinking in astonishment with your hands hanging lopsided by your side.

"Guhhh?" I asked once our lips finally separated. "What the...guhhh?"

"I broke up with Steve," she admitted. "It wasn't working and..."

"Um... and what?" I asked, afraid of the answer.

"And I want to be with you, Ben."

My apartment got very quiet. I didn't know how to answer that. Here was the woman I had been crushing for a long time declaring that she wanted to be with me, and a part of me leapt at the chance, but deep inside I felt guilt at the kiss.

With sitcom like timing, my bedroom door opened and Rachael emerged. She was fully dressed in her own clothes and her gun was on her hip. She took one look at

Elaine, her hand dropping to her gun, and flashed me a look. She marched passed us both and headed for my front door. "I have to go, Ben, work called and I have a case."

"Rachael -- wait?" I begged, but by the time my words tore from my lips, she'd passed us both and was out the door. I glanced at Elaine.

"Let her go, Ben," she whispered. "Let her go."

"Hold that thought," I said and limped out the door. I saw Rachael climbing into her car. "Rachael! Stop!"

She paused and looked at me. I limped over and looked her in the eyes. Her face held an expression that said 'I carry a gun so choose your next words carefully' and *I decided to listen.*

"Elaine kissed me..." I stammered. "She broke up with her boyfriend and wants to be with me. I didn't initiate the kiss nor did I do any--"

She shushed me with a finger to my lips. "It's okay, Ben. You and I are nothing. We are just two people having fun. She is the woman you've been jonesing for and she's throwing herself at you. Go have your *Sixteen Candles* moment." She leaned in and gave me a peck on the cheek.

"I'll see you when I see you, Ben."

"No, wait..."

She looked at me and shook her head. "Sometimes, Ben, you have to man up and figure out what you want."

And with that, she drove away. I stood there for a moment, watching the car vanish in the distance, and found myself wondering why my chest hurt the way it did. Why did I feel pain at this moment? Why did I feel sick, lonely and abandoned? Why did I feel like I'd just had the shit kicked out of me and, most importantly, why did I feel guilty?

My door opened and Elaine emerged, carrying my cane. She handed it to me and escorted me back inside, which was good because it was freaking cold out and I was the idiot freezing my ass off outside without a jacket.

Chapter 16
Was There a How to Mess With Ben Newsletter?

I've come to terms with the fact that being dumbfounded is basically a fact of life for me. I'm not the brightest man in the room -- any room – and that normally leaves me in a constant state of befuddlement. That being said, how I got from my home to being back beneath the scope of Nouri Al-lawi still left me with a state of confusion the likes of which I hadn't felt since the ending of *Lost*.

It started with Elaine escorting me back into my apartment and walking me to the kitchen. I slid onto the stool and just stared at my plate, still numb to what just happened.

"Before all of this goes forward, between you and me, we need to talk about something important," Elaine began. "When you were trying to find Robbie I tagged along. We came across that body. I freaked out but you were okay with it. People shouldn't be okay with dead bodies. The moment things like that *stop* getting to you is the moment you're in trouble. You're in trouble, Ben. We need to get you back to normal."

Normal?

She looked at me with her pleading eyes. "You need to stop throwing yourself into danger. You're not a cop and you're not a soldier anymore but you're still acting like one. It didn't used to be like this, you used to do safe cases but now..." she paused for a moment. "I can't be like the cop's wife or the soldier's girl friend, always wondering if you'll come home safe or even at all. Promise me that it'll all end. Promise me that together we'll get back to normal?"

Normal. That word just stung. Was I so far from the norm that I needed fixing? I knew I was a broken man -- busted leg, busted psyche, busted everything -- but I was healing. Six months ago I started healing and I decided that I wasn't turning back. But despite all that, did I still need fixing? Was I wrong?

"I... um."

"Thank you, Ben," she smiled.

I just sat there, my ass on my stool, and glanced around the kitchen. So much of what had just happened didn't make sense to me. Twenty minutes ago, I was happy and now I was apparently promising life-changes and eternity to my crush. I should have been Pharrell-Happy, but I wasn't.

"I'll clean this up for you." I watched as Elaine scooped up all the pages from my warehouse case and put them in a pile together. She spotted my food and helped herself. "This is good."

"I'm a Thompson," I muttered, quietly at first, then repeating it louder. "I'm a Thompson and I gave up my grip on normality years ago."

"No you didn't, you only think you did," she replied, wiping away the grease from her lips. "Somehow you got it into your head that normal was impossible because you were broken, that normal was tied to your leg. When it stopped working, so did your normality but that's not true, Ben. If you want to be normal, I can help. Let me help you."

"I don't need to be normal, I just need to be me," I snapped.

"Really? And does being you involve getting shot at? Does it involve almost dying? Does it involve risking your life?" Her voice was louder now.

"It used to," I yelled. Then it hit me. I missed it. I missed the danger. I missed my old life. I missed damn near everything about it.

"And look where it got you." She clapped her hands over her mouth and her eyes went wide. She didn't mean to say that, it just came out. "I'm sorry, that's not what I meant. As long as we've known each other, you've been the take no risk guy. Then it changed. I don't know what sparked this change but I just don't want you losing more because you're trying to relive your past."

As I broke it down I had two options. I was basically down to the last round in *Deal or No Deal*. There were two gorgeous women each holding a silver case. I had to pick between the woman offering me my cane and the woman offering me a case file all while Howie Mandel stretched a latex glove over his head and inflated it with his nostrils.

"Sometimes, Ben," Elaine whispered, "you have to man up and figure out what you want."

Why was every woman in my life saying that? Was there a meeting where this was all discussed? Was there a *How to Mess with Ben* newsletter? Was this a meme or something? If it was, I disliked it greatly and I was going to bring back grumpy cat.

What *did* I want?

The answer was easy: Zoey, but that was impossible. She was dead and in the real world dead meant dead. So if she was out, then what did I want? I wanted to be with someone. I wanted someone who cared for me, and I had that, but what was caring about someone? Was it looking after me and helping me fix my life or was it helping me accept who I was and encourage me to be a better me?

May I offer a suggestion?

I mentally shrugged. He was the brain for a reason. He might know something worth knowing. Then again he was my brain. He was probably as useless as my leg.

Never leave fun to look for fun. - Elton John.

I bolted up and limped for the bedroom. I scrambled around until I found my shirt. It was the shirt Rachael was wearing earlier. I reached down and touched it. A shiver and a twitch and I was diving back down the rabbit hole. My vision pulled me from my bedroom, tossed me into the Wayback Machine with a bowtie wearing canine time-traveller and his human companion, and dropped me in the distant time and place of: My bedroom.

Era: twenty minutes ago.

Rachael tilted her head sideways as she trapped her phone between her head and her shoulder as she unbuttoned my shirt. It was that awkward position we all do when we're trying to do three other things while talking to the people we love. Can't we all just stop, take a moment, and enjoy the company of those we love?

"Yes, sir, I'll head out immediately." Okay, it was probably work. "Datlow Center, got it?"

She dropped the phone on the bed and pulled off her shirt. I let the vision linger for a moment longer, evil me, before I hopped back into the Wayback Machine and headed home. Back in the present, I grabbed my phone and called a cab. I limped to the kitchen, grabbed my gun off the counter, and clipped it to my belt.

"Ben?" Elaine whispered.

"I can't do this, Elaine," I explained. "I want to be with you, but I can't just drop my life for you. I'm a gumshoe. I like it and I'm good at it. I'm not normal; I haven't been for a while."

"But, Ben, I..."

"I'm psychic." I reached up and touched her shirt. A shiver and a twitch, and I was transported to Steve's apartment. "You broke up with him this morning. You were at his place. He understood, he kissed you on the cheek and you left. Nobody cried and nobody fought. I think both of you knew it was over for a while now."

She just stared at me dumbfounded. It was the look that was half *how did you know that?* and half *are you stalking me?* I hate that look. I limped to the hallway and grabbed my jacket.

"It's her, isn't it?" she snapped. "You've wanted me for a long time now. I'm not blind, Ben. But here I am, offering myself to you, and you're saying no, for some booty call?" T   hat stung. This wasn't Elaine. She was hurt and she was lashing out. She'd just put her heart out there, offering it to me, and I just smacked it away. I felt like shit. "It's more than that. I'd be lying if I said otherwise. I have to see if this means as much to her as it does to me. I owe myself that."

A cab honked its horn. I grabbed my hat and cane and hobbled to the door. Elaine shook her head in confusion. "Where are you going?"
"To stop a meme."

Twenty minutes later, after a quick stop at my bank, I pulled up to Datlow Center. I threw money at the cabbie and limp towards the building. Nothing seemed to register as I walked past, not the dozens of onlookers, the red Chevelle, or the cops' cars. I was a man on a mission and I needed to get inside.

Datlow Center was an office building. One of those tall building that held dozens of businesses in them. I entered the building and headed directly for the elevator. I ran my fingers over the panel and let a quick vision take over. Rachael was on the ninth floor. A short ride later and so was I. The elevator opened up and a uniformed officer stood before me.

"Sorry. You can't be here."

I reached into my jacket and pulled out a business card and handed it to the cop. "Benedict Thompson: Insurance Claims Investigator."

The cop took the card and looked it over. "I'm sorry, Mr. Thompson, but this section is off limits. You'll have to come back a..." The officer looked up and saw me gone. He snapped his head around to see me hobbling away at top speed. I'm not a patient man. "Hey, get back here."

The cop chased after me, catching up to me almost instantly. It wasn't a difficult thing for him to do, my top speed as a hobbler isn't exactly roadrunner-esque. My top speed is more like the turtle from *The Turtle and the Hare*, the only difference being that I was a turtle and somebody knocked me on my back and pointed and laughed for twenty minutes. Yet regardless of my non-speed, the cop still decided to tackle me to the ground.

"Oh my god, why?" I screamed as I fell to the floor. "He's assaulting a cripple. Why would you hurt a cripple? Why? I'm a war vet. I'll check you cats for worms during a war. It's a horrible business model." I say the most *random* things when I'm scared.

"What's going on out here? Ben?" I recognized that voice. She sighed. "Of course it's you."

I looked up from underneath the police office and force an idiotic smile. "Rachael? Fancy meeting you here; do you Officer Innocent here? I believe his full name is Officer I'm An Idiot Because I Tackled A Crippled Man Who's Totally Innocent. I think that's an Irish name." I looked up at my captor. "Are you Irish? It's cool if you are, I'm just curious. Thompson is an English/Scottish name."

"What are you doing here?" she asked.

"I really need to talk to you," I explained. She rolled her eyes and sighed. She signalled the cop to let me up. She pulled me into a side office.

"What do you want?" she said sternly.

"For a long time, I didn't know what I wanted," I began slowly, picking up speed with each word. "I wanted to be happy and to be with someone, but at the same time I didn't. I didn't want to bring my broken ass into someone else's life. Nobody deserved to deal with me and I didn't deserve anything good. But then you happened.

"At first it was sex. It was *great* sex, but then things changed. Things got weird. You started staying over more. I've always had people looking out for me, but you did more. You encouraged me; you pushed me to be a better detective, to be a better man, and to be a better person. I can have good things in my life and you are the best thing."

I pulled a wad of bills from my pocket and held them in my hands. "I want you, Rachael Puzo. I love you and I want to be in a relationship with you." I tossed a twenty dollar bill onto the nearby desk. "Relationship, relationship, relationship, relationship, relationship, relationship, relationship, relationship, relationship, relationship, relationship, relationship, aaannnnd relationship."

One after another I tossed twenties on the desk, until all fourteen were lying in a messy pile. Two hundred and eighty dollars sat in a pile, staring up at us. "I love you, Rachael, and I want to be with you. Please be with a broken man like me?"

"You're an idiot," Rachael said with a stern look. Her lips never moved or quivered, they just sat there, emotionless, until a small smile peaked through. "Took you long enough." She leaned in and kissed me. The kiss felt wonderful, but somehow I got the distinct impression that Puzo had me completely figured out the moment she first met me. "You're not broken. What about Elaine?"

"I slept with her."

Puzo elbowed me in the gut and I doubled over, exaggerating the damage for comedic effect and not because I was trying to cover up how much her blow actually hurt. Puzo rolled her eyes and then glanced at her watch. "Wow, sex with her didn't take you very long. I might have to reconsider."

"Low... blow," I gasped. I coughed and caught my breath. "Okay, I think I should take you out on a real date or something." I glanced at Puzo as she shoved all the twenties into her pocket. I smirked. "But you're paying."

"If you ask me to the prom, I'll shoot you." She kissed me again. "I love the gesture, but next time, don't pick a crime scene."

"A what now?" I looked out the office door and glanced down the hall. There were cops and CSI everywhere. Off in the distance I could see Humpty, Dumpty and Jason talking amongst themselves. "Ohhh. Damn. Who died?"

"We have four deaths, but it's obvious who his target

was. His name is Jameson Wagner, Senior Project Manager for Homewind Industries."

"Homewind?"

"They're a private military. They operate mainly overseas."

"Why are you investigating this?" I asked. "I know you're not allowed to say a lot about your work, but this isn't missing children. What's going on?"

Rachael pulled me back inside and closed the door. "I'm no longer assigned to missing children anymore, Ben. I was reassigned."

"Why didn't you tell me?"

"Ben, I'm assigned to a task force that has one purpose. We're investigating Croxallé," she explained. "The Bureau didn't take lightly to Ryman being turned. They've always had their suspicions about the medical company, rumours mostly, but Ryman was their first distinct proof. Now it's full on investigation."

"And you're in charge?"

"Almost," she admitted. "For a while my job was on the line but my record, and a testimony from Ryman, cleared me. Then they offered me the job after the way I handled Robby's case. That became high profile amongst the Bureau."

It made sense why she couldn't tell me. It had to be kept secret and my family had some connection to the medical company. The secret had to be kept. It also explained why she was involved in all of this. A high ranker suit from Croxallé's competitor dies so they investigate. "That's why you have the no touching clothes rule."

She shrugged and replied, using a sing-song voice: "Sometimes when we touch, the honesty's too much, and I have to close my eyes and hide."

How has that not been my theme song? That song has many lines that just seem to fit:

> *Romance and all its strategy*
> *Leaves me battling with my pride*
> *But through the insecurity*

Some tenderness survives
I'm just another writer
Still trapped within my truth
A hesitant prize fighter
Still trapped within my youth

"Okay, Dan Hill," I smirked. "Can I help with the investigation? Is it connected to the last?"

She nodded and escorted me out of the room. "We think so. Different weapon, different MO, but we think so."

The crime scene was bad. It wasn't chopped-up-body-pieces-bad but four people dead are still bad. The room was one of those corporate conference rooms with a massive table in the middle and expensive leather chairs all around it. While the room was stunning, I decided almost instantly that I did not like the chosen decor -- I've never been fan of decorating a room with dead bodies. There were two young ladies dead on the floor, another body of an older man slumped over the table, and a guy -- obviously Wagner -- dead in a chair. I also saw Jason in the room and luckily he was still alive. Jason turned and looked at me with a raised eyebrow.

"Ben? I was just about to call you."

"I guess I'm just psychic." I pulled off my glove and knelt by Wagner's body. I touched his suit, his expensive suit, and let my powers pull me back in to the past.

Wagner, a blond haired man with glasses, entered the room with his female assistant following closing behind. He started pointing to different thing around the room and vocalizing everything that needed to change.

"No pitchers of water," he explained as he pointed to the counter. "Make sure our caterers have bottled water. Have you made sure that they're bringing the good coffee?"

"Yes, sir," his assistant cooed. "We'll also have food being brought up, mostly small sandwiches and the sort."

Wagner turned to the second female, a geeky woman with thick glasses and a couple cords slung over her shoulder, and watched as she hooked up the large TV screen to several monitors. "Will the displays be ready? I can't have any tech problems when Mr. Koplan gets here."

"Everything will be re--" Her words were cut off by the startled scream that slipped between her lips. Wagner spun around to see an unfamiliar man, one who wasn't there a moment ago, shimmering into view.

Wagner didn't know who this guy was, but I did. It was Nouri Allawi.

"Who are you? This is a private room."

Nouri stood by the table and smirked. "I'm afraid your meeting is being cancelled." He held up a silenced pistol and flashed an evil-Mel-Gibson-*Expendables-3*-Super-Villain smile. "Director Theodore A. Koplan will not be attending today."

Nouri swung his gun around, levelled it at the geeky girl's head, and squeezed off a round. Her head snapped back and she collapsed to the ground. Wagner's assistant opened her mouth to scream, but never got the chance. Nouri shifted his aim to her and put a bullet through her neck. The older man tried to bolt past, but Nouri was too fast. The assassin spun around, grabbed the man by his collar, and slammed him face first into the table. He pressed his gun to the back of the old man's skull and pulled the trigger. Wagner stood there stunned and terrified. Nouri levelled his gun at the man and approached.

"W... w...why?" Wagner asked. "Why me?"

Nouri just shrugged as he pushed the Senior Project Manager into a chair. "Bad luck mostly. This has absolutely nothing to do with you."

"Then why?"

"I could say how you've lost your way or how you've failed this city. I can lie to you if you'd like, if it'll make you feel better." Nouri pressed the gun to Wagner's forehead. "But the truth is that this will just make a better movie." Nouri pulled trigger. "You always need bait."

I snapped back to reality and twisted around and glanced at Jason and Puzo. "He's here. The killer is still here. It's a trap!"

A second later, four people died: two CSI agents, one cop and FBI agent. Each one fell suddenly with a new bullet hole somewhere on their body but no gunshot to be heard. The rest of the cops reacted quickly, each drawing their personal weapons and diving for cover. Seeing Rachael in action is amazing. In a firefight like this she takes command and instantly starts to assess the situation. But what makes it truly a sight to see is how she does it all without breaking a sweat. In the seconds it took for the four to fall, Puzo had her Glock drawn, dropped to the floor, pulled me with her, and was already scanning the room for her attacker.

"Dorlan?" she called out across the room. "You got eyes?"

Agent Dorlan, an older FBI man, lay on the ground across the room. Everybody was thinking the same thing, *sniper*, and that meant avoiding the windows. "I got nothing, Boss. No shooter and no holes. I'll take the door."

Dorlan climbed to his feet and bolted for the room's only exit. He got two steps when a bullet hole appeared in his head and he crashed to the ground. I snapped my head around the room as I looked for Jason. I found him, and Humpty and Dumpty, on the ground several feet away. Our eyes locked and I cried out for him. That may have sounded more like a rom-com then I intended.

"Kevin Bacon's in the room."

Rachael just stared at me. She had no idea what the hell I was talking about, but Jason did.

"Flash Bang: take cover!" Jason yelled.

Training took over and most of the FBI and cops covered their eyes. Truth was, there was no flash bang but with everybody's eyes closed Jason could do his superhero thing. I watched as he pressed both palms on the floor and felt as if a sudden invisible pulse rippled through the room. It was like the force from a small explosion, pushing everything back except there was no bang and there was no boom. The pulse barely affected anybody in the room, most of us were on the ground, but after I heard a loud thud by the door I realized that anybody who had been standing upright would have been tossed by Jason's psionic pulse attack. I looked at the door to see Nouri shimmer back into view. He had been slammed into the wall and had fallen to the floor. His hand still held the pistol and his eyes were locked on the quickly rising Jason. For a moment I saw a look of panic, a look that told me Jason was not part of his plan. Nouri scrambled to his feet, firing three silenced shots at Jason, and bolted for the door. Jason easily deflected each round with his Neo power before turning to subdue Croxallé's former employee, but he found only nothing as Nouri shimmered out of sight.

Humpty and Dumpty leapt to their feet only to find that Puzo had beaten them to it. She moved to the door and peered into the opening, using the ledge as cover. I'll never get used to just how fast Rachael is. In a way she reminded me of David -- in the awkward fashion of comparing your best friend to the woman you're now in a relationship (wow, the world didn't blow up) with. Both were fast, very fast. They could go from prone to full upright faster than anyone I could ever see. David, however, would do it with a needless twist or spin. The man had reflexes like a cat.

"Primary objective," Humpty began.

"Protect the asset," Dumpty finished. Both moved to protect Jason. Looking back, I find that a little funny. Jason could life a car into the air, with his mind, and toss it further then Tony Romo could throw a football. Yet somehow Croxallé decided that he needed the protection of two men whose names I could barely remember.

"Call for backup," Puzo barked at one of her FBI lackeys. "Everybody else, secure the room and get ready to move people out. We'll take them to the elevator."

I climbed to my feet, slowly, and drew my M9. I hobbled to the door and slid in beside Puzo. "What's the plan?"

Puzo glanced at me and eyed Jason and his bodyguards. "We push forward and clear the hallway so we can get the civilians out of here. Let's move."

Puzo pushed forward, her Glock out, and Jason followed. Humpty and Dumpty went out next. I pulled up the rear with a single thought in my head: Wait, wasn't I a civilian now? Somehow, I was getting the short end of the civilian life stick. I peaked around the corner, glanced down the hallway, and spotted the elevator. It was a straight stretch from here to the exit. There were a couple offices and adjoining hallways, but the path seemed relatively easy if you removed the invisible assassin from the picture. Everything seemed easier when you removed the invisible assassin from the picture, except cooking. I always found cooking difficult.

There is a saying that no plan survives first contact with the enemy. Every day of my military life proved that correct. So when we stepped out into the hallway with the plan being run straight, that plan changed the moment three goons shimmered into view. Each wore a mask and carried a MP5 submachine gun. Two things happened before I could scream out a warning. The first was Puzo putting two rounds in a goon's chest and the second was Humpty and Dumpty tackling both Jason and I down another hallway. Bullets whizzed through the cartoon like afterimage, made entirely out of smoke of course, that remained where I once stood. I scrambled to my feet, furious.

"What are you doing? Puzo!" The idiots saved Jason and I, but left her alone. I limped to the corner and popped out, my M9 ready. I couldn't see Puzo but I did see the two goons marching forward. I snapped off a round and put it in one of their necks. The second goon fell to the floor in a mess of gargling and choking. I snapped off two more rounds, hitting only the wall, and pushed the remaining bad-guy back. He returned fire as he shimmered out of sight. "Puzo?"

"In here." I glanced at an office and saw Puzo pressed against a door. "Is there an invisible man running around?"

"Several if I had to guess." Puzo pointed at me with two fingers and then pointed at the elevator. "Not loving the Kevin Bacon?"

"No clue what you're talking about," she replied, nodding at me. "But I hate super powers."

"That's fair," I nodded back.

Puzo popped out from her cover and opened fire. She snapped off round after round, firing at nothing in particular. Instead she spread her rounds across the hallway. Puzo didn't have to explain it, I knew what she was doing. There was a hostile enemy hidden somewhere in plain sight. Her seemingly random spread of bullets was actually an attempt to clear the hallway of any invisi-bads. I limped forward, holding back my weapons fire until we were side by side. We stopped at the elevators. Puzo glanced at me and tapped her pistol. I nodded at her and she ejected her magazine, fished a replacement from her belt and slapped in a full clip. I quickly did the same.

"We keep ourselves at the ready," Puzo said as she pressed the elevator button. "Then we get everybody out of here. We give them a hallway to run down." The elevator dinged and the doors opened.

I opened my mouth to speak but the words never left my lips; instead I felt the strength of a boot slamming against my chest. The kick sent me flying backwards and sliding across the floor. I cursed loudly and looked up from the floor. I saw Puzo glancing at me surprised and Nouri, standing in the elevator, shimming into view with a gun in his hand. Puzo snapped her head around just in time to see Nouri level the gun at her chest and pull the trigger.

Nouri gave me a smile. "Hello, Ben."

Chapter 17
A Father-Killing Wildebeast Horde?

No, not again. Please not again. My screams drowned out everything else in the world as I watched Puzo fall. Nouri fired twice more into Puzo chest and I felt my own chest explode.

No. First Zoey, now Rachael; I couldn't do this again. I couldn't lose the women I loved.

Nouri stood in the elevator, on the left side by the button, and shot me a cocky smile and he waved with his silenced pistol. That cocky bastard; I want nothing more than to kill him. I glanced to the side and saw my M9. It fell from my grip when I was kicked and now lay only a couple feet away. I looked back as Nouri.

"Go for it," he taunted. "Go for your gun. I'm not going to stop you; I'm not even going to shoot you. I'll even give you a free shot."

I scrambled across the floor and scooped up my pistol. Propping myself up on one knee, I levelled my pistol at Nouri.

"Take your shot, Ben. We both know it won't do a thing."

I stared down my pistol iron sights, and lined both over Nouri's chest. The arrogant prick was just standing alone in the elevator, presenting his body for my bullet. I was seeing red and all I wanted to do was rip this man's heart out from his chest. The only problem was, it would probably grow back. I couldn't beat him, I couldn't hurt him or stop him and he knew it. It was why he did little else but stood in the elevator, alone, taunting me to shoot him.

Standing, alone, in the *left side* of an elevator.

Hell.

I shifted my aim away from him, putting it on the empty side of the elevator, and pulled the trigger three times. Each shot rang out with a bang but instead of the sound of ricocheting bullets or smashing glass, I heard only the sound of a gasp followed by a heavy thud. When you're alone in an elevator you stand in the middle, not the side. Everybody stands in the middle, just like the good old days in the caves.

God bless cavemen and their caves.

A crumpled body, collapsed on the elevator floor, shimmered into existence. From across the floor, I could hear a couple gunshots and the sudden cries of FBI and police doing their thing and ordering men to floor. Suddenly it made sense. This was a light bender. He could bend the light around people. He could make light bend around anything and anyone, and without light, nothing could be seen. That was how he made Nouri, himself and dozens of others invisible.

Ship.

Light bender.

It poured back to me. Moore; this light bender was a WhiteStar dick named Moore. He was arrested on a ship, on the ship that held Robby. Six months ago, this dick kidnapped Robby. Now he'd help Nouri kill Rachael.

Moore looked up from the elevator floor and stared at me, his eyes pleading for help and for forgiveness. It was as if in this last moment, *his* last moment, he realized the errors he'd made and the clemency and absolution he needed. He couldn't speak, there was blood quickly filing his lungs, but he could stare at me and plead, hoping that I'd be the bigger man.

Rachael. Robby.

Fuck him.

I snapped off another round and put the bullet directly into his skull.

Fuck him.

I pushed myself to my feet and twisted my body and aimed my pistol back at Nouri. He just looked at the dead body, nodding slowly. "Well, that will complicate things." He looked back at me. "You have darkness in you, Ben, real darkness. I am--"

I snapped off another round and put a bullet through his neck. Nouri gargled as blood poured from the hole like a twisted Eli Roth version of Niagara Falls, but he didn't fall. He pressed the elevator button and gave me a blood filled smile. I screamed and started pulling the trigger, pouring round after round into his body and then, after they'd closed, into the doors themselves.

I kept pulling until my gun clicked, signalling an empty clip. I dropped my gun and scrambled for Rachael's body. I slid in beside her and gently held her head. I just stared at her, my breathing rapid and my chest beating rapidly. My heart wanted to explode out of my chest and my body wanted to shut down. But I couldn't, I had to be strong. I had to be tough like her. Puzo never showed weakness. She didn't break, she never faltered, and even now when she was on the ground, she still looked stoic and she didn't even bleed.

No blood.

"Oh please, please pull a Clint." I grabbed Puzo's shirt and ripped it open and looked at what lay beneath. I almost cried at the sight I saw. "Oh thank god."

"You're... buying... me... a... new... shirt." A tear swelled up as I saw the Kevlar vest, dented with three bullets, strapped to her body. "It was... Prada."

"Bullshit," I said as I reached down and kissed her. "But I don't care. I'll buy you an entire Prada wardrobe." I kissed her again. "Prada isn't expensive, is it?"

I sat leaned up against the wall and pulled her into my arms. I held her and she just let herself be held. We sat there for what seemed like hours but it was little more than ten minutes. We broke the hold when two cops entered the hallway, each with a pistol drawn. They saw us and lowered their weapons. "We're clear. We've got everybody detained." Rachael smiled and tried to get up; she winced and clutched her chest. "Any more dead?"

"Six more, ma'am. Someone shot up the lobby." The officer cleared his throat. "There was someone else."

"Who?"

"That Croxallé consultant," the officer said. "Jason Daggett is dead."

I stepped off the elevator and stared at the commotion in the lobby. There were cops and FBI everywhere. I couldn't hobble two feet without awkwardly bumping into some form of law enforcement. The floor was littered with little numbered yellow cards that marked where a bullet landed. There were a lot of yellow cards. I reached down and touched a bullet. A shiver and a twitch, and I fell into the past.

I found myself in the elevator watching Nouri. His clothes were stained with his own blood but his body was already healing. His chest ejected the bullets and his neck wound quickly closed itself. It was disturbing to watch, seeing a wound heal itself instantly, but it wasn't nearly as disturbing as what Nouri did next. He reloaded his pistol, removed the silencer and then holstered it. He pushed back his jacket and pulled free a TEC-9 machine pistol. I shuddered as he loaded the weapon and cocked it. Then he pulled free a second one, and repeated

His TEC-9 had a 50 round magazine. That was a lot of bullets and a lot of people in danger.

The elevator dinged and the doors opened. Nouri spat out a mouthful of blood, clutched a TEC-9 in each hand and stepped off the elevator.

Reality returned and I frowned. I touched another

spent case and fell back into the vision. Nouri stepped out of the elevator and fired three rounds into the air. What few people were left in the lobby screamed and ran, but he brought them to a halt as he killed two women closest to the door.

"Everybody freeze," he laughed. Everybody dropped to the floor or stood still, terrified. They watched as the gun wielding maniac walked forward. "Today is my villain moment. Today we make a scene worthy of Joel Silver or Michael Bay. Today we make this building famous." He pointed to a large security office near the reception desk. It had three solid walls and a glass wall that allowed the guards to peer out. "Everybody in that office. Move!"

He watched as the dozen remaining civilians did as he ordered. He glanced at the elevator, as if he was waiting for someone to descend but nobody came. Nouri's body twitched as a pair of round slammed into his body. Nouri turned, his wounds already healing, and smirked at Humpty and Dumpty. He sprayed a flurry of rounds, clipping Humpty's shoulder with one lucky shot. Dumpty screamed in pain and dropped to the floor. Nouri raised a curious eye.

"It's over, Allawi." Nouri glance over at the sound of his name and watched as Jason stood up. Jason scowled as he continued speaking. "Surrender now."

"You can't stop me, Dagget," he laughed. "You know this." He levelled his TEC-9 and fired a burst of five. Jason didn't flinch. He simply raised his hand and stopped each round dead, the bullets floating in the air like a pretty damn good Neo impression.

"Give it up," Jason barked, allowing every round to harmlessly drop. "You know what I'm capable of."

"No, I don't," Nouri smirked. "But I'm about to find out."

Nouri spun towards Jason and pointed both guns at him. He opened fire with both and started walking forward. The TEC-9 was not a very accurate gun, especially when you fire at the speeds that Nouri was, but he didn't need to be accurate. He just needed to be close. It took me a second to figure out what Nouri was doing, I'm not a smart man, but it quickly became apparent. He was trying to test Jason's limits.

Every person had limits and each of our respective powers came with restrictions. If I used my powers too often during any given day of the week, my brain would scream out in pain and misery, kind of like a Whoo-Girl. If you could fly, you could only fly for so long. If you had super speed, you'd run out of energy after a certain point. We were all super-men, but none of us were Superman. Nouri was pouring every bullet he had in Jason's direction because he knew Jason had to catch them all. He couldn't deflect them; there were still the chances that they'd tip through the glass and hit the hostages. He had to catch each and every one of them.

I'd seen Jason catch dozens of bullet and toss a car like a school boy tossed a ball of paper. But Jason had rested in-between, they weren't long rests but they were long enough. Nouri wasn't giving him any rest and he was tossing a crap ton more bullet then I'd ever seen Jason handle. When both machine pistols made the resounding click, Nouri ditched them without a second thought and drew his pistol. He opened fire again, pumping ten more rounds at the telekinetic.

Jason was at his limits. He held in the air nearly a hundred different rounds and his body and mind was paying the toll. Blood dripped from his nose and his eyes, crying blood like a Bond villain, and a muddy liquid dripped from his ears. His body twitched and each vein seem bulge outwards, like they were trying to jump ship and get clear of this body. Jason dropped to one knee.

When the pistol clicked, Nouri ejected the magazine and slapped in another. Jason dropped the floating rounds, each dropping harmlessly, and raised his arm to stop Nouri but no power came. Nouri, now two steps away from the telekinetic, pressed the pistol against Jason's forehead. Jason tried to push him away, but his arms had no strength left.

"You," Nouri chuckled. "You are amazing. I'm seriously impressed. It's a shame you have to die. It's not all bad though. Now, in my movie, you are the tragic death that the fans will clamber to. They'll cry and then they'll beg for a prequel movie. You'll be the cult hero. You will be the Boba Fett for our little 'verse." He smirked. "But you aren't making it out of this movie alive."

Then Nouri pulled the trigger. Jason body fell backwards and collapsed on the floor before the reception desk.

I pulled my hand away and returned to reality. I was speechless. I didn't know what to think. I wasn't Jason's biggest fan, but I wasn't his enemy. He didn't deserve to die like this. I climbed to my feet, finding myself needing my cane more than normal -- the cane Jason gave me -- and hobbled to the desk. I expected to find a body but there was none. There wasn't even that white chalk outline either. There was nothing.

I waved down a cop. "Where Dagget's body?"

"We found him in the bathroom. For some reason he was dragged into the bathroom and killed there. Why do you -- hey!" I hobbled away before he finished speaking. That didn't make sense. Jason was shot by the table. How the hell did he get to the bathroom? I kicked open the door, pushed past a surprised CSI dude, and stared at Jason's body. He was leaning against the bathroom wall as he sat on the floor. A cell phone was in his hand and smile sat on his face. The wall had a bullet hole in it and also had the appropriate amount of blood and grey matter painted upon it. Somehow Nouri had shot Jason by the desk out in the lobby, but the bullet came out here in the bathroom.

I felt my heart race and my chest heave as my breathing became laboured. Staring at Jason's body felt like those days when I stared at the bodies of friends I'd lost overseas. I felt fear, anxiety and nausea all building up. Then I let them overwhelm me.

It was a technique I was taught, a way to super charge my powers. It was dangerous, especially when you hadn't properly named the ability something cool (Power: TBA is what I call it), but it granted me an unparalleled level of access to the past.

I felt like I'd been tossed on a country fair's tilt-a-whirl and I'd been stuck there way too long. The longer I stayed on this ride, the worse it got. My nausea grew to a point where every movement could set me off, and my anxiety become overwhelming as I noticed every detail on this ride. The rusty bars, the missing bolts, the three fingered carney who was supposed to be paying attention to the ride but was currently too busy flirting with a local townie girl who was legally way too young. And then there was my fear. Fear and I have never been on good terms, but when I let it go unchecked, when it stampeded across my body and mind like a father-killing wildebeest horde, it became stronger than I ever imagined, like I'd just killed it with a laser sword and it came back as a floaty ghost that never seemed to shut up. It was at that moment, when I felt like my body was about to shutdown, that's when I grabbed Jason's shirt.

Every inch of my body shivered and every muscle and nerve twitched. I looked like I was having a seizure. It was like the past, present and future was one large intricate stain glass window, millions of feet high and millions wider, and I'd just smashed through it like an action movie freeze frame.

My vision was like a water slide and the waves were forcing me along. I could see the enclosed slide all around me, except the sides weren't made out of the same ugly orange material as the rest; they were made from fractured moments of the past. I saw Jason getting off the elevator, I saw him getting dressed this morning and I even saw a tailor stitching the suit together.

I don't know if words could explain what this moment felt like, or if there was anything in movie-references that could compare, but I'm pretty sure how I felt was similar to what Luke Skywalker must have felt after Mufasa showed up in the clouds to reveal that he was his father.

The only names I've come up with, as lame as they sounds, are the Clarity Channel, Psychic Passageway or Super Subway. None of those were any good, but whatever I decided to call this slide, it was giving me access to everything in every point in time for Jason's suit.

Amongst the slide, I saw what I wanted, the sight of Jason being shot. I reached out and touched it and suddenly I was there, not as a cosmic voyeur, like normal, but as Jason himself. What Jason saw, I saw. What Jason felt, I felt. What Jason pooped -- you get the picture. The important thing was I felt the bullet in our head but we weren't dead. I could feel the bullet in skull, still spinning around as it dug deeper, but we were still alive. It was as if the bullet had been put in slow-mo.

We stood up, our eyes glowing bright white. Nouri was gone. We looked around and let out a sigh of relief. The hostages were still alive. We saved them all. We climbed to our feet, our legs barely strong enough to hold us up, and limped to bathroom. We reached into our suit pocket and fished out our phone. We slid our thumb across the screen, tapped it a couple times, and stared at the name on our screen: Robby Belledin. We tapped the name and held the phone to our ear. It was ringing.

Then I understood. We were using our telekinetic powers to slow the bullet down. We were too far gone to save our lives but we could give ourselves a couple more minutes of life. It was still spinning in our skulls, slowly killing us, but we had given ourselves enough time to do one last thing.

We were going to call Robby.

"Hello?" A tear formed in our eyes (Jason's eyes -- not mine. Cowboys don't cry. I don't care what you think I did earlier) and we smiled. "Hi there, Robby, how are you today?"

"Good. Um...who is this?"

"My name is Jason Dagget," we explained. "We met at the hospital. You called me Mr. Vulcan. Do you remember?" We almost laughed at the question.

"You called yourself Gabriel Summers. Yeah, I remember." There was a pause. "Do you want my Mom or Dad or something?"

"In a second. What do you know about Peter Parker's father?" we asked.

"He was a decorated soldier of the United States Army Special Forces, was recruited by Nick Fury to the C.I.A." He listed this off like he was reading a Wikipedia article. "He had to leave Peter because of an important mission. He left Peter with his older brother Ben to protect him."

"Very good, Mr. Parker," we say with a smile, using my nickname for the boy. "I've had many names but I think from now on you need to call me Richard Parker, okay?"

"Mom!" Robby yelled; his voice cracking. "Mom!"

"I had to leave a long time ago and that was the biggest mistake of my life, Robby," we explained, fighting back tears. "But I always loved you and I'm very proud of you."

"Mom!"

"I love you, Robby."

We listened as Annie rushed into the room, sounding worried, and then desperately asked what was wrong. There was the sound of rustling as the phone switched hands.

"Who is this?" That was Annie's voice, angry and worried all in one.

"Hey, Desert Lily."

Silence.

"G... Greg?" Her voice suddenly lost its ferocity.

"Hi." We needed something else to say but to be honest, we couldn't think of anything. "I'm sorry."

"W... what?"

"I'm so sorry," we began. "Leaving you was the hardest thing I ever had to do and it was also the most cowardly. I'm not as strong as you, Annie. No one is. I love you, I always have, and I always will, but you need to keep on hating me."

"Greg..."

"You need to keep on hating me because I am not worthy of anything else. You powered on, you stayed firm, and you raised our -- your boy. I've kept my eye on him, Annie. You've done an amazing job. I'm so very proud of you, Desert Lily."

"What's going on?" We could hear the tears flowing

down her cheek, impossible as it was we could hear them. "Why now?"

"He's going to be an amazing man and it kills me that I won't be around to see it," we said, tears finally rolling down our face. "I love you, Desert Lily, and I love Robby. I always have and I always will."

"Greg... I..." Annie was full on crying now and it broke our heart.

"I know, Desert Lily, I know," we reassured her. "You were the best thing to ever happen to me and I was the worst thing to happen to you. Don't forget me, Annie, but don't ever stop hating me. It's all I deserve."

And with that we hung up.

We let our arm drop to the floor. We don't even notice the pain as our hand smacked the bathroom tiles. It didn't matter anymore. Nothing did. We forced our other hand up to wipe away the tears; we couldn't be seen crying. We leaned our head against the wall and smiled.

Then we let go.

Fade to black.

Chapter 18
I Still Bought my Groceries with Pelts and Furs

I hate hospitals. Whoever decided that hospitals were good places was freaking insane. How can TV make endless shows about hospitals? Even hospital sitcoms are sad and depressing. Zack Braff can be humorous for only so long before somebody dies and things get boring. That's me being generous by the way; I never found Zack Braff that funny to begin with. Donald Faison, on the other hand, was frickin' hilarious.

I've spent way too much time in a hospital. They are too clean, they're full of death and disease, and worse of all they are a haven for the greatest of all evils that this world holds: needles. There is nothing so barbaric in this world as needles. I mean, who in this world allows some strange man stick something long and phallic into them?

I squirmed as I watched the needle pierce the skin. My heart rate sped up and nausea filled my body. I let out a small scream. I was no good around needles.

"Ben," Puzo said. "What are you doing?"

"I hate needles."

"Yeah, I know that," she said with a raised eyebrow. "But I'm the one getting stuck."

The nurse removed the needle from Puzo's arm and smiled. He eyed me and asked if I was going to be okay. I waved him off. Damn nosey male nurses. I looked at Rachael and gave her a forced smile. She rolled her eyes. The needle didn't faze her in the least. Apparently Puzo had no problem letting strange men sticking long phallic objects into her.

Internal giggle.

Puzo lay in a bed with a small amount of painkillers flowing through her. I approached and leaned in to kiss Rachael Puzo, my girlfriend.

That just sounded right.

Puzo lets strange men stick things into her -- and I'm giggling again.

"You're doing your fretting wife bit again," Puzo mocked. "I'll be okay. It's just a couple of broken ribs. I've had worse."

I tried not to, I tried so god damn hard not to, but I still did. My gaze dropped from her eyes and landed on her neck. Puzo had a thin scar that ran the length of her neck. She never mentioned it and I never asked. She didn't like to bring attention to it; I could dig that. After all, I didn't like to bring attention to the Rorschach Ink Blob of scars that littered my back.

"I know you have," I replied. "Doesn't mean I like when it happens to you."

"Ben," she smirked. "Grow a pair."

For the record, I was not stunned into silence by that comment. Me, Rambling Ben, stunned? Not likely. There wasn't thirty seconds of silence and stammering from me, I was just interrupted by my cell phone ringing and damn anyone else who tells you different.

"Hello."

"Benedict." It was Mia. "I have a link for you."

Puzo gave me a raised eyebrow. I told her I had a break in the case. She asked me to put it on speaker. Spoiler Alert: That turned out to be a mistake.

Sports are a thing. I have no other way of describing it and people spend a crap ton on this thing. So since there is money to be made from it, TV will milk it to death. They make shows that will spend twenty-three minutes dissecting the game you just watched and examine each and every play through super slow replay. If my life was a sports chat show, they would be examining this moment as an All-Time-Disas-ter-Play.

Our lead player, Ben, has been going strong the last couple days. He hasn't screw up, he just made a great romance play earlier, and he's on his way to solving this case. That being said, he's started to slip up.

"Okay, go ahead Mia," I said.

This is where thing start taking a turn. How could he leave an opening like that? Doesn't he know the other team, life, is just going to exploit it?

"Before I say anything, I need you to take me up on my sex offer."

There is the first blow. What a devastating hit.

"Excuse me?" Rachael's voice suddenly became ice cold.

"I'm on speaker phone? Cool. Who's that, Benedict?" Mia asked in her usual jovial tone.

"I'm Ben's girlfriend, Rachael. Who the hell is this?"

Oh. What a follow up blow. This is not Ben's day.

"I'm Mia Roan. Who are you?"

"Rachael Puzo," she answered. "Special Agent in Charge Rachael Puzo of the FBI."

If you notice, life isn't pulling punches. It's throwing out everything its gun. It's going full gun, giving it 110%, and I'm using every tired metaphor to describe it.

"Holy shit, really?" Mia replied. "Wow. I'm an on-air business reporter. My first night is tonight. Benedict helped me get promoted by slipping me info from cases he's been working on."

Ohhh. Wow, what a blow.

"Did he now?" Puzo's voice sounded really pissed. "And you want to sleep with him now?"

"I did." The sound of keyboard clacking filled the silence. "Not anymore. Wow, I just found you in our news database. Forget Benedict, I should be going after you, Ms. Hottie."

If you were paying attention then you'd notice the look on Ben's face. It's part-confused, part-scared and part-holy-crap-can-I-get-a-threesome-out-of-this? Right about here Ben has no options. All he needs to do is stay quiet and let this blow over.

"Ladies please, let's not fight over me," I replied.

Oh damn! That was it. That was the worst thing he could have said.

"Ben," Puzo snapped. "Shut up, women are talking."

And there we are. It's over and Ben has lost. This was just a disaster play to begin with, poorly handled from every angle. All I can say is it's a good thing that a season is eighty-three games and not just one.

"Yes, ma'am," I murmured.

"I do need to talk to Ben about the case," Mia injected. "But seriously Puzo, call me."

"So what do you got?" Puzo asked, her voice calming down.

"Hey," I cried out. "That's my line and that's my contact."

"Not anymore I'm not," Mia said. "Seriously, Puzo, if you need anything, ring me up."

"Seriously, Ben, the women are talking," Puzo said, sticking her tongue out at me. "Mia, go on."

"I looked into the names you told me," she began. Puzo looked at me in confusion. I mouthed the words *Allawi's targets*. She nodded and listened. "At first there wasn't any link, at least nothing visible, but there is a connection. It is well hidden, buried between shell companies and dozens of other legal business loopholes that isn't going to mean much to you."

That wasn't an insult -- which was weird not to get from a hottie-hottie-hot-hot-hottie girl -- it was just the truth. I knew nothing about business or money. I still bought my groceries with pelts and furs.

"Most people couldn't find this connection, but as you know I'm not most people." She was *much* hotter. "But

Skit-Tech is a subsidiary company."

"Yeah, that I know." Whoot! I'm not a complete idiot.

"But so are Leti-Wind Pharmaceuticals and Claymont Development," Mia revealed. "They are both owned by a company called Homewind Industries." I glanced at Puzo. She cursed quietly. They were all connected. Allawi was cutting a swath through this company, one business at a time. "Well, technically Homewind is owned by a Langovo Fiancials, but that's just for tax purposes. All money is funded directly back into Homewind. They use the rest of the companies earning and success to fund their private military."

"It makes sense," Puzo added. "Need new tech for your private army or better meds? Buy a tech company and a pharmacy."

"Exactly. Damn, you're smart too." Mia paused.

"But why target these companies?" Puzo asked. "What is the importance?"

"I have a theory," Mia continued. "It's farfetched, like spy novel farfetched, but I have a theory."

"Spy novel seems accurate these days," I muttered.

"Rumours are Homewind was up for a big government contract. I think somebody didn't want them to get it." My mind raced. Mr. Koplan was the intended guest at the meeting before Allawi shot up the place. The more I thought about it the more I realized that I'd heard that name before.

Need help?

No. Screw you, Brain. I could do this on my own.

I searched my memory, searched it for something that was not right or something that was out of place. I mean everything in this case seemed out of place. A Hugh Jackman-Tom Beringer crossplay decided to shoot up a dozen places and started taunting me with movie quotes. That was weird. That was freaking weird. Or at least it would be for anybody else. Throwing me into a game against a movie quoting big bad seemed like the perfect script for a guy like me. I don't find that out of place. I'm the weirdo who found his TV on CNN and thinks that's out of place.

CNN.

Holy crap.

Took you long enough.

See, see. This is why we broke up in the first place.

Homewind was hosting a meeting with Mr. Koplan, Mr. Theodore A. Koplan, Director of the Centers for Disease Control and Prevention. "Homewind was up for the CDC's AVERT team," I blurted. "They must have been the favourites."

"Holy hell, Benedict," Mia cursed. "That contract is suppose to be huge. It probably is going to take every spare dollar that company has to expand Homewind enough to meet the CDC's needs. I mean the payout will be epic, but still. It's a big risk for a company."

I've got this detective thing down.

"This just supports my theory. It's like someone wants to hit Homewind where it hurts: the pocket. That way they can make their stock price drop so much that Homewind won't be able to pony up the dough. They'll have to step away from the offer and rebuild their holdings."

"Insurance won't be able to help them for months," Puzo explained. "This is Bond villain territory."

"Please don't tell me we're going into *Quantum of Solace* territory. That movie was shit." I threw out my best British accent. "Oh, I'm a rich super spy who just lost some random lady I met three days ago. My life sucks. Emo Dance."

Silence.

"What the hell was that? I think I just lost the connection," Mia cried out. "That was just -- wow."

"No, it didn't cut out," Puzo sighed.

"Really? It sounded like Jet Li doing an impression of Gerard Butler who is trying to do an impression of Tom Hardy's Bane." I am really bad at accents.

"I have a pretty good idea who is doing this," I said, trying to draw focus away from my blunder. "It's WhiteStar. I don't have proof, but it's definitely them. Look, Mia, I've got some more work to do. Thanks for this. I owe you."

"No worries," Mia replied. "Puzo, grab a pen and paper."

Mia read off her phone number and told Puzo to call her. She had a lot she could offer the FBI and they had stuff for her. I rolled my eyes, let my imagination wander for a second, and snapped back into reality. I hung up and looked at Rachael.

"Some things still don't make sense," I explained and I leaned in and kissed her cheek. "I have to go and work."

"Be careful."

I smirked and put my hat on head. "Don't you know crying over a cowboy is just wasted tears?"

"I'm sorry, which one of us was in a bundle of tears last night?"

"I didn't cry," I defended.

"Yes, yes you did."

"Those were Man Tears," I explained. "When men cry, real mean, we cry Man Tears. Those are tears made up of actual meat. We basically cry pork chops and steaks. Imagine a steak tearing its way out of your eye. It hurts like hell, which causes more tears. It's a vicious cycle."

"You cry meat?" she said in disbelief.

"It hurts like hell. Women will never know real pain until you cry meat," I said triumphantly. "Seriously, giving birth has nothing on Man Tears."

Silence.

"Just shut up and leave."

Chapter 19
Some Serious Inappropriate Touching

So there it was: I had my plot laid out before me. WhiteStar was killing people to lower Homewind's stock prices in an effort to rob a contract. Then they bought stock in every company that directly opposed Skit-Tech, Leti-Wind Pharmaceuticals and Claymont Development, so that when the opposition's stock prices rose, they'd made a crap tonne of money which would go directly into WhiteStar's expensive expansion. This was all about money, a butt load of money, but money none the less. But things still weren't adding up. Why would WhiteStar make such an event of this? Why kill all those people? Why make it so public that every cop, fed, and news media would be required to look into every small detail involving this case?

Then I had a chilling thought.

What had to have happened in history to make the term *butt load* a household saying?

My own personal digression aside, one question rang louder than others: Why involve me? WhiteStar and I didn't have the greatest relationship. She was talented Tina Turner and I was Ike -- actually no. I'm not using that reference. I feel dirty from just thinking it. Needless to say, WhiteStar tried to be a big bad-ass and I smacked them down. It wasn't their fault really; who thought a cripple could stop them? They just didn't realize that I was a Thompson. Add those two together and you get a man who has nothing left to lose and makes really bad life decisions: a deadly combination.

Okay, my life officially became a movie there. I can even hear the voice-over guy narrating the trailer. "In a world where..."

I had no more mundane leads so I had to cheat. I had to get psychic on the world. It was time for serious touching, some serious *inappropriate* touching. It was time to go to the morgue.

Oh... ohh... ohhhhh. That sounded better in my head. *Trust me, it really didn't.*

The cab pulled up to the city morgue and I hobbled inside. A young man sat behind the counter and looked at me. "Can I help you?"

"I'm Benedict Thompson," I said, showing my private investigator license and tipping my cowboy hat. "I need to see a body that was brought in recently."

I stared to scan the room behind him. My eyes fell upon a familiar mocha-face with bouncy brown hair. It was the not-yet-evil Doctor Christine Hammett. "I'm sorry, but am I suppose to just let you walk on in? Don't you know--"

"Hey, Christine! Over here," I cried out. She snapped her head over at the sound of her name and I suddenly saw a look of fear on her face.

"Christine?" the man asked. "You are mistaken, that Dr. Trisha Reese."

"Right, sorry. I always get them mixed up. She looks so much like the other girl. You know who I'm talking about, the one with the eye-patch, hook hand, and peg leg. They're dead ringers for each other." A fake name, why did everybody have a fake name? I wanted a fake name. I was tired of being left out.

"Dr. Reese," he waved her over. "Do you know this

guy?"

"Of course she does. I'm Jameson McMorganPants."

"You just said you name was Benedict."

"Good, you were listening," I quickly lied. "I'm here from the city for a surprise inspection."

"You said you were a detective."

"He's here for a meeting with me," Christine/Trisha said. She grabbed me and pulled me into the back. Once we were out of earshot, she glared at me. "You are a horrible liar. What are you doing here?"

"I need to see Moore and learn his secrets," I answered. "What are you doing here?"

"I'm trying to cover up Moore's secrets." Good answer. "I'll let you see his effects first."

She escorted me into the back. She handed me a tablet. I gave it a swipe and looked at the open file. Staring back at me was a photograph of Moore's face. Christine had just handed me his personnel file.

Name: Phillip Moore
Real Name: Stewart McKenzie.
Age: 27
Ability: Light Bending

The file went on and on with his WhiteStar service record. I stared at it in wonder. He was a KyroCorp covert experiment -- a 2nd Choir -- and was one of their favourite potentials. Then, at age eight he was kidnapped, given a new name, made into a child soldier and sent into one battle after another. Phillip Moore was arrested six months ago but escaped after he -- according to the reports -- simply vanished. This man, this dead man, was basically Robby. The only difference was that I saved Robby. There was nobody to save Stewart nineteen years ago.

"How is it someone that suffers like this guy did," I asked out loud, "can then turn around and do the exact same thing to other kids?"

"There is a reason child soldiers are illegal," Christine said quietly. "It messes with their mind. Nobody ever fully recovers from it, not even those that get out. For someone like Moore, he did it because that's all he knew."

We reached the back room and I saw Moore's corpse on the table. I instantly looked away. I didn't want to see the body of a man I just killed. It's a weird feeling, seeing life in his eyes a few hours ago, then to see him as nothing more than an empty husk and knowing the only reason the change occurred was because of you.

Christine handed me a large container filled with Moore's supplies. I opened it up. There were his clothes, blood stained as they were, and his wallet, along with his phone, a set of keys and several piles of money. I pulled off my glove and reached for the most important object, the one no man leaves home without: his wallet.

A shiver and a twitch, and I find myself in some random room, in some house in some random city. The house was built to look normal: it had furniture, art and utilities, but it lacked that lived-in feeling. This was a safe house. Moore sat alone in the living room watching TV as the door opened up. He spun to his feet, grabbed a pistol off the coffee table, and shimmered out of view.

"Moore: I'm coming in," a gruff voice announced. A man walked into the living room holding a brown file in his hand.

Moore shimmered back into sight and put down the gun. He eyed the man but simply nodded. The man was dressed in all black slacks and a black shirt. He covered everything with a long brown duster and topped the entire ensemble with a black cowboy hat.

I zoomed in on the hat.

It was a Stetson, like mine, but his was formed differently. My Stetson was brown and was formed in a Gus Style fashion. The Gus Style, or Gus to his friends, has three steep slopes towards the front of the hat and has three creases. This other cowboy, Mr. Evil Hat, had the Diamond Style. This method of hat forming put a pinch in the front of the hat and a pinch in the back, making a diamond on the top. The only problem was that John Wayne favoured it.

Boo Wayne. Long live Eastwood.

"I have a couple things that will interest you and a couple things that will interest me," he said as he tossed the file at Moore. The light bender caught it and opened it up. He started to read it over as Mr. Evil Hat walked into the kitchen.

"Why him?" Moore asked. "His doctor says he's teetering on the edge. Will it be safe to use him?"

"Yes," he called out from the kitchen. "It'll be your job to keep him in check. We're hoping he goes a little crazy. It will pull focus from us."

Moore sighed. "You give me the worst jobs."

I returned to reality but stayed there for only a moment before I reached in and grabbed his winter jacket. A shiver and a twist, and I went back in the past. I saw Moore and Allawi walking through the snow as they crossed the quiet street. It was nearly midnight, the snow was falling hard and fast, and nobody in their right mind was out in this weather.

"So who is this guy?" Allawi grumbled.

"His name is Sergio Casale," Moore explained. "But we just called him the Item Man."

"That is a stupid name. Fire your writer before you become a Direct-to-DVD."

Moore just grumbled. "He is an astral locator. He can find any object anywhere in the world. He'll help find the item on your insane list."

The two entered a small hole-in-the-wall store. They were quickly ushered into the back room. The two men sat at a table and waited. Their silence was interrupted when a large Italian man entered the room. "Did you bring what I asked for? An object owned by this Ben?"

"I did," Allawi replied and put a spent rifle round, crumbled from impact, onto the table. "He shot this at me."

I returned to reality. With a deep breath, I reached in once more and grabbed the phone. This time the reaction was stronger. The shiver dug deeper and I twitched harder. I was thrown into the past. Moore held his phone to his ear and paced around in the room. He was in another safe house.

"Pick up, pick up," he mumbled.

"Operator."

"Extension: 3652."

"One second."

The line went silent until a new voice came on. I recognized it as Mr. Evil Hat. "Go."

"He's gone off the deep end," Moore yelled. "He's snapped. The death count has skyrocketed. This is no longer a small thing. This is a media storm now. Everybody will be looking."

"I know. We have our funds in the market; we're set to make a lot of money," Mr. Evil Hat said. "This insanity was... planned for."

"Really? 'Cause that's stupid!" Moore yelled. "Worse of all -- he brought the cripple into it. The gimp psychic is involved and not by accident. Allawi called the psychic and started taunting him."

"Good."

Reality returned and I finally had some answers. Nouri Allawi wasn't just insane in the membrane; he was full on bat-crap crazy. He was so far gone that sanity didn't even recognize him anymore. If this assassination plot was a Rolling Stones concert T-shirt, then WhiteStar wanted Allawi to bring back a size medium and Allawi just came back with XXXL. He was the worst personal shopper ever.

"You get what you needed?"

I looked at Christine and just nodded. She was seated at a computer looking over the report files. She froze. "Oh shit, Ben. Get out of here now."

"What's wrong?"

"I was supposed to edit the official file on Moore before it went out to the FBI and such," Christine explained; the panic in her voice was clear as day. "But it got sent out before I got here."

"And that's bad?"

"That is very bad." I spun around at the new voice. Standing in the door way was Humpty and Dumpty, each with a silenced pistol in their hands.

"Containment has been breached," Dumpty declared.

"We must cleanse," Humpty followed.

Christine called out both of their names, and I instantly forgot them. "We can still wrap it up. I'll track down the files and delete them. They won't know about super-human genetic make-up."

"Tech Team is risking expose to cover this up," Humpty said.

"You've already been seen by civilians," Dumpty followed.

"We will make this seem like another kill by Allawi," Humpty concluded. The pair aimed their weapons at each of us. Christine screamed and I reacted. I drew my M9 with lightning speed and fired. It was a draw worth of Marshal Raylan Givens' respect. My aim was dead on, but somehow I still missed. At the last second, Dumpty twitched, moving just enough for the bullet to zoom past him. They returned fire. I dove across the table and landed on the floor, accidently pulling Moore's cold corpse atop of me.

It was official, I hated these two.

Chapter 20
Sorry, Mr. Gift Horse; I Ain't a Dentist

A loud feminine screamed filled the room. Shame filled my body as I realized that scream was mine. I pushed the corpse off of me, promised myself that I'd shower for the next three days, and grabbed my hat. I scrambled to my feet and let my mind race. They were going to kill Christine and me. I couldn't let that happen. Allawi kept calling me the hero of this movie, so I had to start acting like it, and that meant saving the good doctor. I glanced at her. She wasn't the villain in this story; she was the redemption story. I popped up and fired a pair of shots, each one missing as Humpty and Dumpty seemed to dodge at the absolute last second. Christine was on her knees praying for mercy, but somehow neither of us believed it was going to work.

I had to do something; I had to be the hero of this film. I had to be an action hero. I had to be John McClane. What would John McClane do?

That should be on a plastic bracelet.

Focus.

I scanned the room and saw what I needed: a fire extinguisher. I popped up from my cover and yelled the only thing I could if I was being John McClane. "That copyrighted line from Die Hard!"

I fire three shots at the pair, each missing, and for my fourth I fired into the fire extinguisher. White stuff poured from the extinguisher and filled the room with a fog like cloud. I hobbled over to Christine, grabbed her, and pulled her out of the room. We bolted to the front door and passed the now-dead body of the young man behind the desk. Crap.

"What the hell?" I yelled.

"They're going to kill us."

"No shit," I snapped. Looking back, that was rude of me. A part of me once thought I should apologize for that, but not any more, not after what happened. "I thought they were on your side?"

"They're not. It's complicated."

"So is Avril Lavigne," I looked back and saw Dumpty approaching us. "Damn it, Dumpty."

I ducked around a corner and pressed myself up against the wall. Christine looked at me. "Dumpty?"

"I can't remember their names," I explained. "No matter how many times I hear their names, I instantly forget it."

"They're telepathic," she yelled. I froze.

"Like Patrick MacAvoy?" I asked. She stared at me confused.

Christine moved to speak, but I hushed her with a finger. I could hear Dumpty coming up, picking up speed as he moved. I raised my cane and waited. The moment I saw him, I struck, swinging with every inch of training Jack had given me. The aim was good, it was perfect, and would have smashed his Adam's apple back into his neck and out the other side. I never landed a splinter on him. He leapt back at the last second and all I hit was air. Dumpty stepped forward, grabbed the collar of my jacket, and spun my already off-balanced body into the wall. I smashed against it, hard, and crumpled to the floor.

I hate walls sometimes. I understand how they hold up my apartment, and I grateful for that, but when I smash into them, I suddenly become very anti-wall. I mean, I'm not going to march in any anti-wall rallies, but I'll probably just stay at home and mutter vile things about them to myself.

I grabbed my cane and swung again, this time aiming for Dumpty's knee, but he lifted his leg, dodging the blow, and then lowered his shoe into my face.

I hate shoes sometimes. I mean, I'm not going to march in any anti-shoe rallies, but I'll probably--

"Ben!" Christine yelled. "They're psychic. They can read your mind. They can read everybody's mind. They know what you're going to do when you do."

"Next time," I said as I spat out blood, "lead with that."

As I climbed to my feet, it became very evident that Dumpty was playing with me. He had his gun and could have killed me at any time, but now he was watching me get up. "I thought you worked with Croxallé," I spat. "So why kill Christine?"

"We are Visegar," he said without a smile. "She is not. She is simply Croxallé. She has used up her usefulness."

"Oh, I doubt that," I defended. "I can think of a use or two for her. You know what I mean? Actually you read minds. So you totally know what I mean."

"You are thinking of fornicating with her. It is an uncomfortable image for me to perceive. Please cease and desist."

"Dude, I'm a guy," I defended. "Soooooo... no."

I swung again and missed once more. Dumpty caught my staff, slammed it into my chest, and pulled it from my hands. I fell. It was sad. He tossed my cane at me in some form of pity. As I hit the floor, two thoughts ran through my mind:

1. Ow.

2. I needed to outthink the telepath.

That couldn't be hard. I scrambled to my feet. Cane in hand, as Humpty joined the room. I glared at Dumpty and started to think. *Hit Dumpty. Hit Dumpty. Hit Dumpty.* Then I swung at Humpty. The plan didn't work. Humpty caught my punch, twisted my body, and kneed me in the gut. I fell to the floor.

I hate the floor sometimes. I mean, I'm not going to march in any--

Humpty kicked me. He reached down, grabbed me by my belt, and hoisted me up to my feet. He stepped back and pointed a gun to my head. I laughed a little. This was like in *Die Hard* when Karl had a gun pointed at McClane's head. In the movie, McClane spins around and decks the killer with a solid left punch. Then the--

Humpty stepped back quickly as if he was expecting a punch at his head and not just any punch, but a solid left punch. He looked confused. Suddenly I had an idea; I had a theory but I needed to test it.

McClane then grabs Karl by his shirt and pushes him-

Humpty twists his body to avoid the grapple but none came. I smirked. I'd just found a weakness. In order to beat a telepath, to beat someone who could literally read my mind and know what I was going to do before I did it, I couldn't just think about my own movements, real or fake ones, I had to think about somebody else's movements. In order to beat these two, I had to think of movie fights to mess up their powers. These two were screwed because if there was anybody in this world that could think of action movie fights as real life, it was me. Actually it was Lee Archer -- a guy I met in high school -- but since he wasn't here, it was all up to me.

I struck a surprised Humpty in the crotch with my cane and watched him fall. I spun towards Dumpty and mentally switched films. Patrick Swayze was in an office above a bar. Some knife-wielding idiot just called Mr. Dirty Dancing *chicken dick*. He slashes with a knife only to be Road Housed out of the window by a spinning roundhouse kick. Dumpty moved to dodge only to find the horse-handled end of my cane leaping forward and breaking his nose. Dumpty cursed loudly and clutched his bleeding nostrils.

Jack's lessons flowed through me, making me shift my weight as I struck and forcing the cane to become an extension of my arm. I had spent many *long* hours on my back looking up at Jack's smug face (that was dirty). Jack liked it rough; he liked to make me sweat (way too dirty).   He was a demanding teacher, but he got results; results all over my chest and floor (way, way too dirty).

I switched films. Air Force One rocked back and forth as Harrison Ford grabbed a Russian bad guy and slammed him into the wall. Humpty tried to dodge, but caught my cane to his knee. His leg buckled and I stuck across his face.

I switched films. Jackie Chan flipped a metal ladder onto his head and started to spin. Dumpty stumbled back and ducked, not knowing how to properly handle a spinning ladder attack. In truth, I doubt anybody on this earth knew how to deal with a spinning ladder attack. I stepped in and hooked my cane behind his knee and pulled. I swept the legs out from underneath him and watched him fall. A pair of hands grabbed me from behind and threw me back against the wall. I slammed against it and fell to my knees, my cane falling from my grasp. I stared at Humpty as I coughed, Dumpty climbing to his feet to meet his partner. I glanced to my left and spotted my salvation.

I dove for my M9, sliding across the floor and rolling onto my back. I levelled my gun at Humpty and screamed, "I am the Haig!"

It's a line from *Expendables 3* where Stallone blows bad guy Mel away. That was exactly what I planning on doing myself; the only difference was Stallone did it standing up. Humpty knew a bullet was coming at him, but because of my movie-brain he expected it at a totally different angle. Two shots rang out and both found a home in his chest. Dumpty screamed as Humpty fell, eventually falling to match his partner. I blinked, confused, and shrugged.

Sorry, Mr. Gift Horse; I ain't a dentist.

I grabbed everything important in that room, hat, cane and the woman -- in that order -- and hobbled for the door. "Do you drive? Do you have a car?" She nodded quickly. "Great, because a chase scene sucks if you have to wait for a cab."

It was a couple hours later when I finally stepped into my apartment, but my heart was still racing. I'd won a fight. I had won an actual fight. I hadn't done that in forever. The last time I won a fight was back in my two legs days. The closest thing I'd had to winning a fight was shooting a guy lying on the floor and in truth I didn't win that fight, somebody else did. I just made sure there was no rematch.

I hung my hat on the hook and dropped my cane stand. Christine was safe at Croxallé. Apparently the company building was a big home-free zone from their own superiors. I didn't try to figure it out. She was safe and that was all that was important.

I plopped myself down into my chair and let out a loud sigh. The last couple days had just sucked. I'd been shot at, I'd been manipulated, I'd broken down, and I'd lost friends. Also, since my DVR was on the fritz, I was pretty sure I missed yesterday's episode of *Person of Interest.*

Jason.

The guy had been scum in my eyes for years, but now I just felt ill knowing he wasn't around. It also filled me with rage that I very much wanted to direct at someone. Currently Nouri Allawi was my chosen subject.

My phone rang.

I answered it without looking, hoping that it was Rachael calling. It wasn't. "Hello again, Ben." It wasn't even close.

"Fuck you, Allawi."

"Temper, temper," he warned. He chuckled slightly. "This is it, you know. This is the final act of our violent little film and I want us to go out with a bang. I want our ending to be spectacular. So I've decided to ask your opinion."

"I want producer credits," I retorted.

"Do we blow up a roof like in *Die Hard* or do we just

blow up an entire building while Mr. Gibson laughs?"
"When in doubt, watch *Die Hard*," I replied. I sighed. "How about this, you break into my house, I'll drive a car through my own wall and then we duke it out on the front lawn while dozens of cops watch?"

"Classic, but I'd prefer we duke it out on a train by a stolen nuke. I like trains."

"We could fight on-top of a train in Europe. I have face masks."

"Let's fight in a subway terminal with CGI."

"Too much work. I'd rather just shoot you by a lake then quit the force," I spat. For a moment, I was impressed. Aside from Lee Archer, nobody I knew could ever talk films like this. We didn't have to explain ourselves, we just knew. It'd be a special moment if he weren't such a whack-job homicidal maniac.

"Too cliché; how about I fill you with poison and watch you struggle to keep your adrenalin up?" Allawi said apathetically.

"Do I look like Chelios? I'll punch you off the back of a plane."

"You'd never get elected. It'd be more likely you'd kill me on a plane because I won't put the bunny down."

"I'll shoot you while doing slow motion dives with two guns."

"Going Asian are we? Then let's fight over a staff in a temple."

"I'd rather fight on a Nazi Tank. I'm not a church guy."

"I could impale you on a miniature church when we fight in a small replica of a town."

"This isn't a comedy situation," I sighed. "Screw it. Let's just blow up the Death Star."

"Sounds good to me." Silence filled the phone. "When in doubt, watch *Die Hard*. That's sound advice, Ben. I'll keep that in mind."

"I thought I had you figured out," I began. "I thought

this was some reverse *Kill Bill*, and then I thought this was *Die Hard With a Vengeance*. But that's not true either. You are seriously messed up; *Timothy-Olyphant-Scream-2* messed up."

"That's touching, Ben."

"But I still don't know why? You blame me because I shot you; you killed those innocent civilians to me to feel responsible and to make me suffer. But why? Why do any of it?"

"Because my faith has come down to nothing else than money and a TV," he explained slowly. "WhiteStar needed money, so they asked me. I needed something more. I needed my moment. I needed my movie.

"I was found, barely alive, and recruited by KyroCorp. They brought me to the US and nursed me back to health. It took awhile. My healing wasn't at full strength and what power it did have was keeping that bullet from killing me. So I lay in bed, with my hand on a remote, and watched TV. For six long months I learned about your country, its intricacies and its hidden rules, from TV and movies.

"Your Daytime TV is a joke. It's all motherhood pandering or the digital version of the carnival freak show. Prime time is no better. Catchphrases and soap opera drama; I'll pass." Did he just insult TV? Amongst all his crazy, he had to throw a jab in against TV? No wonder I hated him.

"But movies, they were amazing; the action, the needless explosion and cheesy one-liners, the romance, and even the comedy. Movies changed my life, Ben. You ruined it; you ruined my life. I tried to end it many times since that day, Ben; I've suffered so much. Do you know what hanging feels like? What leaping off a building feels like? What a bullet to the head feels like? They all hurt, but not as much as it does when your healing factor reassembles that broken neck and those shattered bones or when your skull slowly pushes a bullet outwards. You ruined my life, Ben, but movies saved it."

Silence. I was terrified. That was me. Nouri and I

started in the same place. We were both soldiers who lost everything. Fighting was all we knew; now we had nothing. We both turned inwards and fell into TV and movies. Then we hit that fork in the road. As much as I tried to push my family away, they kept me from going nuts. I took the right turn because of them. Allawi didn't. His mind broke and he took the left turn, driving down the road, doing 50 mph, to the unfinished bridge and off the edge. It was a shame really. If he'd been going 38 mph faster he would have reached the finished bridge many years later, happy and sane

Great Scott! I had an arch nemesis. If it weren't for the fact that his kill count was higher than Doc. Hannibal's, then TV-Ben would be a little more excited.

"You have a chance to stop me, Ben," he said suddenly. "What type of shitty movie would this be if you didn't? Figure it out, Ben. Be worthy of this finale."

Chapter 21
Stop Quoting *The Simpsons* and Focus

Well, crap.

I was screwed. I had a chance to stop him, to save people, but I didn't know how. Let's face it. I'm a moron. How in the hell was I going to figure out where he was going to strike? I couldn't touch anything but myself, but I was not making that Divinyls song about Nouri and I.

> *I don't want anybody else*
> *When I think about Nouri*
> *I touch myself*

I already created the Jason/Ben slash fanfic, I didn't want to create the Nouri/Ben slash fanfic as well.

There were facts I was missing. I needed to find that little clue. I needed a Sherlock Holmes moment. I needed that other Benedict. In truth I'd much prefer Johnny Lee Miller, but I'd take other-Benedict. Hell, I'd take Robert Downy Jr. I needed high definition black and white flashbacks. I needed a freeze-frame sports show where they draw circles on the screen to draw attention to a player. I'm that much of an idiot that I needed someone to literally circle what I missed. I'm a big, adorable, kind-of-sexy-but-how-in-the-hell-I-have-no-clue idiot.

Seriously, why do people find me attractive? I'm a gimp; I'm a wreck. I'm a broken cowboy who makes really poor life decisions. Do you know I was the other guy on the train with Kenny Rogers? Yeah, I'm the idiot who didn't share his whiskey or his cigarette. That song could have been about me!

It was time to make a good-ish decision. I grumbled to myself and closed my eyes.

I'm sorry.

What?

I'm sorry. Let's patch things up. I need you and you need me. We can work this together.

I was wondering when you'd come crawling back. You've been doing a horrible job of things without me.

You're not allowed to judge me. Nobody is. I judge myself enough for the entire world. Where is he going to hit next? Homewind has literally dozens of companies in the city. Nouri can hit any of them and that's even assuming he's being truthful. For all I know he could pick now to switch up his tactics. He's bat crap crazy as it is.

Think it through.

I have been. It's insane. There are too many options. How do I think like a crazy person when I am -- comparatively -- super sane? I may be a detective, but I'm really not. I'm a psychic who cheats. I touch things and now I'm suddenly out of things to touch.

Because of the restraining order? Ha!!

Alright, Brain, you don't like me and I don't like you, but let's just do this and I can get back to killing you with beer.

Stop quoting The Simpsons and focus.

Mmm. Beer.

You'll be fine, think it through. As much as you hate to admit it, you're pretty good at this detective thing...

But?

No but, I have no but.

Then how do you poop? Ha!

I don't know why you're putting so much attention on this. You're not even getting paid for it.

I'm doing it because the case I am getting paid for does... does... Holy crap.

My brain was a genius. All this time I'd spent arguing with it now suddenly seemed stupid. Okay, there is a part of me that thought me arguing with my own brain at all was stupid to begin with, but that was my colon and he's a bit of an ass.

I bolted to the kitchen and flung open the folder that lay upon it. I quickly gave it a read. What do you get when you start with a mysterious stock jump in your competitors on the eve of your product launch, add a pinch of corrupt guard selling the security layout for some bonus cash, sprinkle in a murderous psychopath, and season with Homewind ownership? You get the answer.

Nouri Allawi was going to hit the Skit-Tech warehouse. He was going to blow up their supply, ruin their launch, and make their stock plummet. Skit-Tech had *everything* in the success of this product. They would go bankrupt. It didn't matter if the other warehouses went off without a hitch, having a stock drop that much before launch would be devastating. Their competitors' stock would skyrocket and all the money WhiteStar made by messing with the stock market would fund the CDC bid.

I could stop him. I could stop Nouri, but not alone. I needed help. Puzo was still out so that left... crap.

A year ago, I had my first-ever future vision: it was of me calling in a favour for help from my super spy BFF. The second future vision I had was of me dying. Since then I'd tried my absolute damndest to avoid either of the future visions from coming true… up until now.

I limped to a living room drawer and pulled it open. I withdrew a white business card and held it before me. It said Joseph Price and had a phone number. I grabbed my iPhone and dialled. My iPhone rang three times before it connected. I heard Price's voice on the other end. "Thompson, what's wrong?"

"I'm calling in that favour. I'm in trouble." And the first future vision had come true.

I open my door to see two familiar men standing before it, each with suits and mystery. It was Joseph Price and the man I knew as Special Agent William Jones. I'm pretty sure that was a fake name. Everybody has fake names. The last time these two stood in front of my door, they wooed me with sensual talk and sexy words like *civic duty* and *serve your country*. A change of panties later, I was doing whatever they wanted me to. I'm a sucker for those sexy words. This time I decided to do things differently. This time we were doing thing at my place, and this time I was going to learn their names beforehand. That's called character growth.

That also sounded incredibly dirty.

"Price." He nodded at me. "Special Agent Jones." Jones laughed. "I don't use that name anymore. Call me Tyrone Straub."

We all went inside. The pair was everything the conspiracy theorists talked about. They were black suit super spies who could take on a different name at a drop of a hat. They acted like James Bond, moved like Jason Borne, fought like Jack Bauer, and had higher kill counts then Rambo. Both of them were dressed like the Blue Brothers, minus the hats, and the only difference between the two was Joseph was taller and had thick glasses, and Tyrone was a man of darker skin.

Black shirt. Black hat. Black tie. This was it. This was my Blues Brother adventure. We were getting the band back together. I was on a mission from God!

Price dropped a green bag on the couch and Straub lifted an e-cigarette to his lips. He took a puff and exhaled, the smoke dissipating almost instantly. I raised an eyebrow. He smirked.

"We have Command grabbing sat-feed of the warehouse," Price said as he unzipped the bag. I knew they worked for something called Oversight and as far as I knew, they were a version of the MIB that dealt with superheroes like me. "They'll send it to us on route. Here, it's clean."

Price handed me a gun. I hesitated. "It's psychically clean as well."

I trusted him. I pulled off my glove and grabbed the gun. I flinched, but nothing happened -- no shiver, no twitch, and no vision. My powers are emotion based and guns were the emotion capitol of a 7-11 drive by shootings. I started my check on the weapon. It was a FN-P90 with a 50-round detachable top-loaded box magazine. It used a FN 5.7×28mm cartridge, had a Straight blowback, closed bolt action, and fire nine hundred rounds per minute.

There were some things a soldier never forgot.

"Each of these is officially registered," Price said as he handed one to Tyrone and grabbed one for himself. I glanced at Straub as he took another puff from his e-cig. "Tyrone's P90 is registered to Jagdkommando special ground of the Austrian Army. Mine belongs to the France GIPN counter-terrorism group, and yours is from the Halifax Regional Police in Canada."

"Why are you telling me this?" I asked more shocked at that then the fact that Canadian cops had a need for guns. Price just shrugged. "Keep your eyes and ears open, Ben. You might learn something that will be important later in life." Price looked at Tyrone as he took another puff and shook his head. "Knock off the bit."

"I barely even realize I'm doing it anymore," Straud laughed as he put the e-cig away. He smiled and sighed; a cloud of smoke came out with his exhale and instantly vanished. I stared at him shocked. Then I clued in. It wasn't smoke and Tyrone wasn't a hipster douchebag. That was breath, the same type of cold breath you saw in freezing winter. I snapped my head to the thermostat and Tyron laughed again. "Relax, Ben. It's not your house. It's me." He held out his hand downwards, his fingers dangling. Suddenly small icicles began to form on the tip of each finger. I blinked again.

"I'm cool as ice," Tyrone boasted, "and that's before

my powers."

"Introductions are over," Price said. "Ben, call your client and warn him."

I nodded him and grabbed my phone. I quickly dialled and impatiently waited as the phone rang. I expected Frederick Déshant to answer; he didn't. Instead, I got the malicious voice of Nouri Allawi.

"It took you long enough, Ben," he mocked. "I was beginning to wonder if you were going to figure it out at all."

"Where is Déshant?"

"He's here with me, at the warehouse. I decided to make our finale have a hostage theme, like strapping a bomb to Sandra B."

I was furious. He was targeting the man who was going to pay me. Was nothing in this universe sacred? "Let him go."

"Umm... no," he laughed. "You can save him, but you can't stop me. When I'm done with him, I'll go after Annie and Alice. Then I'll kill David and then, I'll make you watch as Robby dies."

Then I snapped. He'd killed dozen just to mess with me. He tried to kill Puzo and now he was threatening to go after my family.

"I am going to fucking kill you!" I yelled. I was in full-out scream mode. The type of yelling that causes you to spit as you talk. "I'll put a goddamn bullet in your head and after that I'll put fifty more in! Then I'll fucking put my boot thought your head. I will find a way to kill you, I fucking promise it."

This was different for me. When Robbie was taken, I had no one to lash out at; it was a company taking him, not a person. I couldn't very well go up to the WhiteStar building and yell at it for hours. Allawi was a person, a single person, who was targeting me and my family. I could hate him, I could fight him and for once I could have someone to unleash my rage upon.

I hung up and cursed loudly. I snapped my head at the

two spies. "Suit up, we're moving out."

Price put a hand on my shoulder, nodding for a second, but pausing to speak: "Ben, we'll stop him. I promise. But do me a favour; leave the cane."

There is something badass about three men emerging from an apartment with an ass-kicking look in their eyes. I wanted to move in slow motion as a Daft Punk song played and hold my gun high in the air. Sadly there was no music, it was dark outside, and I don't suggest waving a gun in the air because cops frown on that.

The three of us climbed into Price's black SUV and we sped off. It was a quiet drive; the type of awkward quiet that felt like it did when a first date goes horrible wrong. You end up sitting on either end of a table, staring at the water and debating to yourself on whether or not that water was bottled or tapped. You hope it isn't tap because of that report you saw on 60 Minutes that said people are peeing the city water supply.

"Okay," I said suddenly, no longer finding the urge to think about the urine-water mix appealing. "We need some music. We need some kickass music to rev us up. We used to do it all the time overseas." Before they could object, I leaned forward and punched the radio. Music started filling the speakers:

He said, "Son, I've made a life
Out of readin' people's faces
Knowin' what the cards were
By the way they held their eyes
So if you don't mind me sayin'
I can see you're out of aces
For a taste of your whiskey
I'll give you some advice"

The Gambler by Kenny Rodgers. This was officially the worst hype music ever.

"I ever tell you guys how this song was almost about me?"

Chapter 22
For Once I Was Happy to be Fighting Like a Girl

"This is a dumb plan," I muttered. "This isn't a plan. This is what, twelve percent of a plan?"

We stood by the SUV and stared at the warehouse. We were parked almost a block away. Tyrone put down his binoculars and frowned. "I agree with Ben. This is a stupid plan."

"We can do this."

"Groot could do this." They both looked at me. Yeah, I saw *Guardians of the Galaxy*. According to box office sales, everybody and their mother saw *Guardians of the Galaxy*. "Don't we need an army or something, maybe a SWAT team with a theme song?"

"We can do this," Price said. "And the three of us are an army."

"Command is saying there are forty-plus heat signatures."

"This plan is fine," Price reaffirmed. "Besides, it's Ben's plan."

"What? No, it isn't," I stuttered. "At best this plan belongs to Shane Black, Richard Donner or Joel Silver. It sure as hell isn't my plan."

"You did bring it up," Tyrone shrugged.

"It's not my plan."

Price looked at me and frowned. "Are you sure you're

up for this, Ben?"

"Yes. I am fully capable and completely up for this shitty plan," I sighed. "That is totally not my plan."

"Good, you're driving."

Have you ever been in a car accident? Sure you have. Nearly everybody has. That was a dumb question; forget I asked. Now think back to it, to that moment you looked over your shoulder and thought that car is going to hit me. Time seems to slow down in that moment, not enough for you to get out of the way, but just enough for you to make a funny face and go oh shit. Now take that moment, that brief instance where the crash is inevitable, and imagine it from the other side. Imagine driving a car, or being a passenger, and seeing that moment where your car is about to crash headfirst into something. I was driving the SUV towards the side of the warehouse. I couldn't help but be overwhelmed by that feeling.

This was still not my plan.

The SUV slammed into the side of the wall and everything shattered. The wall had taken a cryonic blast from Tyrone and became a layer of fragile ice. The moment the grill collided with the ice was the moment the wall became nothing more than a flurry of ice shards that rained down on the SUV and its stupid bumper sticker that read How was my driving?

The vehicle came to halt inside the warehouse and the four armed goons just stood there, staring at us with a stunned look on their faces. Two of them slowly approached the car as the windows started to descend.

"Hi," I said with a stupid grin. "My GPS just told me to take a right turn. I think it may be broken. Can I get directions?" I raised my M9 and fired twice, one bullet into each of them. Then hell broke loose.

Price and Straub both poured out of the SUV from the

passenger side and opened fire. I scampered across the front seat and rolled out of the passenger door. With my P90 in hand, I crouched beside the two super spies and smiled. "So, how are you guys?"

"More coming down the hallway." We could hear them running, a group of WhiteStar goons, and we popped up to meet them.

The moment they poured into the room was the moment they were met with a burst of FN 5.7×28mm rounds. The three of us generously sprayed at the oncoming horde of private military douches, not stopping until the entire wave fell.

"Welcome to the party, pal!" I whooped. Tyrone hid a smile as Price just shook his head.

"Thermals show the hostages are further in," Price explained. "Let's move."

"Wait." The pair looked at me. I limped to the broken shelf, grabbed a couple phones and a handful of tablets off the floor, and tossed them in the back seat of the SUV. "What? Christmas is just around the corner."

Moving through the warehouse quickly became reminiscent. It had been years since I'd operated with a team of highly skilled individuals. Recently, I'd been hanging out with fictional ones. There is something special about working with someone who could watch your back and who were trained the same way you were. It's like working in a kitchen and your co-workers always know when to flip the steak or turn down the burner, all without being told.

But to say that I was on the same level as Price and Straub was just grossly erroneous. I used to be a highly trained Special Forces infantry member of the US Army. Now I'm a gimp with a cane -- except I left my cane at home. My two super spy buddies were exactly that, super spies. Everything that

I missed in the military, they embodied. They moved without talking, they reacted without thought -- and always in the correct fashion -- and they protected one another without a breath of difficulty, and all of that was before the powers. Heat vision and cyro-powers, fire and ice; these two were meant for each other.

I'm oddly okay with Price/Straub slash fanfiction. Go figure.

I watched, from the corner of my eye, as the pair moved as one. Their weapons would fire, seemingly constantly, while Straub would freeze a pair to the floor. Price would pop up, blasting another with twin tongues of blue flames that emerged from his eyes. Then Straub would spin around, fire a cone of ice, and send another three crumbling to the ground.

And me, I just shot my gun a lot.

We punched through the warehouse until we reached the back quarter. We saw ten people, including my client Frederick Déshant, bound and gagged. They were seated in a huddle with explosives placed in a circle around them. Here were the hostages. Price pointed the hostages and the three of us slowly moved forward.

"Drop the guns." I glanced up at the sudden voice. Standing on an upper landing was Nouri Allawi. He smirked at me and waved a small device in his hand. "This is a detonator. One click and this entire room goes kaboom like the Nakatomi Plaza."

When in doubt, watch *Die Hard*. I hate my own advice.

"Now I'm pretty sure *I'll* survive this, but will all of you?" Four more goons entered the room, two from one end and two more from the rear. "So if I don't hear those P90s hit the floor: click click boom! Surprise ending, fade to black and roll credits."

I dropped my submachine gun and the other two followed.

"How's your quick draw, Ben?" Price whispered.

"Out of practice but still good," I whispered back.

"Good. You got the front two." He nodded at Tyrone. "Now!"

We all struck at the same time. Price fired twin tongues of blue flames that tore through Allawi's chest. Tyrone spun around and threw up a wall of ice to block any gunfire from the rear and I drew my M9. My pistol seemingly leapt into my hand and fired four shots before I could blink. I was quick, not as swift as I used to be but still quick enough to drop the two in front of me. "The only thing faster is light!"

Then I felt it. It was like it emerged from the gun and rolled up my arm. I felt like Neo after he touched the mirror. This feeling, I hadn't felt this way in a very, very long time and to be honest, I missed it. This feeling was confidence. I used to have a great relationship with confidence when I was younger. We were going steady. We were looking at making permanent. I was going to ask confidence to marry me. Then I met the temptress that would split confidence and I up. Her name was Improvised Explosive Device -- IED for short -- and man, was she a bang to remember.

I bolted for the stairs and made it halfway up when I realized my P90 was still on the floor, a stupid mistake, but I had to catch Nouri. I reached the landing and looked around. There was no Nouri and nearly no blood: fire cauterizes a wound. Worst of all, there was no detonator. I glanced down over the ledge. Tyrone was freezing each of the explosive, disabling them, as Price cut the hostage's ropes. Those two had the hostage situation in check. I had to kill the bad man.

I moved quickly, moving to the sole door. I pushed it open, carefully, and stepped inside. The room was an office with a larger storage room connected to it. I moved to the attached room and glanced inside. I saw rows of filing cabinets, I saw several smaller desks and I saw a gun pointed at my head.

"Ben, Ben, Ben," Nouri panted from across the room. I saw the hole on his shirt and watched as his wound, eerily, healed itself. "Did you call in Agent Johnson and Johnson?"

"No relation," I muttered.

"You've cornered the bad-guy and you saved the hostage," he laughed. "I'll be honest; I did not see you being able to do all of that. I am very impressed. Regardless, there is only one part of this movie left and you know what it is."

"The fight scene," I ducked behind the wall as Nouri snapped off two rounds from his pistol.

"This will be an epic fight scene!" he yelled. "Two men -- two soldiers -- who were at their peak during war are now forced to fight once more as broken men." He snapped off a couple more rounds. "Do you miss it, Ben? Do you miss the war? Everything made sense then, before powers, before conspiracies, and before all of this. It was simple."

"It was horrible!" I called back, highlighting my argument with two 9mm rounds. There was a part of me that agreed with him. My life was simpler back then. Things made sense. But life wasn't better then; life was better now. I flinched as a bullet tore through the drywall and sent dust flying everywhere. I mean, I was still getting shot at by Middle Eastern crazies, but life was still better.

"We excelled at war. We excelled at the worst thing humanity ever does, and yet you and I can't handle peace. How broken are we that we can't handle peace." He laughed again. "That's what makes us perfect as arch-enemies. We are so alike."

Those words were frightening.

"We are both broken," he taunted. I popped out with my gun around and snapped off a burst of three shots, the rounds hopefully enough to shut him up.

I was pissed. I was sick and tired of people calling me broken. Friends called me broken, family called me broken, and now psychotic serial killers were calling me that. I was done. Enough was enough. "I am *nothing* like you!" I screamed. I popped out from cover and fired again, only this time I spotted Nouri charging at me.

He collided with me in a full fledge tackle. We both fell backward and my gun flew from my hands. I hit the ground hard and tried to curse, but with no air in my lungs no sound came out. I gasped for air, begging for reprieve from the universe, only to find a boot slamming against me. "You are a broken man, Ben!" he yelled, "just like me. You have to be broken or it just doesn't work. The movie looses all of its subtext if you're not broken."

I gasped, finally getting air, and looked around the office. I spotted my gun on the floor, just out of reach. Internally, I sighed. My life was a movie and it wasn't a very good one either.

"Fine," Nouri said, releasing me. "If you're not broken now, then I'll break you myself."

I grabbed the desk and used it to pull myself up. I glanced back and saw Nouri grabbing a standing lamp and hoisting it in the air. He spun the base around and aimed it at me. I looked at the desk and spotted the phone. It was one of those high-tech landline do-hickies that had more buttons then Air Force One. I grabbed it and spun around. Nouri was charging at me with the lamp raised. He was intending to slam it into my face, into my moneymaker. Like hell I was going to let that happen. A man has to take care of his good looks. I mean, it's not like a man can make children forever -- oh wait.

I stepped forward, grabbed the lamp with my left hand, and pulled myself forward. I twisted as I slammed the phone into his face, hard. He screamed, let go of the lamp, and stumbled back as the phone fell. I finished my spin, taking the lamp with me, and by the time I had made a full circle, the lamp was in my control and firing at his face.

Reversal.

I slammed it hard into his skull, over and over until I heard that satisfying crunch of his nose. He lunged at me, avoiding my next strike, and punched me square in the gut. I grunted and dropped the lamp, but didn't fall. I slammed my elbow across his face and stumbled forward. He struck again, but this time I was ready. A quick block and I was firing my fist back into his face. With each punch, either received or delivered, I felt closer to the old me, to the young me. I felt closer to who I was. I was Ben. I was kick-ass, I was a bad-boy, I was a soldier, I was a warrior, and I was damned good looking. Seriously, I wondered what younger me was doing later.

Nouri grabbed a chair and swung it my leg, my bum leg, and I collapsed to the ground. Just like that I was reminded of who I *really* was: I wasn't younger me, I was just me. For better or for worse, I wasn't Old Ben or Young Ben. I was Now Ben and there wasn't anything wrong with that. I climbed back to my feet and lunged back at him.

My body moved without thinking. Jack's training took my Ranger training into the back room, had dirty hook-up sex with it and made the Ben that was standing and fighting in the now, kicking the crap out of Nouri. It wasn't a highly choreographed Chan/Lee fight. This wasn't a special effect driven Reeves/Weaving fight either. This was a knock-down, drag out type of fight. This was a Gina Carano versus Channing Tatum, and for once I was happy to be fighting like a girl.

I grabbed Nouri's head and slammed it against the desk. I picked up a cheap-ass iHome clock and slammed it against his skull, over and over, until he knocked me back. He dove at me and slammed me through a wall like a bad Arnie stunt. I kicked his legs, I locked his arms, and I even resorted to biting. I pulled a Mike Tyson and bit the bastard's ear.

Nouri hoisted me off of my feet, slammed me against another wall, and kneed me, over and over, pummelling my body until all I could feel was pain. But I didn't surrender. I didn't tap out. For the past year, my life had been nothing but pain and I was not going to let him take credit for anymore of it. I grabbed his shirt and slammed my fist against him, over and over, until he let go. I grabbed him, spun him, and tossed him back into the office. I limped after him, my limp more apparent now, and saw him about to get up. I slammed my boot into his face. For once, it was good not to be the guy on the receiving end of the face-boot lovemaking. I straddled him and slammed my fist across his face. I spat at him and screamed.

"I am..." I punched him again. "Not..." I fired another. "Broken!" I fired another. I punched him, over and over, until his body went limp. I crawled off of his body and limped to my gun.

"You forgot about this?" he said. I looked back at him. He was already conscious again. Nouri held the small detonator in his hand. "Click, click: boom!"

"Tyrone defused all of your bombs," I said as I reached for my gun.

"Not all." Then he clicked the button.

Chapter 23
No More *Magic Mike* For Me

The building rocked as the deafening sound of an explosion filled the air. I squeezed my eyes shut and quietly said my goodbyes. I never expected to open them again, but when I did, I didn't see the Pearly Gates nor did I see the Burning Gate. I didn't even see the Golden Arches. All I saw was Nouri's fist. The blow knocked me back against a wall.

"All I needed was one single bomb," he explained with a cocky smirk. "Just one."

It made sense. One bomb would blow up a small chunk of high-tech supplies, the cops would show up, everything else would be evidence, and to make matters worse, the stock price would plummet from the bad press. I tried to step forward, but Nouri wouldn't let me. He grabbed me by the neck and slammed me back against the wall. He reached for his belt and pulled a combat knife free. For the first time since all this began, Nouri did the smartest thing he could. He didn't tease me with the knife. He didn't spend twenty minutes talking about its origins or how this knife would make the perfect movie prop. Instead, he just stabbed me. He took the knife and pressed the steel deep into my stomach.

Well, crap.

I could feel my body react, wanting to go into shock while also wanting to trigger a vision, but I fought the urge to do both. Nouri jabbed the knife in deep, then twisted. "I didn't want to kill you, Ben. Not now and not here; but, Ben, do you know how infuriating you can be?"

"Want to know a movie secret?" I said between grunts. Nouri just nodded. "Never forget about the gun."

He narrowed his eyes in confusion but came to a quick understanding when he noticed my M9 in my hand. I pressed the barrel against the bottom of his jaw and squeezed the trigger. The bang rang loud and the back of Nouri's head just exploded. His body fell as did mine. I collapsed against the wall and smiled. At least now I could die in peace. I turned to the door in time to see Straub and Price bolting in. I smiled at them and simply let go.

A shiver and twitch and I fell into the past. I was standing in a warehouse office, pressed against a wall by Nouri's grip. He drew his combat knife from his belt and stabbed it into me. I winced, making a horribly embarrassing face, and fought the urge to die. I took my pistol, pressed it against Nouri's jaw and squeezed the trigger. I decided to take comfort that in the last moments before his head exploded, Nouri also made a horribly embarrassing face.

I watched as I collapsed to the ground, smiling as my two super spies charged in. In all honesty, it was a major bummer that my last vision, the one from the steel of the knife cutting into my skin, was of that exact moment, not five seconds earlier. I was hoping for some super secret vision before I died, like how this knife was really what killed Elvis and JFK when they were both at a party that one time. But, alas, I was given no such secret. My astral form shrugged.

I watched as my body shivered, and twitched, and fell into a vision. This had never happened to me before, a vision within a vision. I watched myself watch as he saw himself standing in a warehouse office, pressed against a wall by Nouri's grip. He drew his combat knife from his belt and stabbed it into me. I took my pistol, pressed it against Nouri's jaw and squeezed the trigger. I slumped to the floor, the spies walk in and then it happened again. My body received a shiver and a twitch and we fell into another vision.

I was trapped. I was stuck in an endless loop of visions. Each vision would throw me into another, which would throw me into another. I needed help. I needed Leonardo DiCaprio or Tom Hardy. I'd take Joseph Gordon-Levitt or even Christopher Nolan. Hell, the Fraggles could enter one another's dreams. I'd even take their help.

Shiver and a twitch. Wall, stabbed, gun, head explosion, fall, smile, spies, and repeat.

Shiver and a twitch. Wall, stabbed, gun, head explosion, fall, smile, spies, and repeat.

Shiver and a twitch. Wall, stabbed, gun, head explosion, fall, smile, spies, and repeat.

Shiver and a twitch. Wall, stabbed, gun, head explosion, fall, smile, spies, and repeat.

Ben!

Shiver and a twitch. Wall, stabbed, gun, head explosion, fall, smile, spies, and repeat.

Shiver and a twitch. Wall, stabbed, gun, head explosion, fall, smile, spies, and repeat.

Ben!!

Shiver and a twitch. Wall, stabbed, gun, head explosion, fall, smile, spies, and repeat.

Shiver and a twitch. Wall, stabbed, gun, head explosion, fall, smile, spies, and repeat.

"Zoey?" I knew the voice. I knew that voice.

Shiver and a twitch. Wall, stabbed, gun, head explosion, fall, smile, spies, and repeat.

Shiver and a twitch. Wall, stabbed, gun, head explosion, fall, smile, spies, and repeat.

I need you, Ben. I need you.

Shiver and a twitch. Wall, stabbed, gun, head explosion, fall, smile, spies, and repeat.

Shiver and a twitch. Wall, stabbed, gun, head explosion, fall, smile, spies, and repeat.

I could see her, clear as day. She appeared before me, a floating form. She looked exactly how I remembered her: that body, those eyes, that face, and that body. I know I said her body twice, but I'd spent a lot of lonely nights remembering her body. I stared at her and cried. Steaks and sausages poured from my eyes. Man tears, they're a bitch.

"Zoey," I yelled over the vision. "I love you. I always will.

I need you, Ben. I still need you. Don't leave me.

"I'll never leave you. Zoey!" I yelled. "But I have to move on. You'd want me to. You'd want me to move past and to live my life. I...I..." More steaks poured out. If I kept this up, then world hunger would be solved. "I have to move on, I'm with Rachael now, but I still love you. I always will."

Don't leave me! I still need you Bright Eyes. Save me, Ben!

"Goodbye, Zoey."

Shiver and a twitch. Wall, stabbed, gun, head explosion, fall, smile, spies, and repeat.

Shiver and a twitch. Wall, stabbed, gun, head explosion, fall, smile, spies, and repeat.

Shiver and a twitch. Wall, stabbed, gun, head explosion, fall, smile, spies, and repeat.

Darkness.

I laughed to myself. I think I finally died.

I opened my eyes to find myself on a stretcher in a hospital. Rachael stood over me, a tear rolling down her cheek. Her face held a relived look and she leaned in to kiss me. "Oh god, Ben. I was so worried." She leaned in and kissed me again.

"What did I say about crying over a cowboy?" I muttered.

"Shut up and get better." She kissed me again. My girlfriend kissed me. Girlfriend. Yeah.

I passed out again. I woke up hours later when a mop of hair and a smile a mile long rushed in and jumped on the bed. "So, are you gonna do something? Or just stand there and bleed?" I seriously love this kid. I hugged him, bit back the pain, and just kept smiling. "I was worried."

"Worried about what?" I laughed. "I tripped and fell."

"Bullshit, Uncle Ben." He hugged me.

"Robby, watch your mouth." David walked in with Alice in his arms. He didn't ask if I was okay, he didn't need to. He just smirked. "Karma's here and she's mad."

I gave him a confused look but as I glanced at the door, I understood. Annie and Puzo walked in next, chatting like old friends. Oh, hell. That wasn't good. The four of us chatted for a bit. Everything was fine until Annie gave Robby a couple bucks and told him to find a vending machine. Then I got really scared.

"What the hell happened, Benny?" Annie snapped.

"It was a case," I explained slowly. "Got into a fight with some guy who decided to cheat."

"And you got stabbed."

"Yeah, but I'm okay." Annie smiled and then punched my shoulder. I screamed. My body was sore. I had bruises from tip to toe and her punches weren't helping any. She punched me again in the shoulder.

Now to clarify, I'm not talking about a slap or a girlish punch. When Annie punches, she punches hard. I never had to give David the Be Good to my Sister speech because I knew if it came to push or shove, Annie would choose neither option, instead she'd just start swinging.

"You idiot!" she yelled, punching me again. She even backhanded my stab wound. "Don't you ever scare me like that again!"

"Help! Help! Nurse!" I screamed. Annie was really hurting me. I glanced at David; he looked the other way. I glanced at Alice, who thought this was a game, and got a happy smile. I gave a pleading look to Rachael. "You're a cop. Stop this."

"Oh hell, no." Rachael held up her hands and just backed away.

"Nurse!"

"What going on?" Robby asked, a half eaten chocolate bar in his hand.

"Your mom is beating up your Uncle," David replied.

"Oh," Robby shrugged. He walked off.

"Traitor!" I yelled. I looked back at Annie and saw it. The lone tear rolling down her cheek. "I'm sorry. I'm fine." My sister and I had a moment, a silent pause where we just stared at each other.

Then she punched me again.

"Why do we keep getting caught up in crap like this?" I bit my lip. She punched me again. "What are you keeping from me?"

So I told her. I told her everything. I told her about Croxallé and KyroCorp. I told her about super powers and I told her about Jason. I told her about Robby's power and how Alice will probably have some herself. Then, I told her about my powers.

I decided not to tell her about my death visions.

There was silence. I didn't know what to expect from any of them but silence seemed to work. Annie didn't call me a liar or anything; she knew from my look that this was all truth. She just listened.

"Say something."

She handed me a small box. "This is for you. I knew you wanted it. So we used a bit of the WhiteStar money and bought you a gift." I took the box and greedily opened it up. Staring up at me was a black ring with dark green inner circle. That was my lucky ring.

My death vision was starting to come true.

It took another day before they even thought about releasing me from the hospital. I spend that day with a body full of drugs admiring my new kick-ass scar. The only trouble with an unsightly scar on your stomach that showing it off in a bar becomes difficult. It also meant my stripper days were long over. No more *Magic Mike* for me.

I watched TV for a bit, and smiled as I saw Mia. She spoke how Skit-Tech had suffered a massive stock drop, but was suddenly saved by a company called Kivian Financials. The tablet and phone were still planning on launching on schedule, but with a different company backing it. Then Mia announced that WhiteStar had won the CDC contract. She cut to a pre-recorded interview. Standing before a pedestal were two people. The male was Jameson Hale and the female was Jessica Hale. At the bottom of the screen read their names and the words Founder of WhiteStar Security.

"We feel very honoured that we will be taking up such a serious mantle to protect the people of our great nation," Jameson began. He was a tall man, with dark hair and piercing eyes. "This is not a position that we take lightly. We are giving the project the highest level of oversight available.

"Traditionally, WhiteStar has been run by myself and my twin sister, Jessica Hale, along with our board. It has led us to be a successful enterprise for the last decade. Our direct involvement in the operation has given our company the immediate touch that is often lacking in the government's branch of the armed forces. We want to bring this touch to the CDC AVERT team.

"Starting tomorrow, when we begin the first steps to take the AVERT team live, I will be diminishing my involvement in WhiteStar's operations and taking direct command of the AVERT project. This will give such a crucial undertaking the required attention and leadership it needs.

"As for my former duties with the remainder of the company, I hand them, and majority leadership, to my sister Jessica Hale. She had proven herself for many years now to be a commanding leader and ruthless CEO. To be honest, I'm frightened of her and I'm just glad I don't have to put up with her as much." A small laughter rolled across the audience as the camera panned in on Jessica Hale. She had dark hair like her brother and the same set of piercing eyes.

I changed the channel and scowled. Was this a win? I mean, I took a killer off the street but I wasn't able to stop his plans. WhiteStar won the contract, they used the stock manipulation to raise the money, and I was in the hospital recovering from being stabbed. It felt like kind of a shitty win. I looked down at the remote in my hand and for the first time in a long time, I didn't feel the urge to watch TV. The idea sickened me a little. Perhaps it was Nouri and his obsession that pushed me away from the boob tube. Perhaps it was looking into the path not taken and being frightened by it. Either way, as I mindlessly flipped through the channels, I found myself not wanting to watch TV, and instead I wanted to just turn it off, let the screen go black, and enj-

"Welcome back to Day Three of the Stallone Marathon on the All Action Super Violence Channel. Up next is *Rocky 3*, followed by *Rocky 4* and *Rocky 5*."

My jaw dropped. Stallone versus Mr. T. Oh, I was not leaving this bed for a while, personal growth be damned.

Rachael parked her car on the sidewalk and nodded at my apartment. My driveway, normally empty, was now filled with a black Honda Civic and a very familiar 1971 Chevy Chevelle SS. Standing beside it was Christine. I climbed out of Puzo's car and limped to the Doctor.

"Hello, Ben." I tipped my hat at her. She handed me a set of keys. "This is for you."

"Um... what is?"

"The car," she said.

"You had my curiosity, but now you have my attention," I said

"There is a letter on the front seat that explains." She leaned in and kissed my cheek. "Thanks for the save."

I watched her climb into the Civic, and waited for her to drive off. I opened the Chevelle's door, found the envelope with my name on it, and tore it open. I read it over.

Dear Ben,

In 1971, my Grandfather bought this car. He saved up for nearly a year and bought it off the line. He was one of the first two hundred to have purchased this car. It was his baby. He taught his son, my father, how to take care of it. The two of them treated this car like gold. One day, my grandfather gave it to my father.

My father taught those same lessons to me. I learned how take care of it, I learned how to love it, and I learned how to treat her right. My father eventually passed this car to me.

It was my hope that someday I would pass this onto my son, onto Robby. I hoped that someday I'd be allowed to see him, that I'd be allowed to get to know him properly. If you're reading this, then that never happened.

After Robby was kidnapped, I rewrote my will. Robby is taken care of and you, Ben, you are a great uncle and a trust-worthy man. So here is what I am bequeathing:

I give this car, my family's legacy, to my only son: Robby Belledin. This car will belong to him on his 17th birthday, or when he's gotten his full license, and when he's grown to appreciate this car and everything it stands for. Until then I give it his uncle, Benedict Thompson, for safekeeping.

Please look after this car for him. Please teach him about it and what it means. And if I can ask one more favour, when the time is right, please teach him about me. Please let him know the truth.

Tell him I loved him but I wasn't brave enough.

Thanks Ben,

Jason Daggett

PS: She needs premium only.

I opened the door to my apartment and forced a smile. Explaining my new car to Rachael was a weird experience. It was another of a long list of weird explanations I had to give today. Between cops, feds, my client and family, I was explained out. What I needed was somebody to explain something to me. As if on cue, my phone rang. I looked up at Rachael.

She smiled back at me. "Answer it. I'll order food. Pizza okay?" Pizza sounded delicious.

"Hello?"

"Hello, Ben." It was Price. I was relived. A mysterious number; I was half expecting Nouri. "How you healing up?"

"Slowly," I muttered. "Where is Nouri?"

"He's in jail," Price explained. "He was pronounced dead by authorities and we had his body shipped out before he healed his head back together."

"So what jail is he in?" Suddenly I'd answered my own question. "Blacksite?"

"Yep."

"Oh." Silence. "Thanks for the save."

"Anytime, Ben." And with that, he hung-up.

I limped into the kitchen and slumped into my chair. Rachael came over and slid into my lap. She kissed me. I kissed her back. It was enjoyable. Our lips parted and Rachael handed me a brown package.

"What's this?"

"I was going to ask you that. It was on your counter." It was the package from earlier. In all the gun fighting based confusion and alcohol fuelled self loathing, I'd forgotten about it. I shrugged and tore it open. I looked inside and raised an eyebrow. Inside was a dolphin necklace, a familiar dolphin necklace. It looked very similar to one I'd given as a gift to Zoey. I reached down and touched it.

A shiver and a twitch, and I fell into a vision. I saw Zoey in the desert, standing beside a man I instantly recognized: Mr. Evil Hat.

"Hello Ben," Zoey said. I froze. Nobody in visions could talk to me. It was impossible. "How are you, Ben?"

"Zoey, wow."

"Is that all you can say? 'Zoey, wow'," she scoffed. "You haven't seen me in years and all I get is a wow?"

"What's going on?" How was I having a conversation in a vision?

"This is a man who can see the future," she said, pointing to Mr. Evil Hat. "He says to call him Van Cleef. I'm not sure exactly how this is working, but basically you see the past, he sees the future, and you two have met somewhere in the middle."

"He's telling you what I say, isn't he?" Zoey just nodded.

"You just stopped Nouri. I know you think it wasn't a big win, but it's still a win. I'm proud of you." She smiled at me. Oh god, how I missed that smile. Slowly the smile faded. "I'm sorry, Ben. Oh god, I am sorry. Van Cleef told me what I'm about to put you through, about how my death is going to crush you." She started to tear up. "I wish you didn't have to go through all that, but I have to. I have to go on this mission."

"No, don't," I begged, just as I did all those years ago. "Don't go. Don't throw your life away for anything this liar tells you. It's not worth it. There must be another way."

"I can't, Ben. I can't turn this down. You begged me last night not to go, and damn it, I almost listened." She wiped the tears from her face. "But I have to go, so much depends on it."

I stood there, motionless. I didn't know what to say. Had fate just brought me back to her just to torment me? I had moved on, I had finally gotten over her death and been able to start a new life without her, and yet here she was, standing before me, talking to me; ripping me apart.

"I have something to tell you about your time, Ben," she said. "You need to pay attention. I need you to do three things.

"One: No matter what happens in the years to come, you need to just be you. Be the Ben I love. Two: When the diamond in the rough shows up, protect her."

"What? You're speaking in riddles." I hate riddles.

"I know, I have no choice. Here's the big one, Ben. Here is number three," she said. "They have me, Ben. I'm still alive and I need you to save me. Help me, Ben, you're the only one who can."

Reality returned and I was left with only one thought: Well, crap.

Epilogue

Thaddius Clay sat in his office and stared at his computer screen. He watched the security feed, studying the screen very closely. He watched as Ben chatted with Jason and his two associates, he watched as the FBI lady worked, and he watched the plan to hunt down and stop Nouri Allawi unfold, but mostly he watched Ben.

Clay tapped his space bar and the feed stopped. He had seen all he needed to. This Ben was an interesting figure. He had brought down WhiteStar's kidnapping programme, at least in this city, essentially on his own. It wasn't bad for an injured soldier; hell, it wasn't bad for a fully fit solider.

Clay stood up and left his office. He rode his elevator downwards, disembarking at the bottom floor. He walked down the hall and stopped at a glass window. He looked inside, staring at the woman trapped in the room. She was a redhead with a stunning body, if you were into that type, but her mind was broken. He didn't blame her, she had been held captive for years. He was doing the same, no sense in denying that, but he was taking much better care of her than her previous captors had. He was even the one that ordered her rescue.

"Mr. Clay." He turned around to see the senior medical officer, Dr. Madison Harper, approach. He looked back at the glass. "What brings you down to this floor, sir?"

"Did you get a sample?" he asked.

"Yes, we withdrew a large sperm sample from Mr. Thompson while he was out cold in out medical room," she explained. "We tested it as well. He is quite fertile. He will make a great donor. All we need is for you to choose a female for us to impregnate with his seed."

"Her," Clay said without hesitation.

"Sir?" Dr. Harper looked through the glass. "She's unstable."

"I know," Clay said, "But her Lycotta gene counts are through the roof. Give her his sample. She will carry Ben's child."

"Yes sir," Dr. Harper said as Clay walked off. She grabbed the chart and started filling up the paper work.

"Congratulation, Zoey Harris," she muttered. "You're about to be a mother."

THE END

Benedict Thompson will return
in
Bedroom Walls that Save Us

WHO IS MAC?

The mysteries of the Visegar Company, Polaris Industries and the Lycotta gene grow deeper with the introduction of the deadly young raven called Mac.

> The Prague Riots
> The Port Alexander Explosion
> The Clockwork Killer

She shows up at each and brings death with her. Who is Mac and what is her connection to all three?

The mystery grows deeper and it all starts here!

Late Night Countdown

There was something about the constant click of rounds snapping into a magazine that drove Mac nuts; it always came to an end after twelve but then he'd eject each one and restart from the beginning. She looked behind her and frowned. It was Marcus Frison; it was always Marcus Frison. There were five of them in the back of the van, her and four men, and each of them were growing impatient. The five of them were each a highly trained special ops soldiers and each of them were currently sitting there with their respective thumbs up their asses.

Many soldiers often spoke about how the worst part of any mission was the calm before it. The military worked on a hurry-up-and-wait system, a tried and true one they had used for years. Various militaries had so much faith in that system that its practice had trickled down to private military companies, government agencies, spies and event security companies. The theory was simple; a soldier would rush to make sure they reached the location on time then they sat and waited, sometimes for hours, until they got the go ahead. The system made sure everybody was ready for the go time but it also made waiting for the mission a long, mind-numbing event.

Every soldier handled that time differently. Marcus Frison, a muscular dark-skinned man who went by Cell, fiddled with his pistol. He'd eject every round from his magazine, then slowly reinsert them, one after another. When he was done, he'd restart the process all over again. Erik 'DJ' Ruckas, a skinny blonde sniper, leaned back in his seat with headphones on and classic rock music blaring into his ears. He bobbed his head and hummed quietly to the music. Jasper 'Zetes' Hill just slept. He would lay his head back, give the team a final wink and then doze off without a care in the world. She never understood how he did it but he just did. That left Rath. He'd read. It was one book after another. He didn't care what genre, all he cared was that it was fiction. He devoured libraries like candy.

Rath was a big guy who had an obscene amount of muscles. He had a gentle voice but always wore a mask. It was a black hood with large white eyes and he never took it off. The men and women of other teams often wondered why and rumours spread. Some said his face was badly burned, others said it was actually filled with technology that kept him alive, but Mac knew the truth. Rath had a really famous face. In order to protect the company and himself, he wore the mask.

Mac shook the off the thought and tried to focus. They were coming up on the drop point. This team, this black-ops strike team, belonged to her. That meant not only were the four men under her charge but they were also her responsibility. Her name was Bailee MacIntosh. He codename was Raven but nobody used that outside a radio. Everybody just called her Mac. She wasn't a spy or a soldier, she was simply Mac.

She tapped her chest and got the team's attentions. "We're five minutes out. Arm up."

DJ turned off the music and switched to his radio. "Command: this is Jericho Team"

"Go for Command."

"We're approaching the first drop point. Begin the recording now." He smiled at the rest of the guys. "Gentlemen, place your bets."

Mac rolled her eyes and let out a groan.

"I'm going with eye beams." Zetes said slowly. "It makes sense. She runs out of bullet and all she has to do is glare them to death."

"A female with an actual death glare," DJ laughed. "That's freaking terrifying."

"Command is giving you 6:1 odds." The radio responded.

They did this every single mission; Every. Single. Mission. Each member on Mac's team had a meta-ability, a super-human skill that set them apart from the common man. Cell could manipulate biological life force. He could heal or injure with a touch. Rath had super strength and durability. He could punch a hole through steel without a second thought. DJ had super-enhanced hearing. If there was a sound, he heard it. Zetes could manufacture and control wind. The team's talker could literally fill a room with hot air. Mac, on the other hand, was a complete mystery. None of the four men knew what her power was. Nobody in Command knew what her ability was and even fewer in the Company's Operations division knew. Each soldier could, and had, called upon their powers on a mission to fight, succeed and survive. Mac never needed to.

"How about telekinesis," Cell suggested. "She could push the bullets faster and further. She could do it without us evening know. It would explain why we've never seen her power."

"Oh, good choice." DJ said with admiration. "Command?"

"Telekinesis is rare amongst females," The voice on the radio explained. "Although when they do emerge they come with a far greater power level."

"It makes sense." Cell said, "Telekinesis is delicate work and I read somewhere that female are better at delicate work than men."

Mac shrugged. She didn't know if she was supposed to be insulted at that or not. "Don't we have anything better to do before a mission?"

"Not likely." DJ mocked. " Command?"

"9:1 odds."

"I'm going to go with pheromone control," Zetes said with an exaggerated wink. "It'd explain why I'm so taken by your beauty, Mac."

"4:1 odds," Command radioed.

"Okay, Rath. Don't disappoint."

"Reality alteration." The three other guys and the driver up front all let out a long unison groan. "What?"

"Every. Single. Time." Cell mocked.

"If you're not going to play, fine, but don't ruin the game."

"Screw you guys," Rath defended, "It makes perfect sense. She moves perfectly on every mission. She never gets injured, she never gets shot and she rarely even gets hit. Nobody's that perfect. She's changing the world around her."

"And Rath throws the same lame pitch," DJ said, disheartened. "Command?"

"Um....632:1 odds?"

The team laughed. All four looked at Mac expectantly. She rolled her eyes and looked away, hiding her smile. Originally this betting pool of theirs bugged the hell out of her but it had actually grown on her. It brought the team together, it gave them something to chat about and to be honest; it was kind of flattering.

"Command: we are two minutes from the first drop." Mac explained, ignoring her team's expectant looks - and Rath' creepy mask. "We need confirmation for a go."

A knock at the door pulled Rhys Polson's gaze from his computer. He eyed the familiar face, a young analyst who served as his assistant and raised an eyebrow. "Yes?"

"They are approaching the first drop, sir." He explained. "They need you in ops."

Rhys nodded. He closed the laptop, grabbed his phone from the desk, and climbed to his feet. Without a word, he exited his office and moved down the hall. The operations room was a large floor with dozens of agents on computers of their own and a series of larger screens mounted at the front of the room. Rhys' office was elevated above the floor; it allowed him to look down at the proceedings if he so desired. He descended the stairs, running his hand through his greying hair. He winced internally. Every day, another grey seemed to sneak into his once magnificent head of jet black hair. They would sneak in, they were unwanted, once they were there they never left and worse still, brought more of their kind with them.

"Command," Rhys spoke for the first time, addressing the senior agent. "We good to go?"

"Yes, sir."

"What do we think their chances are?"

"We're looking upwards of 84% of success, sir."

Rhys thumbed a code into his phone. "You have a go."

The van slowed to a halt on a dirt road. Mac pulled open the door and glanced at DJ. He threw out his trademark smirk and moved to the door. DJ gave Zetes a small fist-bump, pulled his neck bandana up over his face and leapt out the door, vanishing into the night. They were in Korangal Valley, located in the north-east part of Afghanistan. The landscape could only be described as massive desert with patches of trees scattered around. DJ cradled his sniper rifle in his arms and bolted up the hill. He crouched by a tree and stared down at the building below. Looking through the scope, he peered closer. The building looked like a series of cascading brown houses, built into the side of a hill, but that was only a facade. DJ peered closer, adjusting his scope slightly, and spotted two Al-Qaeda guards, each carrying an AK-74. No neighbourhood watch needed that amount of firepower. These buildings were an Al-Qaeda base.

DJ took a prone position and quickly started preparing. He gripped his rifle, adjusted the scope again and waited.

The plan was Mac would lead the rest of the team in an assault on the base while he covered from up here. The US military wouldn't hit a base like this with anything less than twelve men and aerial support. Mac would do it with a team of five. That meant he had to be alert; he was their best cover. No one on that team was a normal soldier and together they were damn near unstoppable, but they weren't invincible.

He heard it before he saw it, he heard everything before he saw it, and reached for his customized headset. "Ladies and Gentlemen, welcome to another edition of *Late Night Countdown.* I'm your host, the magnificent and fabulous DJ." He looked down at the base of the hill and spotted Mac and the team. Each wore desert combats, a brown tact vest, a helmet and a bandana covering their faces - except for Rath who simply wore his creepy mask. They looked like Seal Team Six, the only difference was Mac's team was much better.

"It's been an interesting week on the charts so let's jump right in. Starting at number Ten is *Ain't no Mountain High Enough* by Marvin Gaye and Tammi Terrell." DJ clicked his watch and the music started to play, quietly, over the comms. DJ's life was music. It hadn't always been; growing up he listened to music as much as any other teenager but when puberty hit, and his hearing amplified, music became his release. Super hearing wasn't the easiest power in the world to have; his teenage brain was literally assaulted by every noise imaginable. From the scraping of a pencil, to the clicking of nails, the flapping of insect wings and the whispers of a young boy, two blocks away, DJ heard it all. Music became his only escape; hypnotic rhythms, powerful rifts and thumping bass lines. They proved to be the only thing that could block out the noise and to grant him peace. "We have two on the top, armed."

"Hi, DJ Awesome; long time listener, first time caller," Zetes replied. "What do you think made Gaye such a household name? Drop yours and we'll enter."

DJ closed his eyes and let the noise flood in. Years of practice had taught him how to use his powers, how to take something as seemingly useless as super-hearing and make it a powerful tool. He could hear as every sound bounced off of every tree, every wall and every person. He could pinpoint them with a far greater accuracy with his hearing then he ever could with his eyes and a scope; acoustic location.

DJ pulled the trigger twice and listened as the two guards fell. "Nice question, caller. He did a lot for the music world but for me it will always be *I Heard it Through the Grapevine*. Now let's continue with the list."

The moment the two guard fell was the moment they entered the base. Rath pushed his thumb through the lock, busting it, and opened the door. Mac entered the building with her rifle raised high. She clutched the M4 tightly as she crept down the hallway. The building had wooden floors that seemed to want to creak with each step she took but her footsteps were silent. Behind her she could hear the faint sound of her team moving, Cell was directly behind her, Zetes next in line as Rath took up the rear. They moved in deeper.

"Peculiar," Cell muttered. "This isn't several buildings, it's just one. They dug into the side of the hill."

"Hey, Mac, this ain't Al-Qaeda." Zetes added. "They don't operate like this. They ain't got that type of coin. This is Bond-villain level."

"I know." Mac muttered. "Intel puts the objective in the back. Push forward but keep 'em peeled. If this ain't Al-Qaeda then they will be better guarded."

They came across the first resistance two doors down, another pair of Al-Qaeda guards. Two quick pulls from her silenced rifle dropped each. She waved her team forward. "Zetes, Cell: body search." The pair knelt by the bodies as Mac and Rath kept their weapons up at the ready.

"American. This one has Ranger ink." Cell spoke. "Best guess: WhiteStar."

Mac cursed. She hated WhiteStar Security. They were a private military company owned and operated by Polaris In-

dustries. Mac had no illusions of her employer's moral direction, it wasn't great, but at least her boss had rules they lived
by. WhiteStar did not.

"Okay, no more silent." Mac ordered, "time to keep
them on edge. Rath; go big and go strong. DJ: Drop the needle and start punching holes. We're going loud."

DJ loved those words. Mac had told him to just open
up. If there was a guard or a soldier then he was to drop them.
Any trepidation that existed in taking a life, what little there
remained in his conscience, suddenly vanished. WhiteStar
deserved everything they got.

"This long distance dedication goes out to a beautiful
woman to her long lost man. It reads: Screw you and die."
DJ smirked to himself as he tapped his custom headset once
again. "Wow. Touching stuff; this song is for you."

Ouga Chaka ouga ouga
Ouga Chaka ouga ouga

The primal chanting played across the radio and
quickly drowned out the collective cries of protest from the
remaining four. DJ ignored them as he ran his hand over his
sniper rifle. It was a highly customized weapon. It started off
as a Denel NTW-20 but now it could be barely called that. It
was like how a dinosaur evolved into a bird. It had been up-
graded to give it more punch and power. The Denel NTW-20
was strong. His baby was stronger.

Ouga Chaka ouga ouga
Ouga Chaka ouga ouga

DJ closed his eyes and let his hearing take over. The
sounds waves echoed out as the acoustic location started to reveal the WhiteStar guards. DJ smirked and started to pull the
trigger. The first shot ripped through the building's wall and

slammed through a guard's chest. The second sent another crumpling to the ground as the third round found a place to hibernate for the winter directly between the eyes of an unsuspecting soldier.

I can't stop this feelin'
Deep inside of me
Girl you just don't realize
What you do to me.

The base, once silent, was a frenzy of fear and confusion. As DJ started to kill soldiers - most before they even realized that there was a threat - Rath began to tear the building down. His first kick put a hole into a wall while his punch knocked a door off its hinges and into the next room. Needless to say WhiteStar was scrambling.

Lips as sweet as candy
Your taste is on my mind
Girl you got me thirsty
For another, cup of wine

Mac popped around a corner and fired a burst of three bullets in less than a second. She shifted her aim, fired another burst, and bolted forward. Zetes followed close behind. Cell, covering their rear, flipped his M4 to fully automatic and opened fire. They were being flanked from behind.

"You know some of these guys may actually be Al-Qaeda." Cell cried out over the roar of his rifle. "Just putting that out there."

"This affects things how?" Rath asked.

Cell just gave an awkward shrug. "Just factual."

Rath ripped another door off of its hinges and hoisted it into the air. "Drop."

Cell dropped to one knee and ceased firing. He watched as a door flew over his head and was tossed down the long hallway. Most soldiers knew how to deal with bullets and explosives, those made sense. Nobody know how to react when a door was pitched at 90 mph. It fractured their sense of reality. Most of them just stood there, stunned, while the lucky ones dived out of the way at the last moment. Those that didn't dodge found their daily intake of oak suddenly taking a large leap.

> *Got a bug from you girl*
> *But I don't need a cure*
> *I'll just stay affected*
> *If I can't be sure*
> *All the good love, when we're all alone*
> *Keep it up girl, yeah you turn me on.*

Mac and Zetes paused at a door. They nodded at each other and moved to breach. Mac kicked the door open and Zetes stormed into the room. His rifle snapped off round after round as Mac's came in after. She spun to her left and surprised a WhiteStar goon carrying a rifle of his own. Mac struck first, stabbing the tip of her barrel into the chest of the goon. She struck again, slapping his weapon to the side and thrust her barrel forward a third time. The third strike caught the goon under his right arm. Mac twisted her rifle, drawing her knife from her belt, and used the barrel to pin the goon's arm behind his back. She spun him around with her knife pressed up against his neck. The end result was the WhiteStar goon hunched over with his arms by his back, twisted around her rifle. His body served as a makeshift tripod. She shifted her aim, lining her sights up with another hostile and squeezed off another burst. The ejected shells bounced off the goon's back. She shifted again and fired once more.

"Clear," Zetes snapped as the last guy fell. Mac freed her goon, tossing him to the floor, and knocked him unconscious with a kick.

"Cell: Report."

"Still more coming up the rear; DJ's dropping what he can. We'll get the rest. Go."

Mac eyed Zetes. The elementalist just nodded. "Confirm. No hero bulshit."

"Orders confirmed."

Mac nodded at Zetes and both took off running. The further they got into the base the more it lost its rustic decor. From the outside, and the early stages of the interior, the building looked like its facade: a series of Afghanistan buildings. Yet now, with the wooden floors gone and the hallways filled with neon lights, key-card doors and security cameras, the disguise had ended.

I'm hooked on a feeling
I'm high on believin'
That you're in love with me
I can't stop this feelin' - deep inside of me
Girl you just don't realize, what you do to me

Even with the mask as protection, Rath could feel the heat on his face. The tongue of orange flame flickered and inched before his face. A second later it vanished. Rath cursed loudly and glanced at Cell.

"Oh great, they have a burner." Cell muttered sarcastically. "Push him back; I'll try for the shot."

Rath' mask didn't react, it hid all emotion that his face showed, but despite that Cell somehow knew Rath was glaring at him. "I hate you."

"I know," Cell popped out from around the corner and opened fire. The WhiteStar troops were sending more men their way but now they had sent their own meta-humans as back up. Among the troops was an Asian female with control over fire. She could summon a flame to the tip of her finger and fire it outwards in deadly tongues of destruction.

Rath charged towards the burner, his first raised and cocked to strike. Most super strengths were barbaric creatures. They roared as they fought, channeling anger and hatred into their body. They became avatars of fury. Rath did none of those. He just stayed silent. Rath ignored the heat as a burst of fire was flung towards him, he ignored the pain as the flames scorched his skin and he ignored the cries of protest as his fist slammed against the burner face. One punch was all it took, one single punch. The Asian woman flew backwards into the air, skipping across the floor like a tossed stone. Two new soldiers rushed the masked man. Rath easily blocked an oncoming punch with his left hand and grabbed the attacker with his right. Rath lifted the man into the air and tossed him at the second attacker. Both hit the ground in a heap. Rath panted as his body screamed in pain. The smell of burning flesh - his flesh - reached his nose and Rath fought back the urge to vomit.

"You're a monster." A new voiced added. Rath turned around and spotted a young Mexican man standing there, staring with a confident smirk. Sparks began to form on his fingers, the arcs quickly forming into full on electrical bolts. "It's a good thing I'm a monster slayer. Time for some serious exp points, mother ---"

Cell snuck up behind the boy and placed his hand on the kid's neck. The young man dropped to the floor, uncon-scious. All it took was a single touch for Cell to inflict enough damage into the kid's body. He never inflicted enough to leave any lasting damage but instead he administered just enough to render him unconscious. Cell walked over to Rath, eyeing the blisters and burns on the big man's body, and gently touched his exposed skin. For a moment nothing visible happened, his healing touch working on the internal damage first, then the exterior skin reacted. It was like watching a burn victim in reverse. The blisters shrunk and vanished while the burns retreated into the skin. With a single touch Cell could heal or injure a person. He'd never brought someone back from the dead with his touch but he had killed someone. It was an unpleasant experience, one that had sadly made him into the man he now was.

"Let's find Mac."

I'm hooked on a feeling

And I'm high on believin'
That you're in love with me
I said I'm hooked on a feeling
And I'm high on believin'
That you're in love with me

"That was Hooked on a Feeling by Swede Blue," DJ said over the radio. He pulled the trigger and dropped another guard. "This song has been a long time favourite of mine. Up next is a ..."

DJ paused and listened. Dead Air; it was the bane of the radio world but at this moment he didn't care. There was something more important he had to focus on - that and he wasn't actually on the radio. He tilted his head and focused his abilities, tuning out everything he didn't need to hear and redirecting his ability to the sounds he did.

Three men approached him from the rear. They were spreading out and were going to flank him. A surprise attack was a great tactic but not if the target heard it coming and DJ always heard it coming. DJ let go of his rifle, drew his pistol and rolled to his back. He snapped off two shots, heard a faint grunt and smirked; one down. He rolled to his feet, closed his eyes and aimed to his left. Another shot and he heard the crumpling sound of a second body hitting the valley floor. DJ adjusted his aim a third time. The last attacker decided to forego stealth and just run in, weaving in and out of trees for cover. DJ fired off two shots but each found only trunk or bark. His acoustic locations could pinpoint a person's exact location but he still had to hit them.

DJ tracked the runner with his pistol, his sights following the random run pattern, and fired off a couple more rounds. He got nothing but misses. DJ cursed and ducked behind a tree of his own as a burst of rounds riddled the spot where he once stood. DJ listened. He heard the man go left for a couple feet, then twist right for a few more only to make a mad dash to yet another tree for cover. DJ didn't bother firing, he just listened. He heard the man's heart beat, he heard him breathe and he heard the sound his fingers made and he rubbed the rifle's trigger guard. DJ heard it all.

Increased heart rate, quickening breaths and the sounds of boots digging into the ground like a runner pushing off a starter's block; every sound told a story and together these were telling DJ that the attacker was about to pop out. DJ spun from his tree, leveled his pistol and took one shot. The attacker dashed out from his cover and, unknowingly, ran directly into the bullet's path. The round tore through his skull and dropped him on his ass. DJ frowned. He stood motionless for several seconds, waiting as he awaited his smile to return.

"Sorry about that folks," he laughed into his radio. "The price of fame is everybody wants a piece of the celebrity. Next up is a classic rock song. This one goes out to all of Bin Laden's followers who are having a difficult time with their nine wives."

Shot through the heart, and you're to blame, darling
You give love a bad name.

Mac and Zetes breached a door and stormed the room. She expected a laboratory with test subjects both human and animal alike. She expected wires and fancy equipment tracking every vital sign of a human man, strapped to a table. She expected dozen of guards with big guns and black masks. She didn't expect a room with a giant ass hole in the middle of the floor.

The hole looked like a massive well. It was made from concrete and was pitch black. She could faintly see stair that descended the well in a circular fashion. She couldn't, however, see the bottom. Mac switched on the light attached to the end of her rifle. "I'm going down. Swoop in if I need it."

Zetes nodded as flipped over a table. He took cover behind the table and aimed his rifle at the door. Mac stepped on the first step, testing it and slowly started her decent. Four stories she descended, walking in literal circles, and she had yet to reach the end. She could see it, she was only a floor away, but she hadn't reached it. She could see four prison cells. They didn't have bars like in prison movies; instead each of them was a square room with a massive steel door. It reminded her of solitary confinement. She also spotted a wooden door, one that must have led to some sort of guard's room. She reached the bottom and kept her weapon trained on the wooden door. Something was going to come out of there, something always did.

As she approached the wooden door she noticed a small camera fitted above it. They knew she was here. She paused, debating her options, and then smirked beneath her mask. She raised her right hand and waved her middle finger at the camera. She'd just flipped the bird to whoever was watching from the other side. She heard angry screams and the sound of boots moving towards her. She hated when she was right.

An angel's smile is what you sell
You promise me heaven then put me through hell
Chains of love, got a hold on me
When passion's a prison you can't break free

Mac opened fire. She didn't wait for them to open it, she just shot through it. She heard cries of pain and the sound falling bodies, knowing that she had hit something. Mac approached the door and yanked it open. She spotted several dead bodies on the floor and one body, still living and breathing despite two bullet wounds in his chest, climbing back to his feet.

Tough guys; Mac hated tough guys.

The tough man lunged at her but Mac easily dodged with a quick side-step. The man surprised her, pivoting towards her and fired a devastating punch in her direction. Mac twisted her M4 sideways and used the stock to block the attack. She heard the sound of bone on steel but also heard a cracking sound from her rifle. Mr. Tough Guy was also super strong. He pulled back his left fist and fired with his right. Mac twisted her rifle vertically and used the weapon to deflect the next attack, and then she struck.

> *You're a loaded gun, yeah*
> *There's nowhere to run*
> *No-one can save me, the damage is done*

She flipped her weapon backwards and slammed the rifle's butt directly into Mr. Tough Guy's neck. A blow like that would stop most men cold. It stunned Mr. Tough Guy - barely - for only a mere second but a mere second was all Mac needed. A single second could change the tide of a war; it could alter the course of mankind and could be the difference between victory and defeat. For Mac, a second was all it took for her to turn this fight into a win. She drew her pistol - using speeds unmatched by most - pressed it against the man's skull and pulled the trigger. The side of his brain exploded outwards and Mr. Tough Guy was no more.

Mac turned away as the body crumpled to the ground. She aimed at the camera and snapped off another round. The bullet ripped through the high tech surveillance equipment, transforming it from top of the line device to a paperweight. "Clear."

Mac pulled off her mask and helmet as Zetes floating down the hole. "So what did you use? Was it eye beams? Please say eye beams?"

"Nope, I used something better," Mac said as she showed Zetes her pistol before holstering it. She ran a gloved hand through her shoulder length hair as she eyed the doors. Three seemed unused, they had cobwebs and spiders, but the remaining one showed signs of use. "There."

Zetes pressed his palm against the lock and filled it with air. Each tumbler clicked and the door slowly opened. They saw a human form, covered in torn rags, scramble to the back of the cell. Mac handed Zetes her busted M4 and slowly walked into the cell. The woman began to mutter, spouting random words.

"Zoey?" She asked, "Zoey Harris, are you Zoey Harris?"

"Bright Eyes?" The female prisoner asked back. "Ben, is that you? I'm sorry, Ben. I'm sorry." The woman began to sob. Mac knelt by the woman and brushed the long, unkempt red hair from before her face. She looked at the woman, studying her features. She glanced back at Zetes and nodded.

"I'm not Ben," She explained. "We work for The Visegar Company and we're here to rescue you."

Shot through the heart, and you're to blame
You give love a bad name
I play my part and you play your game
You give love a bad name

Rhys had seen enough. They had their objective. He glanced down at his phone and thumbed in another code. "Get them out of there. If things get bad, hack a nearby drone and use it for aerial support." Rhys didn't listen to the reply; he just walked back to his office.

"Wow, that Ops team is amazing, sir." His assistant said as the pair walked. "Especially Mac."

Rhys looked up and shrugged. To most of Visegar, Mac was just another tool. Rhys knew she was more, as Director of Field Operations he knew just how important she really was.

"She went through that entire mission without using her powers." The assistant admitted. "That's kind of insane."

Again, Rhys just shrugged.

"So which one of the guys was right?" Rhys paused, looked at his assistant, and raised a confused eyebrow. "Her powers, which one of the guys guessed right?"

Rhys resumed walked, ascending the stairs to his office. "None of them."

"But, sir, they've been running this betting pool for

almost four years. You mean nobody has ever guessed it in all that time?"

"Not a single one." The pair paused at Rhys' office door

"Then what is it, sir?" He asked carefully. "What power does she have that she can out-soldier everybody here?" "She doesn't have any powers at all." Rhys said, cracking a small smile. "That girl is one hundred percent powerless."

THE END

Mac will return
in
She Who Train Under Death

ON SALE NOW!

FROM THE AUTHOR

I had a vison that the world ended. When I did I learned tow things. 1: Thanks the people in our lives while we have the chane and 2: Even the apocalypse wont stop my bill collectors from hunting me down.

Friends: Thanks to Cliff, Lenny, Matt, Jay, Mr. DeYoung, Chelsea, Kayla and Megan. The only reason I climb so high is because each of you gave me a bump up.

To the Gentle Girls (seriously, is that name still a thing?). You have all been there for me and helped in ways I never thought possible. Thanks MM, CL, KF, KC, SC and of course the other MM.

To my family: you are my biggest supporters and critics and somehow that works!

To my Mom: I wouldn't be here without you. Seriously. Not at All. I love you and thanks.

To my wife: With each book I write I'll try to thank you a little more. I may write a thousand book but there will never be enough words to properly thank you for all you've done. You've truned a sad scrawny boy into an author man and for that I can never thank you enough, not even with cookie, but I'll never stop trying.

And to the most important: Zid

All Hail

My name is Benedict Thompson and I am a superhero. With a single Touch, I can read an item's past. I can tell who used that pen before you, I can describe how that shoe was made and I can describe everything that has been done on that motel room bed.

The problem with having superpowers is that people want you to actually use them.

I just want to watch TV but here I am dealing with a movie-quoting assassin, murderous celebrities, kidnapped children and secret government conspiracies.

My family's in danger, my life is in ruins and worst of all, my TV is being ignored.

I miss my TV.

THE BENEDICT FORECASTS

Author **Larry Gent** transports you into a world spies, espionage and superpowers. Each book is an action-packed thriller that'll keep you on the edge of your seat.

Winner of the silver medal in the *Best in Halifax* award, the Benedict Forecasts deleve deeper into the ever growing Lycotta mystery

WHAT'S WORSE THEN BEING STUCK IN A VIDEO GAME AND NOT BEING ABLE TO LOG OUT?

My name is Rake and I'm stuck in a MMO. It wouldn't be so bad if I was in my max level main but I'm not. I'm stuck as my level 1 Rogue. I'm stuck in my bank alt.

Now I'm running for my life, I'm fighting to stay alive and I'm trying to figure out how the hell to get out of here.

Where's a GM when you need one?

HELP!

BEING STUCK IN YOUR BANK ALT!

Vörissa's Catalyst

—ONLINE—

Patch 1.01: New Game+
Patch 1.02: Escort Mission
Patch 1.03: Corpse Run
Patch 1.04: In Another Castle
Patch 1.05: Silent Protagonist

In this new series by Award Winning author Larry Gent, we dive in the action and mystery of the *Stuck Online* genre.

Follow Rake and company as they fight in a harsh digital world. If they're smart, they'll keep their lives. If they're lucky, they'll keep their sanity and if they're both, they just may find a way to log out.

TO ARMS, SOLDIER

LIGHTYEARS TO GO
BEFORE I SLEEP
ON SALE NOW

Allana Guiver was the Legendary Soldier that all of history knew. She won the great war but lost everything she knew and loved doing so.

400 years later, Major Guiver wakes up from cryo-sleep to find a world she doesn't reconize.

Earth is gone, humanity floats through space on a massive ship, searching for a new home and a new alien threat wants to rid the universe of every human.

Humanity needs their Legendary Soldier but how do you ask a woman who gave up everything to give up more?

YOU'RE NOT DONE YET

Photo by Lisa Liteplo

ABOUT THE AUTHOR

Larry Gent is a is a bottomless well of know-legde on historical wars in worlds that are, sadly, fictional.

Larry is a enthusatic gamer whose dreams as a child was to be either a detective or a TARDIS Repair Man (it's like a VCR repair man except you just see the ending of the movie first). He got into writing to give back to the worlds he's enjoyed so much from.

A Perth, Ontario native, he lives in both Ottawa and Halifax where he works as a freelance writer and full-time dreamer. He lives with his wife Valérie and his owner Zid the cat.

Website:	Larrygent.com
Twitter:	@42webs
Instagram:	@xan_in_the_hat

www.ingramcontent.com/pod-product-compliance
Lightning Source LLC
Chambersburg PA
CBHW070426120726
47910CB00003B/672